REAPER GAMES

BOOK 11 OF THE ANGELBOUND OFFSPRING

CHRISTINA BAUER

COPYRIGHT

Newton, MA 02464
www.monsterhousebooks.com
ISBN 9781956114591

First Edition

DEDICATION

**For All Those Who Kick Ass, Take Names
and Read Books**

CONTENTS

ALSO BY CHRISTINA BAUER

APPENDIX

BONUS IMAGES

AUTHOR'S NOTE

$\mathcal{D}$ear Reader,
      Previous books in the Angelbound Origins series have been true stand-alone installments. However, when it comes to my writing, the unexpected is often routine. For instance, remember when I went back and added Myla's wedding into Angelbound Origins? I fought that addition for a long time. But now, I can't imagine doing anything else. If I'd just tacked a short chapter onto the first Angelbound book, many great stories would have been lost.

Which brings me to *Reaper Games*.

This book wanted to be something different. After battling against myself for a while, this novel is set to become part of the Angelbound Abyss Saga (Angelbound Abyss books 1-4). They'll also be co-numbered as Angelbound Origins books 10-13, which are *Lady Reaper, Reaper Games, Angry Gods* and *Phantom Corsair*.

Here's the deal with the Angelbound Abyss Saga. It tells the tale of Cissy's wedding which, as it turns out, is way too big to shove into one book. Tons of questions arose during writing.

Why did Cissy and Zeke wait ten years to marry?
What really happened to all those ghosts in 1857?
Who's lurking in the Abyss?
What's the story with Cissy's future family?

The tale dives into the Dark Lands in new ways that include

Greek gods, lost orphans and undead soul pirates. I can't wait to share it all with you.

Full disclosure: I'll release the Angelbound Abyss Saga as a box set someday, so you may want to wait for that.

Now, let's get to the good stuff. I hope you enjoy *Reaper Games*!

Best,

Christina

REAPER GAMES

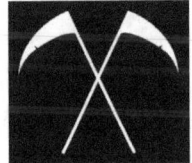

MYLA

AGE TWENTY-NINE

I'm about to spend another six months in Purgatory.
Color me happy.

Sure, I like living part-time in Antrum (aka the underground home of the demon-fighting thrax.) Still, I miss Purgatory's rain... All the ghosts... How the landscape combines the charm of a strip mall with the rusted gloom of an abandoned mine... And, of course, it's home to my best friend, Cissy, as well as my parents.

What's not to love?

Happily, I'll be back there in short order. Which is why my husband, Lincoln, and I step along a fancypants passageway of Arx Hall, our castle in Antrum. Did I mention we're king and queen down here? *We are.*

Lincoln's a tall guy with broad shoulders and loose brown hair that always looks expertly tousled for some reason. We just left a ceremony marking our relocation to Purgatory, so Lincoln sports his *formal best* as king. In Antrum, that means leather pants, tall boots, chain mail and a velvet tunic.

In case you're wondering, there are certain advantages to ruling a people who remain stuck in the middle ages. Leather pants on my husband—that's one of the biggies.

For my part, I wear fitted white robes with a black, medieval-style over-gown. The colors highlight my amber skin, long auburn hair and black dragonscale tail.

All of a sudden, my husband adds a new accessory to his ensemble: *a frown.* Not that most people can tell this, mind you. My guy is a vault when it comes to emotions. But after a decade together, I know what it means when his lips thin ever-so-slightly.

I whisper from the right side of my mouth. "What's wrong?"

Quick aside. At this point, you may wonder if it's totally appropriate for a queen to go around whispering in odd ways to her husband. Here's my take. Queen or not, I never give a flying fart what other people think. Plus, my husband enjoys my sass. Which is why he answers right away.

"Your tail is at it again."

Eep.

Lincoln's a thrax, meaning a part-angel demon hunter. I'm a quasi-demon from Purgatory, so I'm mostly human with a little demonic DNA. Being a quasi gets me powers across the seven deadly sins (mine are lust and wrath, the two bestest.) Most of all, my quasi-ness results in a tail that's long, black and covered in dragon scales.

And that tail has a mind of its own.

I glance over my shoulder. Sure enough, my tail's causing trouble. In this case, it's alternating between frantically waving at the guards and using its arrowhead-shaped end to point to at the back of my head. Taken as a whole, the movements say, *help her, please!*

I crook my finger in its direction. "Up here, buddy."

My tail slinks around so the arrowhead-shaped end points at my face. *Yeah?*

"Stop scaring the guards," I state.

My tail dramatically scans from left to right. A pair of warriors in armor stand at every closed door, which means they're spaced about twenty feet apart. Although most guards have the visor of their helms pulled down, there's no missing the low rattling noises—they're literally shaking in their metal coverings.

"Am I right or am I right?" I ask.

In reply, my tail points toward Lincoln. Its question is obvious. *Do you think I should stop?*

"I agree with Myla. You're worrying our people."

My tail gestures to my face before fake-jabbing at my heart.

"Let me guess… you think I'm still at risk?"

My tail bobs up and down its version of, *Hells, yes.*

This isn't the first time my tail has gone around my back—literally—to try and convince the guards that I'm in trouble. The last few days, this activity has become my tail's favorite pastime.

I roll my eyes. "You know, I got the whole 'arrgh you're gonna die' concept the first four hundred times you warned me. But honestly, there's nothing to worry about."

My tail loops around my ear in a gesture that says, *you, Myla Lewis, are bat crap crazy and about to face mortality.* And it won't stop until I confirm that indeed, I face imminent death.

But I won't.

Because I'm not.

What I *am* is the warrior queen of the demon-fighting thrax. Kicking ass and taking names? That's my bag. Besides, in Purgatory I'm also the Great Scala, meaning the only being who can move souls to Heaven or Hell. I sum it all up to my tail.

"Trouble should worry about me, not the other way around."

"Huzzah," agrees Lincoln.

Still, the arrowhead end keeps circling my ear. It's not giving up.

I roll my eyes. "You're such a drama tail."

Lincoln and I round a corner which leads to yet another gilded hallway. All the while, my tail keeps circling my ear, only now it moves at triple speed. It'll get a kink at this rate.

"Fine," I state. "I'll stay open to the idea that I'm in some minor level of effed-up-edness."

At last, my tail slinks down to hang by my ankle. *Success!*

Lincoln and I make the last turn in our journey. Before us, there's a—*surprise, surprise!*—long gilded hallway, along with more guards. The big difference? This passage ends with a round portico. On the floor of this alcove, there sits a circular metal disc. Once Lincoln and I stand on that spot, we'll get transported to Purgatory.

All of this is to be expected.

It's who stands before the metal platform that's a surprise: our son, Maxon, and Lincoln's mother, Octavia.

The four of us just left the same ceremony… and at the same

time. So how did Maxon and Octavia get here so quickly? There are hidden passages throughout Arx Hall, but some routes trade off stealth—meaning no one knows where you're going—with the amount of time it takes to reach your destination. Long story longer, these two should not have gotten here first.

I whisper from the side of my mouth once more. "Is there a quick secret passage from BARF to this pulpitum?"

True fact: BARF is the name of the last ceremony we just left, not anything that splattered on the floor.

"Ah, no," replies Lincoln.

"Then how did Maxon and Octavia arrive first?"

Lincoln replies with two words. "Thumb ring."

Here's what that means. The after-realms have five parts: Heaven, Hell, Purgatory, Antrum and the Dark Lands, which are the home to ghoul kind. Of all these realms and peoples, only ghouls can set up portals. A black thumb ring means my honorary older ghoul brother, Walker, set up a permanent transport between two spots inside this palace, enabling Octavia to speed around like a sneakypants.

How very Octavia of Octavia.

And truly Walker of Walker.

Maxon steps closer to his grandmother. He's ten years old with brown hair and a cherub-like face. His formal tunic hangs loose on his lanky frame. For her part, Octavia looks pristine and lethal in a black gown. She rests her hand on Maxon's shoulder. As Lincoln and I step closer, we share a long look. There's no need to speak. We're already thinking the same thing.

Clearly, there's a secret scheme between Octavia and Maxon.

Is this plan why my tail's so worried?

I'll find out soon enough.

LINCOLN

THIRTY

*S*eeing Mother and Maxon is unexpected, yet not surprising. Octavia is forever playing multiple games of interpersonal chess at once. Showing up at unforeseen places is one of her more classic moves. On an added note, I've long suspected that my friend Walker creates shortcuts for Mother inside the palace. *Something to ask him about later.*

In classic Octavia style, my plan is guessed at before it can be enacted. "Please, son. Don't bother Walker regarding my new portals." The edges of her mouth quirk up in a slight smile. "Allow your mother to have a few secrets." She looks to Maxon. "Shall I begin or would you like to do so?"

"I got it." Maxon taps his chest. "G and I talked after you left. We both have gifts for you. We were going to wait and everything, but we changed our minds."

Octavia gently squeezes Maxon's shoulder. "Don't you have something else to say first?"

"Oh, about my gift." Maxon stares at the floor. "I know I shouldn't have been sneaking around without permission."

"No," corrects Octavia. "The other thing."

"Oh, right. Thanks for letting me hang with G."

"You're most welcome," I state.

Maxon is staying behind in Antrum so Octavia can train Maxon and his friends for an upcoming battle test.

Myla narrows her eyes. "Let's circle back to the *sneaking thing*, hun."

"Right." Maxon huffs out a breath. "I know I promised not to go on adventures behind your backs, but in this case, I couldn't help it. That Austin guy told me about a hidden book. The idea got stuck in my mind. I just had to find it." He looks between me and Myla as if our heads will explode at this news.

Myla and I share a long look and a short nod. There's no need for us to chat. After so many years, we can read each other's expressions. And in this case, our faces are silently saying the same thing.

We trust Octavia completely.

I refocus on Maxon. "Your mother and I weren't happy when you broke into the magical pyramids without permission. However, it appears you enlisted your grandmother's help while searching for this book."

"That he did." Octavia smiles indulgently at our son. "Why don't you show them what you found?"

Maxon reaches into his pocket and pulls out a small leather volume. Some words are stamped on the cover: *Trash Category XJ-94. Burn immediately.*

"Categorizing trash?" asks Myla. "Only ghouls have ninety-four ways to classify junk. That book must be from the Dark Lands."

On reflex, I pat the note that's hidden in my pocket. Back at the ceremony, Austin handed me a rather cryptic message. I picture the words.

> For King Lincoln: what the Oligarchy see as trash will become your treasure. Give the second part to your queen.

> For Queen Myla: Zelene, Zelene, Zelene.

Austin gave me this message only minutes ago. Now, Maxon volunteers a related book. *That can't be a coincidence.*

I hold out my hand. "Thank you, Maxon. I'm certain the book will be useful."

Maxon sets the tiny volume on my palm. "I found it in a forbidden cave deep under Striga territory."

"Striga," repeats Myla. And the way she says that one word is packed with a lot of meaning. The House of Striga is made up of powerful witches and wizards. "I'd almost rather you'd gone back to the pyramids."

"Maxon and his friends went there on my suggestion," clarifies Octavia. "Therefore, it's not entirely forbidden."

"So..." Maxon winces. "Am I in trouble?"

Myla and share another look. This time, my wife is the one to reply.

"No," she says. "We trust your grandmother."

Maxon sighs. "Good."

I shoot Octavia a sideways glance. "It seems as if you've begun Maxon's training in more ways than one. If I'm right—*and when it comes to you, I often am*—then this little trip to a forbidden cave was all part of your master plan for our boy."

"Of course," confirms Octavia. "There's no point in stifling my grandson's curious nature... Only in directing it." She clears her throat. "Moving on. Since Maxon had something to give you, I wanted to share a present of my own." Octavia pulls a small letter from her pocket and hands it to Myla.

"This is addressed to Cissy," says Myla. "What's it for?"

"For when the time comes," answers Octavia in her classic cryptic style.

I enjoy a good puzzle. My thoughts whirl through possibilities as to what 'time' Mother means. One option quickly rises to the top. "Could this concern a wedding, perhaps? After all, Cissy and Zeke have been dating for years."

"That's not possible," counters Myla. "Cissy would have told me." She rounds on Octavia. "It's something about how Cissy's Senator of Diplomacy, right?"

Mother's face stays unreadable. "As I said, you'll both know when the time comes."

Myla sets the envelope into the inner pocket on her over-gown and pats the spot. "For that moment."

Maxon rushes up to give us both hugs. "I'll miss you guys."

This is a big admission, so Myla and I work hard to play it cool. "We'll miss you as well," I state.

"Love you, baby," whispers Myla.

"And we look forward to seeing you both in two weeks," says Octavia. "That's the test date."

Maxon looks at us. "You both are coming back for that, yeah?"

"We wouldn't miss it," confirms Myla.

Octavia lifts her chin. "Now, give me a swift goodbye." I step up and kiss Mother's cheek.

And I inhale something strange: the scent of cedar and honey.

I step back. Much as I try to remain calm, I can't help but frown. "Do I smell cologne?"

Mother retreats at double-speed. "Must be the Earl of Striga. We held a planning session this morning. The man reeks of lemon."

"Actually, Lucas always wears patchouli oil," I report. "And that scent is something entirely different... cedar and honey, if I'm not mistaken."

Octavia waves her hand airily. "I really wouldn't know."

There's no missing the sly gleam in Mother's eyes. Protective energy rises inside me. Mother is a lonely widow. Is some enterprising earl taking advantage of her?

While I glower, Mother embraces Myla before standing beside Maxon once more. Her 'goodbye smile' is gone. Now, Octavia wears a steely look that says one thing: *stay out of my personal business.*

And perhaps she's right.

Time to go.

3

MYLA

*L*incoln and I step onto the round metal disc set into the floor. A smooth female voice sounds from hidden speakers. "Hello, your Highnesses. We have you scheduled for transport to Purgatory. Are you ready?"

"Yes, Wilhelmina," confirms Lincoln.

At this point, it may appear that my husband's focused on transfer central. *I have my doubts.* If my bet's right, then the *great cologne mystery* still presses on my husband's mind. Lincoln's worried about Octavia.

"On your mark," says the woman.

There's no reply from Lincoln—just a lot of glowering. *Better step in.*

I rest my palms on my husband's shoulders and call out the countdown. "Three, two, one."

Above us, the ceiling dissolves into darkness as the platform lurches upward. The metal disc rocks from side to side as we hurtle through the ground.

"Lincoln?" I ask.

He keeps staring off into space. "Hmm?"

"Safety first." The platform rocks to the right, highlighting why it's best to hang on to someone while traveling by pulpitum.

"Of course." My husband rests his hands on my waist.

"Liiiiiincoln."

This time, I get some actual eye contact. "By chance, do I seem a tad distracted?"

"Ding, ding, ding."

His mouth leans into a lopsided smile. "I'm concerned about the prospect of Mother dating again."

"Understood. But guess what? For the first time in years, you and I are heading to Purgatory with no kid... *and* no obvious disaster hanging over our heads. We can do all sorts of stuff."

Lincoln pulls me a little closer. "Such as?"

"Oh, hang out naked and eat demon bars."

Lincoln's grin widens. "I vote no on the second part of that concept."

My husband hates demon bars, saying they are only candy... and not the *granola meal* as written on the label. For my part, I refuse to waste the gift of a demonic metabolism by stuffing myself with carrots.

"And the first?" I ask.

"Nakedness is a brilliant concept."

"*That's* what I'm talking about." I go on tiptoe and brush a kiss across his mouth. Lincoln nips my lower lip in his teeth. His scent— pine trees and musk—fills my lungs. A spike of desire moves through my core. Suddenly, I ache to feel his bare skin against mine.

Lincoln grips my waist more tightly, pulling my body against his. I sense every place where the firm planes of his chest and thighs press onto my soft curves. Our kiss deepens.

Slam!

With a jolt, the platform comes to a halt. Humidity presses in around me, along with the scent of fresh rain. A deep male voice sounds. "Welcome to Purgatory. Please step off the transfer pulpitum."

Lincoln presses a gentle kiss to the corner of my mouth. "Soon."

"I'll hold you to that," I whisper.

"Myla!" A familiar voice echoes across the room. Stepping away from Lincoln, I scan the familiar interior of Purgatory's official pulpitum—it's a round chamber made from dark stone. A single archway marks the only way in or out. About a half dozen guards stand nearby. All of them wear the traditional purple armor for my home realm.

Cissy rushes toward me. She's tall and lithe with blonde hair that hangs in ringlets to her shoulders. Today, my friend sports her violet senatorial robes and a huge smile. Her golden retriever's tail wags behind her as she approaches.

"Hi, Myla!"

"Hey, Cis. What has you so blissed out? A new treaty?"

In reply, my bestie hold up her left hand, showing off her engagement ring. The thin platinum band holds a big round diamond. In turn, that stone is encircled by a family of little baby diamonds. Very Cissy.

A jolt of happy moves inside me. "You're engaged?"

Cissy's boyfriend—*correction, her fiancee*—steps away from the cluster of guards to stand right behind her. Zeke is a slim guy with slicked-back blond hair and a monkey's tail. His guard uniform includes the platinum emblem that signifies the rank of Captain. Stepping behind Cissy, Zeke rests his hands on her shoulders and beams. "She finally said yes."

"Sheesh." Cissy mock-frowns. "I didn't take *that* long."

Zeke kisses the back of Cissy's head. "You're worth any wait."

All through school, Cissy pined away for Zeke from afar. Once they got dating and a-near, Cis was in no rush to walk down the aisle. And Zeke is a patient man.

Cissy throws her arms wide. We share a big hug. The moment seems to freeze in time. Part of me is thrilled for Cissy and Zeke.

But there's more to this.

Clearly, I missed the actual *asking to get engaged* part of the process. Years ago, something as big as an engagement would've involved lots of discussion between us. Now, my best friend is wearing an engagement ring.

And I missed it.

Sure, I was buried under miles of dirt in an underground castle, but Cissy and I used to send messages between realms all the time. Questions echo through my mind.

When did that stop?

How did I miss this engagement was coming?

Why do I sense danger?

At this point, I realize that Cissy has stopped hugging me back and things are getting awkward. I set my questions aside and release Cissy from what was quickly becoming a death grab.

A long moment of silence passes. Then another. Both Cissy and I know something is off here. Neither one of us knows what to do about it.

Thankfully, Lincoln steps into the conversation. "Don't you have something for Cissy?"

"Right, the envelope." Reaching into my pocket, I pull out the letter. "Octavia gave me this for you." I hand to Cissy.

My friend opens the envelope and reads the message aloud.

My dearest Senator,

I hear congratulations are in order. My sources told me about your recent engagement. I'll ensure Maxon and I are there for the big day, whenever it is. You've been such a great ally to Antrum; I wouldn't miss your nuptials for anything.

Warmest regards,

Octavia

Cissy frowns. "What does that mean?"

"I believe," injects Lincoln. "That is my mother conveying the concept that you couldn't keep her away from your nuptials."

"Oh, sure!" Cissy beams. "I'll be thrilled to have Octavia there, assuming she can make it on such short notice."

The slightest chill creeps up my spine. *Something about this feels off.*

"Short notice?" I ask.

Again, the silence hangs heavily around us. Lincoln turns to Zeke. "How about we chat with your guard friends?"

"Uhhh." Zeke shifts his weight from foot to foot. *Poor guy.* His mortal sin power is *lust*, not *detecting interpersonal tension.* "But you met them already."

"I assume they're all groomsmen?" asks Lincoln. "Perhaps we can discuss their plans for the wedding. It will give Cissy and Myla a chance to speak alone." My husband accents this last sentence with a pointed look.

"Ooooooh, sure," says Zeke. "Let's go chat up the guys."

As Zeke and Lincoln walk away, a little thought bubble appears over my head that reads, *short notice, short notice, short notice.* I force a smile. "So when's the big day?"

"A month from Saturday."

Suddenly, it's a chore to maintain my forced smile. "So, this isn't a 'finally, we're getting around to this' kind of thing. It's got a sense of urgency."

Cissy rolls her eyes. "I'm not pregnant."

"I wasn't even thinking that. I just figured that if things were moving more quickly, then I'd... you know..."

"Myla, we haven't talked in months."

"Because I've been saving the world from at least three apocalypses."

"Which I totally appreciate."

"So, let's talk now. What's the reason behind getting married so quickly? I know you. That's not your style."

"Oh, that's..." Cissy shifts her weight from foot to foot.

"It's okay." I step closer. "You can tell me. What's wrong?"

"Nothing. This isn't just about me and Zeke, you know. We need to take *other people* into consideration."

I try to process this bit of information. *Total fail.*

"Is this about your mother?"

Mrs. Frederickson is a rather high-maintenance mom. She almost lost her mind when Cissy moved out to live with Zeke in downtown Purgatory.

Cissy winces. "Not really."

"So who's behind this? Because I know it's someone."

"This is all Regina-na's idea." Her eyes widen. "I mean, Lady Reaper."

In reality, I know Cissy just stands before me. In my mind, a red whooper light starts flashing over my bestie's head, along with a male monotone voice.

Warning... Warning... Warning...

"Hold on," I state. "Are you talking about Lady Reaper, as in the she-ghoul *heroine*—" I make little finger quotes as I say *heroine* "—who supposedly saved the last Great Scala in 1857?"

"Myla, it's that..."

Cissy's mouth keeps moving, but I don't hear any more words. Which is why I keep talking. "Millions of ghosts disappeared that year, Cis. I still haven't found out what happened to them."

"Myla!"

I raise my pointer finger. "And back then, there were hundreds of Reapers and Weavers who built ghost wells for any number of scalas. When the first ghost towers were built in Purgatory, then the Reapers and Weavers went out of business. There's no reason Lady Reaper should be a big deal. Well, except that our old ghoul overlords shoved her down our throats."

"MYLA!"

I pause. Cissy's face is flushed. The room is back to being super quiet. Clearly, my speech about Lady Regina Reaper is not helping.

"You know what? I take it all back. Tell me more about Regina... Na." That last *na* cost me a lot to say. My parents still call me Myla-la sometimes. Years ago, Cissy refused to use the name anymore, saying Myla-la is baby talk. Now, she's calling this random ghoul Regina-na? *What the actual Hell?*

I realize Cissy has been talking for a while again without any real attention being paid by yours truly. I refocus on the conversation.

"... And Lady Reaper has been my ally in the Dark Lands for years," says Cissy. "She's kindly offered to hold a traditional ghoul carnival for our wedding. There will be pavilions and all sorts of cool stuff. It's a big deal in terms of mending relations with the Dark Lands. The Oligarchy have been reaching out to me directly with requests for the big day. *The Oligarchy*, Myla. They rule every last ghoul."

I bite my lips together.

Don't say it.

Don't say it.

Don't say it.

Crap, I have to say it.

"Oh, you mean the same Oligarchy that wanted to chuck me out as a blood sacrifice to the King of Hell? That Oligarchy?"

"You're carrying a grudge," warns Cissy. "That battle happened ten years ago. People change."

"Sure, *people* change. Ghouls? not so much."

"This is why I didn't want to tell you anything. There's a new generation of quasis in Purgatory who don't remember ghoul rule. Most of our people are excited to have a ghoul carnival. We'll even have reaper games as part of it. I'm Purgatory's Senator of Diplomacy. This is a big deal for me. You're happy, right?"

Cissy looks so hopeful, I can't burst her reaper games bubble. "I'm working on it."

"Remember those festivals we had growing up? Ghoul carnivals are like those… only on steroids. It will be so much fun!"

As I hear the word *festival*, an old memory knocks around my head. It's a recollection of me and Cissy at a high school lust festival. Something important happened there with Lady Reaper, only I can't tell what it is.

A moment later, I can't even recall what I was trying to remember. *Must be that dreaded disease: mom brain.* I actively ignore the deeper feeling that something else may be at work. Like magic.

Cissy taps my shoulder. "Are you paying attention?"

"No, you lost me."

And because Cissy's awesome like that, she just catches me up.

"I said," repeats Cissy. "The festivals back in high school were fun, correct?"

"Sure, they were."

"And my wedding will be like those old festivals, but with reaper games added in. Plus, it will be totally safe. You know how the ghouls are. There are tons of rules about when, where and how the carnival takes place."

"Hey, isn't a month from Saturday your birthday, too?"

"With so many rules, something is bound to happen on my birthday. This will be my big achievement as a senator of diplomacy. I need your support, Myla."

"You know I'll be there. It's just happening so fast and I can't shake this sense of danger." My tail arches over my shoulder to start speed-nodding. "See? I'm not the only one who's concerned."

"I get it. You need the whole story." Cissy lowers her voice. "Only, it's not something we should talk about here. Maybe you can stop by soon? I'll explain it all then."

"Sounds great," I declare. "You're still living with Zeke, right?"

"No, I'm back with Mother."

Now, Lincoln addresses Octavia as 'Mother' all the time. And the way my husband speaks that word, there's a real regal vibe. But when Cissy says Mother, it's one Christina short of a Mommy Dearest situation.

"Come over and talk," says Cissy. "We'll have tea. It'll be fun."

I do a double-take. "Tea?" Cissy's always been a *coffee girl* like me. Something tells me that tea is yet another Lady Reaper thing. Which means I should refuse on principle. Only, as I understand it, tea always includes snacks…

Cissy winks. "Yes, there will be cookies."

And like that, Cissy makes everything normal. It's her superpower.

We share a quick hug goodbye. Cis walks over to Zeke, who's still chatting away with his guards and Lincoln. My bestie works the crowd like a pro before sauntering out the main archway.

And she's engaged.

I should be happy.

Then why can't I shake the feeling that something terrible is coming?

4

LINCOLN

*W*hile Cissy and Myla chat, I spend time with Zeke and his buddy-guards—meaning these warriors are old friends from high school. They all sport chiseled looks, lust powers and monkey tails. Myla calls them Brad-Chad-Tad-Other Tad, since that covers their names. Over the years, I've adopted this shorthand as well, if only in my mind.

My conversation with Brad-Chad-Tad-Other Tad involves a lot of discussions on how to party between now and the nuptials. As it turns out, Cissy is getting married a month from Saturday... and with none other than Lady Reaper organizing the event.

In a word, this news is *strange*. And not just because Brad-Chad-Tad-Other Tad keep talking about some opportunity to get discount coupons for strippers.

In point of fact, the oddness concerns the careful nature of Myla's best friend. For instance, Cissy spent a full year debating over whether to change her senatorial robes from purple to lavender. She's not the type to get married with less than two years to plan. Then again, we haven't seen much of Cissy for ages. People do change.

While the guys push on the party discussion, Zeke gives sketchy answers to their plans. One thing becomes clear, at least to me.

Zeke is doing something between now and his wedding day, but it's not partying with his buddies. The way Zeke talks about Lady Reaper, I wonder if his time will be spent in the Dark Lands. We'll see.

Eventually, Cissy steps up to say her goodbyes to Zeke and his friends. Afterward, I return to Myla. One glance at my wife's face and I know something is off.

"What is it?" I whisper.

"Cissy's getting married in a month and Lady Reaper's planning everything."

"Zeke just mentioned that as well. I find it unusual on two levels. First, *my* people marry young. Quasis tend to wait."

"I know, right? Plus, Cissy was really vocal about being on the slow boat to wedding town. And now... *a month from Saturday?* How did I not know this?"

"Do you want an answer or sympathy?"

"Answer," says Myla. "This is freaky."

"It's been ten years since we started splitting time between Antrum and Purgatory. When we first made this change, you and Cissy kept up a regular stream of correspondence."

"I know, right? Remember when Cissy sent that emergency letter because she thought her cat, Tiny, was dying? I rushed to Purgatory and everything."

"And then, Tiny coughed up a fur ball."

Myla kicks at the stone floor. "Yeah, Cis and I used to talk constantly. Now, we don't. It's way depressing." She shoots me a sideways glance. "You said there were two things. What's the other one?"

"My second concern is how Lady Reaper is organizing this event. She's married to the Grim Reaper. I never liked that fellow. Grim and Walker used to work together at a laboratory in the Dark Lands founded by none other than Eli, the greatest ghoul engineer of all time. And the way Walker won't say anything about Mister Reaper? Something happened there."

"You once told me that you almost-not-quite-remembered how Walker took you somewhere in the Dark Lands to meet Grim."

I blink. "Right. I'd forgotten about that." Another memory appears. "Do you recall meeting Lady Reaper with Cissy at a Lust Festival? You told me about it last week."

"Huh. Now that you say it, Cissy and I did hit that festival in high school." Myla purses her lips. "It's not like us to forget stuff. Do you think it's a magical memory block?"

In reply, Myla's tail pops up, points to her nose, and bobs up and down. *Hells, yes.*

Myla focuses on her tail. "Is this what you've been worried about? Grim and Regina Reaper?"

Even wilder nods are the reply.

I look to Myla. "Perhaps your tail remembers things that you don't."

Yet more energetic nodding.

Myla pats the arrowhead end. "Slow down, buddy. You're still attached to my ass, you know." Her tail calms. Myla rounds on me. "That settles it. We have magical memory blocks on us. I didn't realize anyone can do that."

"It would require a unique kind of supernatural power. Something our current scans don't know how to detect." I look to Myla's tail. "Am I correct again?"

The nodding resumes, only with less vigor, which I'm pleased to see. *I am rather a fan of Myla's ass.*

"What else can you tell us?" asks Myla.

Her tail goes from side to side. *Nothing.*

"So if we look into the Reapers, we've got it," recaps Myla. "No need to extract hidden memories?"

Her tail nods once more.

Across the Pulpitum, a new set of figures appear under the entrance archway. It's Myla's parents, Camilla and Xavier. My heart lightens. The President and First Gentleman of Purgatory are always a welcome sight.

Myla's mother comes over. Camilla an older version of Myla, from her auburn hair to her dragonscale tail. "Hello!" She scans the Pulpitum. "Oh, I missed Cissy giving you the big news."

Xavier steps up as well. In reality, Xavier's an archangel who's been alive since the dawn of time. In appearance, he's a middle-aged man with cocoa skin and a warrior's build. While Camilla dons a purple skirt and matching jacket, Xavier wears a gray suit.

"Sorry we're late," says Xavier.

It's not like them to miss such an important moment. Since Myla's mother is President of Purgatory—and Cissy is the Senator of Diplomacy—they spend a lot of time together. Myla's parents see Cissy as their daughter. And when it comes to family, Xavier and Camilla never miss things like engagement announcements. It all adds up to one conclusion... and Myla knows it, the same as I do.

"What's the emergency?" asks Myla. "What kept you away?"

A better question I couldn't have asked myself.

"Nothing at all," says Camilla brightly.

"You're a crap liar, Mom." Myla swings her gaze toward her father. "Dad? Anything?"

"There are some minor technical issues with the ghost towers," replies Xavier. "Nothing to worry about."

Ghost towers are how souls are stored in Purgatory. Before those buildings were created, spirits were kept in ghost wells on Earth. Both were creations of the aforementioned Eli.

"There are a few minor glitches to the older towers," adds Camilla. "We truly wanted to be here when Cissy told you about her engagement, but little snags are all part of being President. We try to keep the realm stable."

Myla's mother is being modest. As Purgatory's president, Camilla has done much to rebuild after the old ghoul overlords were kicked out.

"You've done much more than maintain things," I state.

"This isn't about me today," says Camilla. "Isn't it great news about Cissy?"

Camilla's eyes light up with joy. It's the same expression Myla and I wore when Maxon first learned to summon lightning. *Ah, parenting.*

"It is," agrees Myla. "But I don't like Lady Reaper being involved."

"She's not that bad," says Xavier. "Regina and Grim are the last of the Reapers... which means they're the final connection to the era when Purgatory and the Dark Lands had a more healthy relationship. The Reapers and Weavers built the old ghost wells, you know."

"I've heard the stories," I say.

"Do you know about Lady Reaper's plans for Cissy's wedding?" asks Xavier. "It will be a traditional ghoul carnival that includes reaper games. Most of our citizens are looking forward to it."

Camilla and Myla share a look. They hate any mention of ghouls in a positive light. Not that I blame them. Both suffered under ghoul rule. Xavier notices their mutual glare, the same as I do. Since he used to be a diplomat himself, Xavier knows when to change the subject.

"Enough about ghouls." Xavier turns to Myla. "Give your dad a hello hug."

Myla smiles as she embraces her father. "You know, you don't need to meet me at the transfer station every time I come back from Antrum. I'm not twelve."

Xavier pats her back before stepping away. "Hey, I missed every day when you were twelve. And your mother missed having me *with* her through your childhood. How could we skip this now?" He rubs his palms. "So, where's my grandson?"

"Maxon wants to stay in Antrum," I reply. "He'll continue his battle training."

"Under the guidance of Lincoln's mother," adds Myla.

"Octavia is a tough teacher. That will go well." Xavier focuses on Camilla. "What do you say? We have that *very important thing* to examine."

Myla and I share a knowing look. *A very important thing to examine?* Chances are, Camilla and Xavier need to check the ghost towers again. They appear to have everything under control, though. In some cases, extra help can be a hindrance. We say our goodbyes.

As Myla's parents step out the exit archway, the crowd outside cheers. I turn toward Myla and say three words with a smile.

"Let's go home."

5

MYLA

*D*on't obsess about Lady Reaper.
Don't obsess about Lady Reaper.
Don't obsess about Lady Reaper.
Hells bells. I'm totally obsessing about Lady Reaper.

As I march out of the pulpitum with Lincoln, I keep focusing on that she-ghoul. Lady Reaper's smug grin flashes in my mind as I rush through the crowd and make for our SUV. A guard waits by the vehicle. This is Zeke's old buddy Tad… and does this guy ever look ready to chat.

And by *chat*, I mean *gossip*.

Normally, I enjoy spilling a little verbal tea with Zeke's posse. But, this time? Not so much. Tad does talk *at* me, mind you. Sadly, the whole conversation registers in my mind as something-something *reaper games* something-something *Zeke and Cissy*.

I nod and make polite noises while slipping into the SUV. Lincoln gets behind the wheel and we speed away. All the while, my mental train of thought rolls back to Lady Reaper. Only now, I contemplate how to best accuse this ghoulette of stealing my nickname.

When did you start calling yourself Regina-na?
Did you REALLY think I wouldn't find out?
Or did you KNOW I'd discover this… and you're trying to monkey with my brain? Well, the joke's on you because my mind's already screwed.

"She calls herself Regina-na?" That's Lincoln.

"Oops. Have I been talking out loud?"

"More like yelling, but yes."

"In that case, yeah. She calls herself Regina-na."

"That's an odd coincidence."

"You don't know the half of it. Not only is Lady Reaper calling herself Regina-na, but Cissy is calling her that, too."

"I thought baby nicknames weren't appropriate for adults."

"Exactly my point! Or rather, that used to be *Cissy's* point. This sucks."

At last, my anger cools enough to realize a critical fact. In my rage, I slipped right into riding shotgun—with no drama involved. There are some things a woman just can't let slide.

I round on Lincoln. "Hey, it was my turn to drive, right?" As always, it's important to say this with confidence, especially when I'm ninety percent sure I'm supposed to be shotgun.

"It's not. But good try." He beams.

I wink. "You're welcome." My guy appreciates a battle, whatever the form.

Let the record show that at one time, Lincoln found the fact that you could roll down a car window to be something of a marvel. Now, he drives like a pro.

In no time, we're back home. Although since Walker updated the building's exterior, the place looks a little more like a Mars settlement than a traditional house.

Love it.

CHEZ SCALA

6

MYLA

*O*nce we're inside Chez Scala, Lincoln and I have our respective rituals. To kick things off, I always seek out some *bad for me food* in the kitchen freezer. Lincoln lurks nearby, watching my pursuit with royal disapproval.

That makes everything taste better.

All of which is why I now open the freezer and yelp with joy. *Nothing but microwave pizza pockets.* Sure, the boxes are covered in weird freezer fuzz, but who cares? I've been eating vegetables and lean meats for six months. *Bring it on.*

"Find anything?" That's my lurking husband.

"Yes." I pull a fuzzy box from the freezer and scrape off enough ice to read the label. "Hello, Cheesy Pizza Product Pocket."

"Expiration date?"

After more scraping, I have the answer. "Two days ago."

"Eew."

"Agreed. I can do better." It takes me a while to fish through the whole freezer, but I soon find the ultimate in crap. "Lookie here! A Meat Lover's Pizza Product Pocket." In celebration, my tail does a happy dance behind me. Like me, it enjoys the odd rush of chemicals that comes from downing this particular treat.

Lincoln stalks closer. "I didn't realize we had any of those left."

I hug it to my chest, a motion which has the extra benefit of melting more of the freezer fuzz away. "Well, we do."

"Chef Purgatory doesn't make those anymore."

I shrug. "I don't see what that has to do with anything."

"What meat products are in that concoction?"

After a little more scraping, I'm able to read the label aloud. "Sausage product, pepperoni product, cheese product and other food stuffs." I rip open the box, grab my meat product fiesta and head for the microwave. "You've no idea how yummy these are."

Fast as a whip, Lincoln scoops the discarded box from the counter. "This expired *two years* ago." He fixes me with his most serious stare. "You are not putting that into your head."

I hit some buttons on the micro. "Let me just warm it up a smidge and we'll see what happens."

"Fair enough." Instead of continuing to fight me, Lincoln leans against the counter. *This is not a good sign.*

Moments later, the scent of dead fish fills the kitchen. I gag. "Open the windows!" I approach the mini countertop microwave as if it were a nest of demons. Smoke now billows from the vent-slits on the side. "We may need a new micro."

Lincoln is enjoying this way too much. "I think so."

"Okay, I'll clean it up. You go be you, only somewhere else."

"No," says Lincoln smoothly. "Allow me to assist."

"False. You'll go really slowly because I have it coming."

"True." Lincoln winks before sauntering out of the kitchen.

I get to work.

Using with my tail, I whip out a super-sized garbage bag—*I keep these around for just such emergencies*—and place the little microwave inside. Then, I put that whole thing in *another* mega bag (because I saw something moving beyond the little microwave's window). And I chuck *that* whole concoction into the trash.

After that, I vow to finally clean out the fridge.

Tomorrow.

LIBRARY

7

MYLA

$\mathcal{A}$fter my kitchen adventure is over, I find Lincoln hanging out in the library. While the house's exterior is pretty modern, our library is all things old fashioned. Comfy chairs. Lots of leather-bound books. Massive his-n-hers desks. I want to get a rolling ladder in here one of these days, just to finish out the look.

Lincoln has parked himself at his desk. He's pretending to review papers. In reality, My husband is trying hard not to laugh his ass off. "Everything set?"

"Sure. You know me. I have a system." There's a reason why we only buy microwaves that are used, super-cheap and crazy-little. This isn't the first time I've liberated odd stuff from the freezer.

"Of course." Lincoln sorts through more papers on his desk.

My desk sits across from Lincoln's... and I store my demon bar stash in the bottom-right drawer. After plunking onto my swivel chair, I pull out a treat and chow down. Because I'm polite, I nod toward my horde. "Want one?"

"No, thank you." After sorting through more messages, Lincoln pulls out the small book Maxon gave him and flips through the pages. "These are demon patrol notes." My husband keeps reading. And the way his jaw clenches? This is about more than the stinky mess I made in the kitchen.

"What is it?"

"This is the final patrol log from the House of Minos."

"Hold on, don't tell me. I know the thrax specialty for the House of Minos." I drum my fingers on the desktop. "Okay, I got nothing."

"They watched over all ghost wells on Earth."

I stop my fingers mid-drumming. "That explains why the Dark Lands got that book. Ghoul Reapers and Weavers made ghost wells."

"There's more." Lincoln pulls out another slip of paper from his pocket. "As we were leaving, Maxon mentioned someone named Austin."

"Right. Austin's that kid you saved years ago. He tipped off Maxon to find the book."

"Austin also has the power of foresight. He gave me this note at the ceremony." Lincoln hands the sheet over. It doesn't take long to read.

For King Lincoln: what the Oligarchy see as trash will become your treasure. Give the second part to your queen.

For Queen Myla: Zelene, Zelene, Zelene.

"The trash must mean that book." I set the sheet onto my desktop. "What does the patrol log say?"

Lincoln slips through more of the tiny tome. "To my eyes, the most important part of this log concerns Winston, the Earl of Minos." He stops at a particular page. "It says here, Winston wanted my father to inspect a particular ghost well in England."

I hiss in a low breath. "England was demon patrol territory for the House of Acca." *And Aldred, the Earl of Acca, was a total creep who puppeteered Lincoln's father, Connor.* "Acca would never have allowed another house on his territory, even if Minos were just checking out a few ghost wells. And if Aldred refused it… then, your father would have, too."

"Worse than that. Father closed Minos down."

My eyes widen. "Closed down? Aren't there ghost wells across the Earth? Didn't the other houses complain?"

"Ghost wells were already being replaced by ghost towers, so Father decreed that Minos was no longer needed." Lincoln sighs. "Minos asked me for help at the time."

I lean forward. Lincoln gets the message. *Keep going.*

"The Earl of Minos approached me about a year before you and I met. Winston wanted me to visit a particular ghost well. I refused. Father said it would annoy Acca and at that point..." Lincoln leaves the logic out there. Because back then, Lincoln had to choose his battles carefully when it came to Connor and the House of Acca.

"I know every pulpitum station on Earth," continues Lincoln. "I can't think of any near a ghost well. Which brings us to the second part of the prophecy." Lincoln flips to the back of the book. "This also discusses emerald ghosts. When someone spends their early years with the Scala Heir, their spirit turns green while their body gains some scala powers."

"That's right," I confirm. "We saw that green spirit back at Antrum. I'm going to go out on a limb and guess her name is Zelene." My tail pops up to point at my nose. "Is this part of what I forgot?"

My tail nods.

"Did I meet Zelene at the lust festival?"

This time, my tail nods and points to Lincoln.

"Ah," says my husband. "And I met Zelene as well? Perhaps when I saw the Oligarchy with Walker?"

My tail gives one final nod and slumps to hang out my by ankle. This is its way of saying, *the conversation is over.*

Lincoln flips through the pages again. "We need to find out more about Zelene. My guess is that we'll discover additional answers at Winston's ghost well. Do you have any ideas where that might be?"

I screw my mouth onto one side of my face. "I got nothing."

Lincoln leans back on his chair. "So, what's next?"

"Two options. We could go to Limbo Town Pizza for dinner because the kitchen should really get fumigated. Or, we could get naked and stay that way for hours... because Maxon's in Antrum and there's no one else here."

A slow smile rounds Lincoln's mouth. "I like the second idea." Little by little, he rises from his chair. My pulse speeds. In a single swift move, Lincoln pulls off his tunic and chain mail. Now, my husband has leather pants and a bare chest. Yum.

I take one step toward him.

Then, it happens.

One moment, I'm in a cheery library lit by candles. The next second, my igni appear as bright little lightning bolts. This kind of thing happens all the time.

It's what takes place next that's a shock.

My igni transform from bright lights into so many tiny black holes. The room becomes inky-dark as well, except for a strange blue light that shines through a nearby window. Someone stands on the other side of the glass. *A woman.* Alarm spikes through me. Somehow, I know this intruder is supernatural. My inner wrath demon awakens inside me. Every nerve ending in my body feels charged with alarm.

Danger!

Run!

Sadly, my feet feel rooted to the spot. The shadowy woman sets her palms against the glass. A warped voice echoes through the room. Is it a woman who speaks? A child? I cannot tell. But what she says is unmistakable.

"The darkness surrounds me."

My legs turn wobbly beneath me. Those four words—*the darkness surrounds me*—shouldn't tear at me so deeply.

Yet, they do.

THE DARKNESS

8

LINCOLN

*S*omething's wrong with Myla.

We've been discussing the puzzle of Austin's note and Maxon's book. Later, we moved onto more intimate topics. I saw Myla's irises spark red with demonic lust power.

It's one of my favorite looks on her.

Now, Myla stands frozen before me, staring out the library window. I follow the line of her gaze. There's nothing beyond the glass except the regular view of yellowing grass under a cloudy sky.

Myla shivers. Her eyes widen with fear.

I've seen this kind of reaction from my wife before. Most likely, Myla's igni are appearing to her. Sometimes I can see the tiny lightning bolts that empower her to move souls to Heaven or Hell. Most often, they're something that only Myla can detect. She'll witness their searing brightness and hear their ear-splitting voices.

And it pains her.

Over the years, I've figured out ways to help my wife. All of which is why I scoop Myla into my arms, shuck off her over-gown and set her into bed. Once she's under the covers, Myla's scala robes come alive. The many threads twist and spin off her arms to pool on a nearby chair. Once there, they reweave into a shift once more.

I place a bottle of water and some demon bars on the bedside table. Then, I peel off my clothes and slip under the covers too. Myla does best when I hold her with her back against my chest. My right arm serves as my wife's pillow. With my left hand, I gently brush my fingers through her long auburn hair.

"I'm here," I whisper. "You're safe."

Minutes tick by while Myla lies still beside me. Her breathing is low and steady. I'm unsure how much time passes. At last, she stirs again. When Myla speaks, her voice is rough.

"Well, that sucked." Myla blinks. "We're in the bedroom now." She angles her gaze to the bedside table. When she next speaks, my wife's voice cracks with emotion. "And you did that *thing* again."

"I did."

From this position, I can't see Myla. Still, there's no mistaking the smile in her voice when she speaks once more. "Water. Demon bars. Thank you."

"There's no need to thank me. I wouldn't wish to be anywhere else."

Myla's voice comes out rough again, but with a different kind of wobble. "You know how everyone talks about romance?"

"I do."

"Not that there's anything wrong with candles and moonlight... but what's just as important as romance is something that I call shit-mance."

I can't help but smile. "Shit-mance?"

"Yes. As in, *oh, shit, I'm having a freaking episode from the supernatural beings messing with my head.* And then, your partner takes care of you with bottled water and demon bars." She nods toward the side table. "Right now, those look as lovely to me as roses."

My heart feels so light, it's as if I could soar. Growing up, I was raised to rule my kingdom, not share love. Even now, these moments with Myla are an unexpected gift.

"Tell me what happened."

"This is a new one, but I think my igni formed a person. She was outside, pounding on the window and saying *the darkness surrounds me.*"

"That's awful."

"I'd rather my igni went back to just screeching at high volume, honestly."

A recollection flashes in my mind. "In Maxon's book, the Earl of

Minos wrote about the Laboratory of Darkness."

"Most ghoul stuff includes the word *dark*. My igni could be talking about a lot of things."

"There's one person who'd know what your igni mean."

"Walker." Myla sighs. "But he's been MIA for months."

Walker is a friend to me and an honorary older brother for my wife. He's also a ghoul of many mysteries. It's not unusual for Walker to disappear for months at a time.

That said, Myla and I do have ways of contacting Walker. We just save it for special emergencies… And a random book passage about darkness and the Oligarchy doesn't qualify.

For a moment, I soak in more of the sensation of lying quietly with Myla curled against my chest.

And I brace myself for some fun.

Because I know how my wife's mind works. She only needs a challenge and a little bit of silence before she comes up with a plan.

Sure enough, Myla twists about to face me. Her blue eyes glisten with excitement. "Oh! I've got it! Do you know what we should do?"

"Let's hear it."

"We need info about this *mystery darkness* along with Winston's ghost well. So, let's break into the greatest storehouse of ghoul knowledge ever."

My brows lift with surprise. "You mean Opus X? That's the ghoul record repository in the Dark Lands. Normally, it takes months of paperwork just to get permission to step through the door."

"Paperwork, shmaperwork. We have all those charms from demon patrol, like invisibility pins, transport rings, the whole smash. We'll be in and out before they know it."

"I like this plan. Ghouls aren't really big on magical security systems. With those charms, I'm sure we can get in and out without being detected. That said, there may be advantages to being *seen* as entering the building."

"And what would those be?"

"Ghouls love their rules. And if you or I are detected as traipsing around Opus X…" I leave the logic out there.

"Then it's regulation for our nearest ghoul relation to be alerted. That would be Walker."

"And I believe we still have some tracker charms." Myla and I keep a stash of thrax demon patrol magic here in Purgatory. We haven't replenished our stock in a while, but trackers are tiny. There are usually a few extras lying about. "When we see Walker, we can attach a tracker and find out what he's up to. Because if I know Walker, it's got something to do with Winston, darkness and ghost wells."

"Love it."

Growing up, Myla and I didn't know each other... but we both knew Walker. "I've always wondered. When did you first suspect Walker knew that Xavier was your father?"

"Pretty much from birth. There was no question that Walker and Mom were in a secret cabal about Dad's identity. But the fact that my father was an archangel and that meant I'd become the Great Scala? I had zero suspicions about that."

"I'm impressed. It took me a while to figure out when Walker was being cagey."

"Did I ever tell you about the time Walker snuck me into the arena to watch a Hell mammoth horde fight against a starfish fiend?"

With that, we launch into an extended discussion about battling demons. Hours pass with Myla cocooned against me. At length, our words dwindle into silence. We both fall asleep.

In my dream, I'm back on Earth. I've returned to the demon patrol where I saved the young version of Austin. It's dark and raining. Austin's old farmhouse is a pile of kindling that grows to be as tall as a skyscraper. I tear through the planks of wood, searching for the child. Austin's cries sound from under the pile, but I can't get to him.

Cloaked figures appear. *Necro hunters.* These ghoul warriors wear black robes while their faces are half-covered in metal masks. Dozens of these fighters crawl across the pile of wood and ruin. I know they're in search of Austin, same as I am.

A woman's voice echoes through the night. "They're not after Austin."

I pause. "Who do they want, then?"

The voice never answers, though.

She only laughs.

Necro Hunter

9

MYLA

*L*incoln has a crap night of sleep. I know this because he tosses against me. Once morning comes around, I let my husband sleep in.

And I use this *me-time* to engage in one of my favorite rituals. While Lincoln snoozes, I slip into the kitchen and crack open my stash of sugar cereal. With my bowl overstuffed to the brim, I plunk in front of the television and engage in what every queen wants to do with her morning.

Watch cartoons.

I'm halfway through bowl number two when Lincoln comes into the living room. He wears flannel pajama bottoms only. I have on a long *sleep shirt*. My husband pauses by the couch.

"I'm not sure what's worse for you, the cereal or the cartoons."

"This is my second bowl of Toasted Sugar Bombs and my teeth feel like they're vibrating in my jaw... so I'm going with cereal." I wink.

"Ah." Lincoln smirks. "Good to know."

"What? No additional warning about how I'm filling my head with crap?"

"Not yet."

Lincoln saunters into the kitchen. A few minutes later, he walks out with a bowl of something called muesli (I saw it in the cabinet but it looked very brown.)

My husband sits down beside me. With a flourish, he points his spoon in my direction. "You, my dear wife, are filling your head with slop."

"Thank you. I was starting to worry I was losing my touch."

On screen, Casper the Friendly ghost meanders through a cartoon town.

Lincoln squints at the screen. "I don't get it."

"Allow me to enlighten you." I gesture at the TV. "Over the years, I've given this a lot of thought. Casper is a very deep cartoon. It expresses the existential dread of a ghost who's unable to leave Earth for Purgatory. See that bird Casper's talking to? It symbolizes freedom."

Lincoln chews thoughtfully. I take this as encouragement to continue.

"And the other ghosts in town are not really spirits... they're actually ghouls who are holding Casper back. This entire show is a complex allegory for how Purgatory was subjugated by the Oligarchy."

Lincoln silently considers this for a full minute. "Did it ever occur to you that humans made this with zero thought about Purgatory?"

"Maybe, but what's the fun in that?"

On screen, the show turns over to a commercial break. Upbeat music blares from our television's little speaker. "Don't miss the ghoul carnival!" cries the announcer. "There will be all-new pavilions for every deadly sin. Plus, you don't want to miss the reaper games. And let's not forget the President Lewis Ride. Just kidding."

Here the screen shows a really nasty old Ferris Wheel. At the same time, a sad trombone makes a wah-waaaaah noise.

This part of the commercial is so upsetting, I stop stuffing my head with sugar bombs.

"How did that nasty old Ferris Wheel get renamed the President Lewis Ride? That's just mean."

"And best of all," continues the announcer. "You can meet Lady Reaper... savior of Purgatory... host of the ghoul carnival... and creator of the reaper games!"

The screen shows a bunch of cheeseball fireworks and people cheering. Some tiny type appears at the bottom of the screen while the announcer speed-talks. "Lady Reaper will marry Senator Cissy Frederickson and Captain Ryder during the special ghoul ceremony for a Hallowed One. Only one marriage per realm. No other nuptials will be accepted."

The commercial ends and Casper comes back on. Only now, I can't appreciate the existential beauty of this animated creation. That commercial has me all mixed up.

"Hallowed one?" I look to Lincoln. "Is it me, or does that sound totally made up?"

"We should add that term onto our research list for today's visit to Opus X."

"Sure thing."

And with that, it's time for me to move on from the commercial and segue into planning our trip to Opus X.

Not happening.

I hop up and pace the room. Sugary energy and rage course through my body. "The President Lewis Ferris Wheel, my ass!" And since it can't resist a chance to take center stage, my tail swoops around to gesture at the screen as well. "Thanks, boy."

Lincoln finishes the last of his muesli. "Why do I feel there's a speech coming on?"

"Because there is." In my mind, solemn trumpet music plays as I announce the following. "No more shitting around. We must hit Opus X and find out about Winston's ghost well. Oh, and research the Hallowed One, too. Because I've had it with all this sneaky crap where ghouls sneak around my realm like a sneaking sneaker."

I might need to buy a thesaurus, but Lincoln raises his hand in a gesture of approval. "Testify."

"And if Opus X can't get us answers..."

"Then Walker will," finishes Lincoln.

I put on my scala robes. Lincoln slips on his demon patrol armor. We load up on various charms for the mission. I claim that we need to use the tracker stickers that can only be read in Antrum because they're more accurate, but Lincoln totally shnaggs me in that I just want to check on our kid.

Because he wants to see Maxon, too.

Once we're all set, we make our way to the main pulpitum. And I talk my sweet self onto the driver's seat even though I'm sixty percent sure it's not my turn.

No doubt about it. This will be a good day.

10

LINCOLN

*I*t *is* Myla's turn to drive, but it makes her happy to think she's getting away with something. Therefore, I play dumb.

Who am I to ruin her fun?

At noon, we reach the pulpitum, a round temple-like building surrounded by a stone courtyard. Normally, the place is packed with folks calling themselves *worshippers of the Great Scala*. In truth, they land somewhere on the continuum between *motivated fans* and *even more dedicated campers*.

As we step closer to the building, it's clear that the courtyard is mostly deserted. Many tents are empty. I've never seen the place so quiet.

A girl skips up to Myla. She wears a blue dress, white ankle socks and patent leather shoes. She has brown skin, braided hair, and a lion tail that sways slowly behind her.

"Hello, Great Scala." She looks toward me. "Hi, you."

"Greetings." And I smile. It's a genuinely good thing to receive a *hi, you* from any member of the quasi population. When I first married Myla, children would scream and run, crying out that I was a demon hunter who meant to kill them.

Myla kneels on the cobblestones. "Hello. What's your name?"

"Tanya."

Myla grins. "Nice to meet you, Tanya."

"Is it true you're going to die and the Hallowed One will take over?"

I pretend that I need to scratch the bridge of my nose. In reality, I'm hiding my grin. I remember this age with Maxon. *The filter-free zone.*

"Actually, that is most definitely false," answers Myla. "Where did you hear that?"

"Carol Cheevers says it on the news. And my mom says it. And my friend Martin's dad says it. And my teacher says…

Myla holds up her hand. "I get the idea."

"Oh. So you know, I don't want you to die, but it would be nice if we had more ghoul carnivals." She looks to me. "And I guess we'd miss you, too."

With that, Tanya turns and skips away.

"Well, after seeing that TV commercial, that kind of encounter was bound to happen, right?" asks Myla. "Now, it's over with."

From the corner of my eye, I catch Zeke's guard buddies lurking under the entrance arch. They all wear the kind of expression that humans save for rubbernecking at highway accidents.

"I fear we have a few more Tanya-style conversations to go." I rest my hand at the base of Myla's spine and guide her toward the pulpitum entrance.

Once there, we're greeted by the Brad-Chad-Tad-Other Tad coalition. They wear the same purple military-style uniforms with vastly different skin tones and identical haircuts.

"Duuuuude!" exclaims Chad. "You just missed Zeke."

"Oh, he's off duty?" asks Myla.

"No." That's Brad. "Zeke had to visit the Dark Lands. It's this Hallowed One wedding thing. The man must prepare."

"All sorts of spa treatments or something," adds Chad.

"Yeah, Zeke can't party with us or anything," injects Tad.

Other Tad gets into the mix as well. "That's a whole month wasted, man. And Chad finally found us stripper coupons. Those aren't easy to get."

Brad-Chad-Tad-Other Tad stare at me expectantly. This is some kind of male ritual I'm missing.

"I'm very happy for you, Chad," I declare.

Myla raises her hand. "And I'm standing right here."

Brad-Chad-Tad-Other Tad keep staring at me. It's like Myla doesn't exist, even though she has the power to sort their souls into Hell one day. As Myla says, you can take the guys out of high school, but not the high school out of the guys.

It's Brad who finally recalls Myla's supernatural status.

"Whoa, Myla," says Brad. "Are you going to kill us?"

"Possibly. Eventually. Not now. Did Zeke *really* go to the Dark Lands to prepare for his wedding?"

"Sure," says Tad. "You mean, you weren't expecting to meet him here?"

"No," replies Myla.

Brad-Chad-Tad-Other Tad all exchange wide-eyed looks. The air turns heavy with unasked questions.

"Is there something else you'd like to know?" I ask.

"Oh, we don't want to bug you two." That's Brad.

Myla shrugs. "Bug away."

"We understand what's happening," says Tad. "Cissy is going to become the Hallowed One. You're moving on to do something else. Like *whatever it is you do* when you're not killing stuff. The guys have a bet going." Tad steps closer to Myla. "Will you live in Heaven now?"

It's getting really hard not to laugh. "Myla can't do that, Chad. My wife isn't dead."

"Brad, tell him how her father is an archangel."

"Shut up, Tad. He knows who Myla's father is."

Other Tad throws up his arms. "I didn't say anything."

Myla raises her pointer finger. "Guys, do you know what this Hallowed One situation is all about?"

"Oh," says Other Tad. "It's another way of sorting souls, but with Reapers and scythes instead of, you know…" He gestures at Myla. "You."

Chad raises his pointer finger. "I've got a question." He focuses on me. "After Cissy becomes the Hallowed One, will Zeke turn into a companion be like you?"

"And *how* am I, exactly?"

"You know: someone who's standing around, holding Myla's purse and looking swole."

I consider this carefully. "No idea."

Myla pales. "I can't believe this. You guys have known me since forever. Do you really think Cissy is about to replace me"

The guys look around, rock on their heels and refuse to make eye contact.

"Come on," urges Myla. "Brad? Chad? Tad? Other Tad?"

"Oh, man." That's Chad. "Look at the time. It's shift change. We better go."

With that, the Brad-Chad-Tad-Other Tad complex rushes out the door.

Myla shakes her head. "Ten seconds with those guys, and I'm mentally back at lunch during junior year of high school."

I nod toward the transfer platform. "Let's go cause trouble with ghouls. It will make you feel better."

"Good thinking."

Myla and I step on the metal disc. A voice comes to life on hidden speakers.

"Greetings, your Majesties."

"And to you, Justin," I reply.

"We don't have you slated for transfer today. Where would you like to go?"

"One moment." I turn to Myla. "I have a new plan. While the guards were chatting, I had extra time to ponder. "

"Oh, let's hear it."

"Let's arrive at Opus X. But when it comes to leaving, I believe by that point we'll have drawn some attention."

"Only if we're lucky."

"Therefore, we'll require an alternate transfer station for the return trip." On reflex, I twist my black thumb ring. It's a transport totem I brought along for today's mission—and it can open a portal to any transport station with the same realm, so long as I know the name.

"Good thinking," says Myla.

"Did you hear that, Justin? We need some options for departure sits from the Dark Lands."

"Sure, let me check." Justin hums while typing away. "I have it. You can return from Red Court, Skullscape, the Whispers and the

Abyss... just kidding. The Abyss is locked down. A little transport humor there."

As jokes go, that one is true, even if it isn't particularly funny. The Abyss is essentially the dumping ground for all misfits across the after-realms. And the ghouls have the place locked down tight.

I look to Myla. "What do you think about Red Court?"

"That's the Oligarchy throne room. Either it will be empty or crawling with ghouls. I like Skullscape. No one goes there."

I nod. "Justin, we'll return from Skullscape. Keep the channel there open so you'll know when we arrive. For now, please send us to Opus X."

"As you command."

We give the countdown and speed through the ground. Within minutes, Myla and I stand before the greatest citadel of rules-keeping and random knowledge in the after-realms: a massive round building made of concrete, glass and spires.

Opus X.

Opus X

11

LINCOLN

The Dark Lands are trapped in eternal night. Even so, Opus X manages to catch enough moonlight on its strained glass windows to create the effect of some daylight.

The courtyard around the building is both vast and empty. My wife is not pleased.

"How long will it take for some bureaucrats to show up and hassle us? We're dangerous warriors, for crying out loud."

At last, a series of low hums sound. Only ghoul portals create those particular noises. Within seconds, a trio of tall black doors appears before us. These are rectangles of black which look solid enough from the front, but appear paper-thin from the side.

Three ghouls step out. All are at least seven feet tall and wearing long black robes with the hoods pulled low over their faces. The center ghoul raises his arms, showing off a one-inch thick stack of paperwork.

"Great Scala and Companion. You must fill out these forms in order to enter the Dark Lands."

Another ghoul lifts an even taller stack of papers. "And complete these to visit Opus X."

"Oh, that's fascinating," says Myla. My wife beams as she attaches a small safety pin to the wrist of her robes. I do the same to my body armor.

Only these aren't regular pins—they're demon patrol charms.

Once in place, the magic makes me and Myla visible to each other, and by that I mean semi-transparent. But to everyone else? We're undetectable.

I march toward Opus X. Myla grabs my wrist. "I have to see this part."

A full minute passes while the ghouls hold out the paperwork and wait. Then, all three start speaking at once.

"Where did they go?"

"What's the regulation here?"

"We must check with the district communicator in charge."

"Who's their nearest ghoul relation?"

A fresh set of portals open. The ghouls step through and disappear.

Myla places her hands over her heart. "That was just the best part of my day."

"Yet," I state.

MYLA

I spent years being forced to fill out stacks of paperwork like the stuff those ghouls just toted around. So how much did I enjoy vanishing and leaving them without a single completed sheet?

Very much, indeed.

Inside, Opus X is just as monumental as its exterior. The place is all stained glass and marble everything. As an extra bonus, there are very few ghouls around. Even so, Lincoln and I stay invisible. *No point attracting attention.* The ghouls may be sticklers for process, but it's because the stuff works.

In other words, they'll find us sooner or later.

In the meantime, I soak in the central hall. It's an egg-shaped chamber that towers three stories above our heads. In the center of the room, there stands a massive statue of a bolshy guy with lots of hair product and a toga. The placard reads:

EL-1, "Eli"
Designer of Opus X
"A monument to knowledge lives forever."

The statue's a little over the top, but the building around it is stunning. "Ghouls can be total douchebags," I say. "But this Eli guy knows his stuff."

"Agreed. Walker always that Eli taught him everything about engineering."

"In my mind, Walker's a great warrior, artist and honorary older brother. I always forget about the engineering side of his life." I screw up my mouth and consider. "Maybe it's because that part includes guys like Grim. How did Walker share a lab with that clown?"

"It's a mystery."

Lincoln and I explore the first floor, which turns out to be a lot of drafty hallways and not much else. The second floor holds a maze of stone shelves that hold nothing but record books. Want to know how many times sweeping services were required at the Skullscape in 1932? There's an entire ledger dedicated to the topic.

We keep going.

The third floor is all metal cabinets with extraordinarily long drawers that hold unbelievably large charts. There are ones for death and taxes, of course. But there's even one that helps calculate how many times a ghoul should get haircuts. *Whoa.* It seems that hair keeps growing after death. Who knew? I thought ghouls were stuck with the style they wore when they kicked it.

The top level is where we finally get to the good stuff. And by that, I mean actual books about topics other than rules and regulations. Here everything is made of oak. Tall panels line the walls. Freestanding wooden shelves cover the floor. In short order, Lincoln and I find a section for Reapers and Weavers. Lincoln checks for anything about the Hallowed One. I look for information on the darkness.

As with everything between us, we make it into a contest. Who will uncover useful information first? Will it be me and my super-broad category of darkness... or Lincoln and the mysterious Hallowed One? We agree to a wager—and Lincoln takes what is certainly a sucker bet.

After all, how hard can it be to find out something about darkness in a realm called the Dark Lands?

All of which is why I went ahead and upped our regular bet. This time, whoever wins gets to *definitively call* the next kiss. That means the other person has to wait.

Lincoln is such a badass about sexual tension. Now, I'm lining up some serious payback. *Oh, yeah.*

Sadly, I've barely scanned my first tome when Lincoln raises his hand. "I have it."

"That's not fair."

"I know. You thought I was taking a sucker bet."

"It's not over until it's over. Tell me what you found and I'll tell you if you won."

Lincoln clears his throat and reads aloud.

The Hallowed One Prophecy

When there are two reapers, two scythes and two emerald ghosts, then the Hallowed One shall appear, ignite the great tower and imprison all souls.

"That sucks," I announce.

"Are you perturbed by the prospect of all souls getting imprisoned… or losing your current gig as the Great Scala?"

"No, I'm bummed because I'm part lust demon and you command the next kiss."

"I do, don't I?" His voice gets all sultry… and Lincoln *knows* what that does to me.

"It's very important that we focus on serious things here." That's what I *say*, but even *I* don't totally believe me. "I don't see why people might think the Hallowed One is the next Great Scala. I don't just chuck souls in a prison, I move them around."

Lincoln skims through his book. "This Hallowed One prophecy is rather vague. It's unclear if there's ever been a Hallowed One before." He snaps the book shut. "It appears as if like my work is done. Need any help?"

"Hardy har har."

"Then, I take that as a no? Nothing to be found on a topic as expansive as darkness? How about shadows?"

I'm trying hard not to smile (and doing a crap job of it.) "Nobody likes a sore winner, Lincoln."

A low hum sounds. *Walker time!* A moment later, a ghoul portal appears. Sure enough, Walker steps out. He's tall and pale with a shaved head and sideburns. He scans the room with his all-black eyes.

"I know you're here," says Walker. "Don't ask me how, but I know. Please remove the demon patrol safety pins so we can talk like adults."

I unhook my pin and wrap Walker in a big hug, mostly because he hates that kind of thing. Plus, it's a nice distraction because at the same time, Lincoln is materializing while patting Walker on the shoulder (and attaching the tiny tracking sticker.)

My husband and I really do make a good team.

I do that thing where I aim to kiss Walker's cheek—but actually kiss his ear—and follow up with the kind of inhale-kiss that sounds like air squeaking out of a balloon. This will blow out Walker's hearing for at least five seconds.

"Myla," says Walker in his low voice. "Ouch."

Truth time: That was over the top, but I wanted to be sure we'd fully distracted Walker. Because we definitely need to know what he's up to… and we won't discover a thing if he takes that tracker off.

"Greetings, brother," says Lincoln.

"I was very busy," intones Walker.

"Well, we were wondering if you could tell us anything about Grim and Regina Reaper," I state.

"No."

"What about the Hallowed One?" asks Lincoln.

Let the record show that Walker is working his best poker face right now. "Never heard of it."

Lincoln sighs. "Walker, even I can tell you're fibbing."

Walker purses his lips while rocking on his heels. That means he's totally lying his ass off here.

"Honestly, Walker." And I give him the kind of wide-eyed look that always got me snuck out of the house as a kid. "Do you know what's happening?"

"Yes," replies Walker. "But at this point, I can say nothing… because it *is* nothing."

"Meaning," says Lincoln. "You promised someone secrecy and whatever this is, it isn't yet dire enough to break a confidence."

"At last, I can say yes."

"Come on," I urge. "Whatever you know, we'll uncover the truth eventually."

"Then why would I spoil your fun?" Walker mock-bows. "And if you'll excuse me, I have to go fill out about a thousand forms because of you two." He sighs. "Good to see you. Stay out of trouble."

He opens another portal, steps through and is gone.

Creeeeak!

A long wooden whine sounds, snapping both of us to attention. Turning around, I see that a wooden panel has swung open on a nearby stretch of wall. My thoughts race.

Did someone follow Walker here?

Are we about to be ambushed?

My tail goes on alert and arcs over my shoulder. Before, I had unhooked the safety pin on my wrist. That way, Walker could see me. Now I reset the pin in place and vanish.

I glance behind me. Lincoln has done the same.

Now that we're both invisible to outsiders, we stalk toward the door. Every cell in my body strains, trying to hear what's ahead. Once we're close enough, I wait for a signal from Lincoln that he's in place and it's safe for me to check the room.

Lincoln sets his hand on my shoulder. That's the signal.

I leap into the room and find… zilch.

Actually, it's not total nothing. There are some leather chairs around and paintings on the wall. "False alarm."

Lincoln checks the door. "Someone failed to lock the door. What an interesting opportunity."

Creak. He closes the door.

Snick. Lincoln turns the lock.

And I smile.

13

MYLA

*I*n life, there comes a time—*hopefully, not too many of them*—where you lose a bet and can't actually make the first move on your own husband.

This moment is one of those times for me.

In such cases, I find it's helpful to act super-casual. To that end, I pretend that it's mega important to scan the paintings in this little room. The first one I find is a watercolor of the Oligarchy. It shows the four ghoul rulers in their red robes. They seem as boring and useless as in real life.

Maybe Cissy was right. It's been ten years. Perhaps I shouldn't be carrying this Oligarchy-centered rage about how they tried chucking me at Armageddon.

Or, I can keep hating them because I like to and it feels good.

Option number two, please!

I step over to the next painting in line. Lincoln sidles up behind me. I love how his body warmth radiates down my back and between my thighs. Lincoln leans in close enough to almost-not-quite kiss my neck. I bite my lower lip to stop myself from moaning.

Little by little, Lincoln slides his hand up my stomach to cup my breast. His thumb toys with my nipple. Heat and desire twist through me.

"Did I mention how I locked the door?" Lincoln's voice sounds low and growly in my ear.

"No, but I noticed that anyway."

Lincoln sets his free hand on my hip. He walks his fingers down my outer thigh. Each slow movement raises my scala robes up my legs just a little bit more. Heat pools behind my eyes.

Then I see it.

The new painting before me shows none other than Eli and Walker. They stand in a laboratory that's filled with metal boxes topped by round glass globes. Eli looks as bolshy as his statue, only in addition to his toga he also holds a swath of golden fabric in his hand. The threads seem to shimmy and writhe.

A realization hits me. *Eli made my scala robes.*

"Damn," I whisper.

Lincoln pauses. "Why do I think that whatever you're thinking about does not involve the concept of lust?"

"Seeing this painting, I just remembered something. You know how Walker practically worships Eli?"

"You mean El-1, the first and greatest ghoul engineer and architect? The one with a statue in this building? The ghoul who taught Walker everything about engineering?"

"That's the guy."

"Never heard of him."

"A few months ago, Walker was going on and on about how Eli built this beautiful ghost well just a few yards from an old Acca patrol pulpitum in England... and Aldred never appreciated this beautiful, gorgeous and brilliant creation."

On a side note, Walker talks a lot about Eli these days. Years ago, Walker used to go on about his brother, Drayden. But ever since Drayden got sprung from his job as an eternal prison warden, Walker has moved onto reminiscing about Eli.

"The Earl of Minos, Winston, wanted you to visit a ghoul well by a pulpitum station."

"I call that. The memory is a mood-killer, but I'm with you."

"Back in the library, you said you know every pulpitum station on Earth, and none of them fit the profile for Winston's *pulpitum-n-ghost well combo*. Were you *only* thinking of the active stations?"

"That I was." Lincoln shakes his head. "I can't believe I didn't consider the closed ones."

"Neither can I. You miss zero. We should buy lottery tickets or something."

Lincoln nips at the juncture of my neck and shoulder. "Maybe later."

Turns out, Lincoln means that phrase—*maybe later*—in more ways than one. He steps away to pace the room.

Sometimes, it's no fun being part lust demon.

"Ghost wells are only built in rural areas," announces Lincoln. "As I recall, there's only one defunct pulpitum station in England that's not in a city center. That must be where the Earl of Minos wanted me to go."

"Which means we need to check it out."

"That we do."

Footsteps sound outside, followed by a trio of voices. It's the same three ghouls who met us outside Opus X.

"Where are they?" asks one.

"Maybe we should wait," suggests another.

"Haven't you been paying attention?" asks the third. "It just came through on Group Think. Walker submitted paperwork for their respectful removal."

"And Walker's portal residue was tracked to this room." That's the first one again. "They must be close by."

"Open all doors!" cries the second. "Inspect every corner!"

"We better leave," whispers Lincoln.

"Agreed."

Lincoln moves to stand before me. Our bodies are almost-not-quite touching. Leaning in, he nips my earlobe with his teeth. "Anticipation, Myla."

"You're a rotten bastard." *But I say the words without any real anger.*

"Correction. I'm a rotten bastard who's making you wait in the best possible way."

"Ugh. That only makes it worse."

"Or better." Lincoln twists his thumb ring while whispering the word, *Skullscape.* A portal opens. Our adventure in Opus X closes.

Hand in hand, Lincoln and I step through the portal and into the oddly beautiful desert that is the Skullscape.

SKULLSCAPE

14

LINCOLN

$\mathcal{T}$he Skullscape is an empty stretch of land that even the ghouls find too creepy to inhabit. The ground here is so parched that it hangs in jagged clumps. Tall stones take the shape of screaming and emaciated faces.

I wouldn't stay here for any period of time, but for a place to depart the Dark Lands, the Skullscape is rather poetic. I set another charm onto the pulpitum platform. This one resembles a wad of gum. Once it's set onto the metal disc, the ghouls won't be able to track us. Unlike our entrance, I'd prefer it if the place where Myla and I depart remains a secret.

It only takes a moment to apply the anti-tracking charm. Myla and I step onto the disc; a gravelly female voice sounds.

"Hello, your Highnesses."

"Greetings, Inaya," I call.

Myla shoots me a quick look of surprise. No matter how long we're together, it still amazes her how easily I recall names. Which is why I display this skill as much as possible.

"We'd been tracking you to appear at this station," says Inaya. "Are you looking to return to Antrum?"

"Not this time," I reply. "There are a number of closed transfer stations in the human realm of England. We'd like to visit one. How many are there?"

Clicking noises reverberate through the desolate air as Inaya checks for pulpitum. "I see seven retired stations."

"Is one out in the middle of nowhere?" asks Myla. "We're looking for a station that's by an old ghost well. Those are usually in fields."

"Ah, yes," announces Inaya. "I have a decommissioned pulpitum stop that meets this description." More clicks follow. "And it's still in working condition. I can activate it as your destination, if you like."

"Please do," I state.

"The destination is now live," says Inaya. "Ready to transfer on your countdown."

Myla and I move to stand in the center of the metal disc and place our hands on each other's shoulders. Since this transfer path hasn't been used in a while, this journey is likely to be a bumpy one.

"Ready to go," says Myla. "Activate transfer in three, two, one…"

The platform lurches into the ground. Dirt and magma stream past us as we magically speed to our destination. The disc rocks so violently, the motion reminds me of a sailing ship being tossed in a storm.

Boom!

The entire platform rattles as we come to the end of our journey. We now stand inside a snug wooden space. The exit is an oblong hole that's about half-way up the round walls. Myla and I step outside.

Turning around, I see that the pulpitum journey ended *inside* a massive oak tree. From the exterior, the odd-shaped exit is a huge knot in the trunk.

This arbor is one of many that form a line to my left. The rest of the landscape is a field of wheat. A cloudy night sky arches overhead. Countless green stalks sway in the breeze. Insects chitter nearby. The scent of fresh earth and dried flowers fill the air.

There's no sign of the ghost well. Yet.

"In his notes, the Earl of Minos said the ghost well would be visible from the pulpitum station," says Myla.

A fresh breeze rolls across the field. Cloud cover breaks. Direct moonlight reflects across the stalks of wheat.

Then I see it. *A crop circle.*

"That's the sign," says Myla. "Ghost wells are always dug into a field and topped by a crop circle."

I have mismatched irises. I cover my blue eye, which represents my angel power, and gaze at the field with my brown eye, meaning my human sight.

"Looking with my brown eye, this place seems to be a regular field."

"Most days, humans won't see the circle," confirms Myla.

A memory appears.

I stroll along a passage of Arx Hall. My eighteenth birthday just passed, along with the confirmation my court must relocate to Purgatory in just two weeks. As a result, Arx Hall is a flurry of activity. Palace workers march off in every direction, their arms laden with supplies and their faces tight with worry.

There's so much chaos, I barely notice a skeletal figure limping toward me. It's Winston, the one-time Earl of Minos. He raises a withered hand. "Your Highness."

I pause. "It's good to see you." I'm so unsettled by the upcoming journey to Purgatory, it takes me a moment to recall the man's name. "What brings you here, Winston?"

The man shivers as he lifts his chin. There's no missing the deep worry lines across his face, the gray stubble across his jawline or the warble in his voice.

"I'm the Earl of Minos."

"Pardon me. It's good to see you, my Earl. What can I do for you?"

Winston grasps my hand. His skin feels papery and cool. "Please. Come with me now. There's a pulpitum you must see. It's on Acca demon patrol territory."

"That doesn't narrow it down. Aldred's region of control expands daily."

"But this is about the ghost wells and the Reapers. I've recorded something for you." The earl tugs at my hand. "Come see the ghost well. It won't take long."

I rub my chin and consider this. Winston is right. It's only a matter of minutes to make a quick pulpitum journey. And poor Winston lost his house due to Acca. The least I can do is indulge him in this.

All the while, the hallway has held a steady stream of workers. Now those folks stand aside as my father strides up. He's a barrel-chested man with white hair and an oversized personality. Like me, Father wears a black tunic along with black leather pants and matching boots.

"Winston, my friend!" booms Father. "Come along, give Lincoln some time to finish his duties. We've a big move coming up."

Winston shoots a nervous look in my direction. Although his eyes are milky with age, there's no missing the look of worry in his mismatched irises. "But the ghost well... it's important."

Father wraps his hefty arm around Winston's shoulder. "Please. Purgatory hasn't used those old spirit pits in years."

"But this concerns the Reapers," adds Winston.

"They're gone, too," counters Father.

"There are a few Reapers left, and they've created followers made of magic. Necro hunters."

That gets my attention. I've run across necro hunters before while on demon patrol. "How many necros have you seen?"

"None," replies Winston. "But I know they're out there. Necro hunters search the earth for a special person... someone who's good friends with the scala heir."

Father pats Winston's shoulder, a movement that almost makes the elder man topple over. "Let's discuss this over a glass of mead."

"It's ten o'clock in the morning," says Winston.

"Ah, two glasses then." Father shoots me a sly look. "The Great Scala is safe in Purgatory, moving souls as we speak. We don't even know who the scala heir is, let alone whether he or she has any friends."

"But I must talk to Prince Lincoln!" urges Winston. "You're only ignoring my request to see the ghost well because you fear the Earl of Acca."

A tense silence hangs in the air. Father's shoulders slump. That means one thing—my father is afraid of Aldred. And ashamed of having brushed Winston aside.

Father looks to me. "What do you think?"

A dozen worries weigh on me at once. Where will we live in Purgatory? Why is the angel Verus sending us there in the first place? Who will manage demon patrols while we're gone from Antrum? With so many concerns, one thing is clear.

I can't waste time with Winston.

Besides, Father's been king for ages. He must know whether Winston's story could really pose a risk.

I round on Winston. "I think it's best if you share that glass of mead with Father."

The conversation ends. Winston and Father take off. I continue on my way, confident that whatever the problem is with Winston, Father can work it out. And I ignore the part of my heart that says I'm very wrong.

Although I'm the kind of person who forgets nothing, I hadn't recalled this conversation until this very moment. I'd say that it's some side effect of whatever magical memory block is on my mind. Still, I know the truth. It would only have taken minutes to visit the pulpitum with Winston. And it was my responsibility to go. I pressed the memory aside out of regret.

Myla laces her fingers with mine, snapping me out of my thoughts. "I know that face. Something's wrong."

"Is it that obvious?"

"To me, yes. If my guess is right, you're feeling guilty about this Winston guy."

"I was so close to coming to this spot before. I always think about Mother as having a blind spot for Father, but I did as well. It was easier to take Father's word that there was nothing to worry about."

"Hey, you're here now." Myla smirks. "And if anything, you should feel guilty for getting half-naked around me before. And I'm holding you to that anticipation thing."

I cut her a sideways glance. "Really?"

"Really-really."

Myla gestures across the field. "And check out this crop circle. It says *adventure* to me." She bobs her brows. "Focus on the fun, honey bunches."

I can't help but smile. *This woman.* "You do realize that without you, my life would be Sparta?"

She winks. "You're welcome."

And I turn my attention to the adventure ahead.

15

MYLA

*N*ot all battles are with swords.

Take Lincoln, for instance. My husband could being angry about having to basically run a freaking realm of demon hunters at the ripe old age of eighteen. Instead, he doesn't lean into excuses. He's doing his part to make things right with Winston. In my opinion, that's what makes him a real king.

Lincoln and I step nearer to the crop circle. As we close in, an electric sense surrounds me, making my hair stand on end. The chemical-sweet smell of ether fills the air. Magic is at work.

The world stops.

Wheat stays half-swayed in an invisible breeze. A nearby oak leaf pauses in its floating journey to the ground. The chittering insects become silent.

Lincoln checks his wrist. "My watch has stopped."

I nod. "Some spell has paused time here." Cool light pools behind my eyes. "Whatever it is, it's pulling on my angelic power—my eyes are glowing blue." I scan Lincoln's face. "It's happening to your blue iris as well."

"The spell must be launched by our proximity to the ghost well."

"In that case, let's get even nearer and see what this thing can really do."

Before actually stepping forward, Lincoln and I take out our baculum rods. These are two small silver bars that we can ignite into any kind of fiery weapon. With our baculum in hand, we slip up to the crop circle.

Suddenly, a line of blue light flares to life on the ground. I've seen humans line up wires beside each other. Something like that happens now, only with magic. Those lines wind out through the crop circle, illuminating its pattern. A round maze of blue light shines up from the ground.

With careful steps, I move closer to the circle. "This maze is so intricate. It's one thing to know that ghost wells are all capped off by crop circles. It's another to see this."

"It's a map of the minotaur's maze. That's how the House of Minos got its name."

I kneel down for a closer look at the threads. "This magic reminds me of my scala robes. Those threads are alive with magic, too."

Lincoln crouches beside me. "Winston talked about some kind of communication that he'd left here for my father and me. I wonder how we activate it."

Together, Lincoln and I try to launch Winston's hidden message. We test different incantations while touching the grass or pulling on the illuminated threads of the maze. Nothing works. At last, Lincoln sets his palm flush against the glowing lines while stating the words, *in thrax sic hunt.* It's our all-purpose password.

And it does the job.

The maze lights up more brightly. While the rest of the world stays frozen, a hologram of Winston appears. He's an old guy in thrax gear—meaning a loose tunic and pants—and such stooped shoulders, the bones of his spine are visible. He hovers above the center of the crop circle.

"Hello, your Highness," says Hologram Winston. "Thank you for coming to see this ghost well." The hologram glitches in and out of focus. Winston calls to the side. "Is the spell working, Maurice?" The earl looks to us. "One moment."

While the image flutters, I ask Lincoln a question. "Who's Maurice? We can't see him in the recording. Tell me this is one thrax you don't know."

"Sorry to disappoint, but Maurice is Winston's older brother."

Lincoln frowns. "I should have bet you on that. Too bad. This situation has me off my game."

The image of Hologram Winston stops glitching. The earl addresses us once more: "As thrax, we focus on saving humans from demons. At the House of Minos, we protect the earthly ghost wells where human spirits are stored before being moved to Heaven or Hell. As you can see—" Hologram Winston gestures below "—these wells are marked on the surface by a round maze, just like the one which originally held the mythical minotaur. When this well was being used, the interior would attract ghosts. Activate the well, Malcom!"

Before us, the maze cover vanishes. A deep, round pit appears below us. Hologram Winston snaps his fingers. Lines of blue magic wind down the inner walls of the well, still keeping to their intricate maze pattern.

"That's it, Maurice," says Hologram Winston. "Now, start up the ghost simulation." He pauses while listening to his brother. "It is not a waste of time, Maurice. We're making this recording for the High Prince of the Thrax. He doesn't understand soul processing. We must show him."

Ghosts appear in the well below us. "Ah," announces Hologram Winston. "There we go! And don't worry. As I said before, these spirits are all simulations."

More fake ghosts appear in the well. All of them fly around in circles. This is one of the problems with ghost wells, by the way. They're the equivalent of hamster wheels for souls. Eventually, the spirits get cranky. That's why ghost towers place spirits on pretty landscapes where they lie in the sun and snooze.

More simulated souls fly into the ghost well as part of Hologram Winston's demonstration. The earl beams. "Thank you, Malcom." Hologram Winston turns back to us. "Ghost wells are no longer in use, but that doesn't mean they aren't use-*ful*. My house has studied these wells for hundreds of years. The magical strands inside them have many purposes. For instance, strand magic is recording me right now."

Hologram Winston continues: "Even better, the magical strands also captured what happened on this very spot in the past. I've reviewed these records. Based on what I've seen, I believe there's a serious threat out there to the next scala heir... and more importantly, to their closest friend."

All this while, I've been having a sweet time. Hologram Winston and Maurice are a couple of personalities—they could have their own talk show. Plus, watching a ghost well in action is a total treat.

But knowing this is all about the *friend* to the scala heir—about my bestie Cissy—being in trouble? That's something else. My stomach decides that now is a good time to hang out by my toes.

Another realization hits me. "This isn't just about Cissy. Maxon's best friend is Uther."

Hologram Winston goes on. "The bottom line is this: terrible things took place at this very ghost well. I've put together the next bits into a magical recreation. I no longer trust that King Connor will take this seriously, so this next part can only be viewed by the High Prince. Lincoln, set your palm onto the threads of the crop circle. You'll see the recreation and gain a little magic, too."

Lincoln frowns. "I liked everything except the *gain a little magic* bit. What do you think?"

"It's not the craziest thing you've done. I'm living proof of that."

"True." Lincoln grins.

Leaning forward, my husband sets his palm against the glowing blue threads of the crop circle. The bright lines twist up his hand and lower arm. While flashing with light, the threads spin about until congealing into a solid shape.

My skin chills over in awe. Sure, I've seen my scala robes form body armor. It's a different deal to watch that happen to Lincoln.

My husband holds up his arm. A loop of blue metal now covers his forearm. "It's a gauntlet."

"Does it hurt or anything?"

"No, just tickled a bit when it took shape."

"That's how my robes work, too."

The gauntlet glows blue on Lincoln's forearm. At the same time, my husband's azure-colored eye also flares with blue light. "It's pulling some energy from me to power whatever Winston has planned next. I was not expecting that."

I scan the fields. The grasses are still frozen in place. Everything is silent. The scent of ether turns intense. My inner wrath demon stirs inside me.

Something's about to happen. And whatever's coming, it's a doozie.

Below us, the ghost well lights up again. Points of brightness shift along the individual threads, highlighting the intricate maze paths set into the round walls below us. Adrenaline courses through me. My tail arches over my shoulder, ready to attack.

Boom!

A blast of thunder sounds as the ghost well lights up more brightly than ever before. A column of blue light reaches up into the cloudy night sky.

Before, the light had created a single blue hologram: Winston.

Now, the brightness rolls out across the ground.

Everywhere the blue light touches, the wheat field vanishes. A three-dimensional scene is created in its place. There are stalls, games and musicians. The ladies wear gowns with bustles along with tiny hats. The men don suits with bowlers. A three-dimensional world surrounds us, all of it in color.

A sign arches above us, reading Ghoul Carnival 1857.

This is the year Lady Reaper supposedly saved the last Great Scala. And a ghoul carnival? That means Regina-na is somewhere close by.

Color me happy. Again.

LADY REAPER

16

LINCOLN

Clearly, Winston was a man of hidden talents.

Who knew the Earl of Minos could manipulate strand technology in order to create this kind of simulation... let alone my new gauntlet? Before, I felt guilty for *not* taking a quick trip with Winston. Now, I regret having missed the chance to learn strand magic from a master of the art.

Myla and I now stand in the middle of a full-color recreation of the Ghoul Carnival of 1857. Humans step toward me. I'm so caught up in thoughts of Winston, I don't step away quickly enough. Turns out, that's not a problem. The humans pass right through me as if I were a ghost.

Myla reaches out to touch the wooden pole that holds up one side of the ghoul carnival sign. Her hand passes right through the wood as if it were mist. "This sign announces a ghoul carnival. Lady Reaper is putting on one of these for Cissy's wedding."

I offer Myla my hand. "Let's see what this festival entails, shall we?"

Myla goes to lace her fingers with mine, then pauses. "Do you mind if I touch the gauntlet thing?"

"Not at all."

Myla gingerly prods the gauntlet with her pointer finger. "It's solid. Just like when my robes make armor." She looks at me and smiles. "Now we can go into battle all matchy-watchy."

"I came here with no other goal in mind."

More humans step past us. We follow the crowd into the carnival itself. A great midway opens before us. This wide path is lined either side with wooden stalls and games of skill. Carnival barkers announce the chance to toss a hatchet at a target. Others challenge men to strike a metal circle with a sledgehammer in order to ring a bell. Still another stall holds a line of sacks painted with images of green-faced women. A man in suspenders and a frayed bowler hat calls out as folks pass by. "Toss a ball, hit a witch, get a prize!"

What a bad idea. I hope this man never encounters a real witch with *that* speech. He'll get a prize alright, but not one he'll enjoy.

We move past the games. Long white tents loom along either side of the midway. A woman stands at a small podium. "Enter the freak show! See the two-headed lady! Meet the man with a tail!"

Myla winces. "Sometimes, quasis get stuck on Earth with their tails visible. It never ends well."

I spot a row of fancy golden tents ahead. Ghouls stand outside the entrances, their black robes edged in gold ribbon. There are no barkers on this row. When we reach this part of the midway, the humans all speak in hushed and reverent tones.

A human family walks nearby: a mother, father and young boy. The child points to one of the guards. "Are those real ghouls?"

His father chuckles. "Of course, they are!"

"Don't frighten the boy." The mother focuses on her son. "No, child. This is all part of the ghoul carnival. It's just in fun. If we wanted to have our fortunes told, we could pay gold coin to have the Weavers show us our fate."

The father nods toward the tents. "They're the descendants of Greek goddesses who spun the fate of all mortals—Clotho, Lachesis and Atropos."

"How did you know that?" asks the mother.

"It says so on the sign," replies the father.

Sure enough, there is a wooden sign near one of the tents. I read the words aloud. "Meet the Weavers—magical creators of fate who can tell your future."

Myla points to the end of this row. "There! Those tents look like crap."

I lift my brows. "And that's of interest because?"

"Weavers were the rock stars of the *ghost well show*," replies Myla. "They made all those intricate mazes. But Reapers were the stage-hands. It was their job to clear away the grass and dig the pits. If Lady Reaper is here, she's hanging out in some rundown spot, not these golden tents."

"How right you are. Let's check it out."

We pass a dozen golden tents that are set in a neat row. Then, we enter another area that's set up past the midway itself. Raggedy black tents dot the ground. A ghoul waits outside each tent, only this time, their robes are torn instead of decorated with ribbons. And each one holds a wooden scythe in their right fist.

"Bingo," says Myla. "We're close."

Another human walks by. She wears a simple white dress and her hair in braids. The moment I see her, a shock of alarm runs down my spine.

"I know her."

"So do I," adds Myla. "That's Zelene."

We trail Zelene through the maze of black tents. Ghouls call out to her as she passes. "Reapers have magical powers of all kinds. Enter the tent to get your friends cured and enemies killed!"

A cloth sign is pinned each tent's exterior. Names are written on the fabric in sloppy letters. I read them aloud as we pass. "Blood and Lady Gore Reaper… Death and Lady Destruction Reaper… Shadow and Lady Darkness Reaper…"

"Do you notice how the scythes here are the same?" asks Myla.

I nod. "They're all made of wood. Chipped. Filthy. No sign of magic."

We reach the last tent in the area. I read the name aloud. "Grim and Lady Regina Reaper." Zelene stands outside. I realize the last time I saw her, Zelene was a green ghost. It's odd to see her in human form.

Myla steps up to the Grim Reaper. "That's a nasty face."

I take a close look as well. Sure enough, the Grim Reaper's visage is little more than a skull with pronounced eyeballs. As Zelene approaches him, Grim's face changes. Strands of red light twist across his bones. Skin grows back. His eyes no longer bulge. The expression turns warm and familiar. A chill crawls over my skin.

Grim looks a lot like Walker.

"Are you seeing what I'm seeing?" asks Myla.

"Yes, and I don't like it."

"That must be strand magic on his face, only how is he casting it? That scythe isn't doing anything."

A long moment passes before Myla and I speak the same name. "Walker."

"Dollars to donuts, Walker fixed Grim up somehow. You said they shared a laboratory or something."

"And it's the kind of thing Walker would do for a friend." I bob my head and consider. "He'd even do it for an enemy, come to think of it."

Zelene pauses before Grim-Walker. "Hello, again."

"How fares your brother?" asks Grim-Walker.

"The same," says Zelene. "He keeps drinking that tea from Lady Reaper. He's coughing up blood these days, but just won't die. Must be that scala heir magic. I need something stronger."

Myla gasps. "She's talking about her brother, the scala heir."

Anger twists inside me. "I know Zelene isn't talking about the current scala heir. Still, Maxon has that role now. I can't help but feel…" Although I don't say the word *rage* aloud, the heat of anger still pulses through my soul.

Myla's eyes flare with demonic fury. "I'm right with you."

"You've come to the right place," says Grim-Walker to Zelene. "Few understand how to handle a scala heir. Regina can aid you." He gestures toward the entrance flap. "Step inside." When he next speaks, he lowers his voice. "She's waiting for you."

"Thank you," says Zelene.

She saunters inside the tent.

Myla and I follow.

GRIM REAPER

MYLA

*L*incoln and I trail Zelene into the tent. Inside, we find a snug space lit by a pair of hanging lanterns. Lady Reaper sits at a small round table whose surface is covered with tiny glass bottles.

Zelene stands before the table with her arms across her chest. "Your poisoned tea didn't work."

Lady Reaper pours herbs from various bottles into a stone bowl. She picks up a pestle and starts to crush them.

"Did you hear me?" asks Zelene. "It didn't work."

"I heard you."

"I did all three steps of the ceremony, just like you asked," adds Zelene. "First day, I gave my hair. Second day, I gave my blood. Third day, I gave my word. You're supposed to kill my body and make my emerald ghost the Hallowed One already."

"I don't see why you're in such a rush to get murdered," counters Lady Reaper. "After all, you're the one who wanted your brother killed. It's rather tricky to do so without a physical form." All this time, a white walking stick has been leaning against the table. Lady Reaper now grips that rod and slams it against the ground. Light and smoke erupt from the spot. When the mist clears, the walking stick is now a fancy scythe. A round red stone gleams in the blade.

I let out a low whistle. "That's not like the other scythes."

"It's the work of someone who knows the supernatural," adds Lincoln.

"I summon the power of strand magic," announces Lady Reaper. "Zelene's emerald spirit must appear."

A puff of green smoke surrounds Zelene. When the haze is gone, Zelene has split in two.

In one version, Zelene is a human with dark braids and a white dress. The next moment, her physical self stands beside a green ghost whose skeleton is clearly visible under her semi-transparent skin. At the same time, all the expression and life seems drained from the physical Zelene—she seems more like a robot than a person.

Ghost Zelene stomps her foot. "Put me back together!"

"Of course." An evil grin winds Lady Reaper's mouth. She swipes the scythe again. "I summon the power of strand magic. Place the emerald ghost back inside Zelene."

Another puff of green smoke materializes. When it's gone, the two Zelenes are one person again.

My body turns numb with shock. Magic prickles across my skin. White spots cloud my vision. When the spell clears, I recall having seen Zelene before as a green ghost—it took place back with Cissy in the woods when we were visiting the high school lust festival. I look to Lincoln. "I remember everything now."

"Same here," says Lincoln. "Walker took me to see Grim and the Oligarchy years ago. Zelene wiped my memory. Something about this magical display is unlocking our recollections."

All this time, Lady Reaper has been holding her scythe in one hand while glaring at Zelene. "Are you ready to listen now?"

"Yes, Lady Reaper." Those are the words Zelene says, but they're spoken with a clear edge that means, *I hate you.*

"You came to me," says Lady Reaper. "And you said how your brother was too proud. You wished him dead. I brewed you a poison to do the trick. This is my kind favor to you. It has nothing to do with your status as the Hallowed One."

Zelene frowns. "So when will I become the Hallowed One?"

"You know the prophecy. We've only one scythe and emerald ghost, so the second scythe and ghost must be procured first. You're an immortal now, Zelene. You must learn patience."

I remember the words Lincoln spoke back at Opus X.

The Hallowed One Prophecy

When there are two reapers, two scythes and two emerald ghosts, then the Hallowed One shall appear, ignite the great tower and imprison all souls.

Lady Reaper is telling Zelene the truth. They have more to do before the prophecy can come true.

"This is a great honor," says Lady Reaper. "It is the destiny of ghouls to take over all parts of the after-realms. The Hallowed One will destroy the physical form of all souled beings and place their spirits into a great tower. Then, every corner of every land will be ready for ghoul occupation under a new ruler. That could be you, Zelene. Just be patient."

I do a double-take. There's a lot to hate in that speech, starting with the idea of killing every living being… going on to the concept of imprisoning all souls forever… and ending with world ghoul domination under a new leader. Growing up, the ghouls would complain how it was unfair that others had both a body and a soul while they only carry a physical form. When ghouls die, that's it. No spirit.

I didn't realize that the undead had a master plan to fix that situation. *Shame on me for my lack of imagination.*

"I don't think we need to wait," says Zelene. "I heard that prophecy is something the Oligarchy made up. They have other plans. You should try to turn me into the Hallowed One now."

Lady Reaper stuffs herbs into a packet. "Continue to whine and I'll murder all of you before you become anything. Another emerald ghost will cross my path eventually. Unlike you, I am patient."

Zelene's defiant posture melts into a show of subjugation. It involves lots of slumped shoulders and sniffles. "You're so right. I can wait. I just can't stand the fact that my brother thinks he'll be better than me one day. Can't you help me again?"

"I'm a kind woman," says Lady Reaper. "I'll get you a fresh dose of poison as well as someone to help you administer it." Lady Reaper stands and raises the scythe high. This time, the candlelight highlights the stone in a new way.

I gesture toward the scythe. "There's a rune on that stone."

"I've seen those carvings like that before," says Lincoln. "It's a maker's mark."

I step closer. Sure enough, the red stone is marked with a spiral made of jagged lines. "That's Walker's symbol."

Lady Reaper swipes the scythe across the ground once more. Where the blade touches the earth, red filaments rise up.

"I summon strand magic," intones Lady Reaper. "Bring me Noras."

The many lines climb higher as they twist into the form of three women in white robes. All of them wear elaborate masks that contain a third blue eye.

Zelene gasps. "I've never seen anyone like this before. Are these angels?"

"No," replies Lady Reaper. "They're magical recreations of a particular ghoul, Nora. When she was alive, Nora was an inventor who designed this headdress to give her ghoulish self the illusion of three blue eyes."

"Grim told me about this," says Zelene. "They're clones."

Lady Reaper sniffs. "Grim talks to you too much." She glares at Zelene. "He's my husband."

Zelene stares at the floor. "Of course." Her cheeks burn red.

Huh. Methinks Zelene and the Grim Reaper are getting it on. *Talk about your bad ideas.*

"These automatons are made from strand magic." Lady Reaper sighs. "A friend imbued my scythe with the power to summon their forms. I call them Noras."

I narrow my eyes and think this through. "Let me get this straight." I tap my chin. "Walker created a scythe that makes magical copies of the same person, over and over?"

"That appears to be the case," says Lincoln.

"Wow. What I don't know about my honorary older brother is a lot."

And I have the sinking feeling it's only about to get worse.

18

LINCOLN

*A*s a demon hunter, I thought I'd seen every kind of being in the after-realms. That said, I've never seen anyone like these new ladies. And I'm not the only one.

Zelene's eyes widen with shock. "I don't understand. Who are they, really?"

"Think of them as statues brought to life," replies Lady Reaper. "As I said, you may call them the Noras."

Lady Reaper stares at the first Nora in line. "Go with her." The Nora steps over to stand beside Zelene.

"I'm not feeding this thing," says Zelene. "I'm short on gold as it is."

"Don't be daft," says Lady Reaper. "Magical beings don't need your food." As she speaks, Lady Reaper scoops a small packet from the tabletop. "This is the fresh poison that I promised you." Lady Reaper offers Zelene the packet. "Now, go kill your brother. Nora will help you. Once the Scala Heir is dead, come back and I'll murder your body."

Zelene doesn't move. "We had a deal. There's a prophecy."

"I'm aware," says Lady Reaper smoothly. She recites the prophecy aloud.

When there are two reapers, two scythes and two emerald ghosts, Then the Hallowed One shall appear, ignite the great tower and imprison all souls.

Zelene rolls her eyes. "I know that prophecy." She sets her fists on her hips and starts talking nonsense. "I'm the Hallowed One. That's why this is all wrong."

"Let's revisit the facts, shall we?" asks Lady Reaper. "You grew up with the scala heir, so your body took on some of his power to manipulate souls. Your ghost is green and—when combined with my scythe—you can direct spirits into ghost wells. When I perform the final ceremony, you'll take your final form."

"Then, I'll command souls?" asks Zelene.

Myla rolls her eyes. "Oh, honey. Moving souls is not the bonus you think it is. It's hard work and the concept makes certain people cuckoo. Last year, someone tried to sell jars of my farts at a county fair."

I do a double-take. "I hadn't heard that one."

"True story," replies Myla. "And according to this follower, my farts smell like orange sherbet, so there's that."

I stifle a grin. "Far be it from me to disagree."

"Every being will heed you one day, ghosts included," declares Lady Reaper. "If you do everything I tell you."

"But I'm the Hallowed One. I should take my final form now."

"Ugh." Myla bends her knees while looking upward. "Where do you get your ideas from, Zelene? Run, honey."

All this while, Lady Reaper's mouth has been slowly curling into an evil grin. "That poison won't stay potent forever."

I scan the ghoul's smile. "Why do I get the impression Lady Reaper thinks she's the real Hallowed One?"

"And let's not forget Grim," I state. "I wouldn't be surprised if he thinks the prophecy refers to him as well."

"Good point," I say.

Lady Reaper slams her scythe against the ground. The weapon turns back into a tall walking stick. "Why don't you run along now? The Nora will help you."

"She better," says Zelene.

"Oh, trust me," counters Lady Reaper. "She will. The original Nora did wonders for me and Grim."

I rub my neck and consider this last statement. "Do you think Walker knew this Nor—"

Suddenly, the entire tent glitches. It's like what we saw before with Hologram Winston, only now it's with a full-color illusion around us instead of just the earl.

When the tent comes back into focus again, Lady Reaper is at her table, crushing more herbs. Zelene stands before her. Today, the human wears a different dress and a triumphant smile. The Nora from before stands behind her.

"Is the deed done?" asks Lady Reaper.

"My brother is dead," answers Zelene in a flat tone. "Now, I want what's mine."

"Of course." Lady Reaper rises. "I always keep my promises."

Zelene rolls her eyes. "Finally."

Lady Reaper slams her walking stick against the ground. Once again, it transforms into a white scythe with a blood-red stone on the blade. Lady Reaper swipes the weapon high and brings it down. Based on the angle of descent, the blade is aimed for Zelene's throat.

I wince, knowing what will take place next.

Only that's not what happens. The scene glitches once more. The tent, Lady Reaper, Zelene… everything vanishes. Myla and I are back on the field. The crop circle is dark. Wind rolls across the many stalks of wheat. Insects buzz. Cloud churn across the night sky.

I glance at my wrist. "My watch has started up again."

"Someone stopped the simulation." Myla scans the field. "Any ideas?"

I've been a demon hunter since I was a child. I've learned to check every blade of grass and wisp of mist. Tonight, I catch the barest sign of a figure in the trees.

Lady Reaper has been watching us. No doubt about it. She's the one who stopped the simulation. A ghoul portal opens behind her. Moments later, she's gone.

For hours, Myla and I try to restart the simulation. Nothing works. Whatever Lady Reaper did, she ruined Winston's creation. When the skies lighten, we realize it's time to go home and get some sleep.

Tomorrow, we'll return to solving the riddle of the Hallowed One prophecy.

19

MYLA

*I*n my dream, I stand before the famous Castle Xanadu. It's a fuchsia palace that sits atop a cliff on the very edge between Purgatory and Heaven. The sky is always painted in shades of pink, orange and red... the perfect mix of hues for dawn and sunset. It's the nicest vacation spot in the after-realms... and it's one place I've never been.

Supposedly, Castle Xanadu is the perfect honeymoon vacation spot. Or so the commercials say. And since it doesn't involve any nunchuck throwing contests or disembowelment exhibitions, you'd think I wouldn't want to visit this place.

But my dreams take me here on a regular basis.

Birds soar by. The scent of spring flowers fills the air. My hair is in a very rare state I call frizz-free. Best of all, my husband stands beside me. I've made the fabulous decision to wrap my legs around his waist, so now we're pressed chest-to-chest as our mouths meet in a rough kiss.

Dream life is getting good.

Ring, ring...

A familiar sound echoes through the air. Not sure how I know this, but I'm certain that this noise is from my waking world. In other words, reality is breaking in on sexy dream time. Not okay.

Dream Lincoln's hands tighten at my waist. Our kiss deepens. There is no way I'm allowing reality to screw this up.

Ring, ring...

The noise continues. The pretty pink clouds lower until I'm surrounded in a rose-colored haze. Dream Lincoln turns blurry. The night vision fades.

I open my eyes.

Rolling over, I spy the rotary phone on my bedside table. I asked my honorary older brother, Walker, to install a *bat phone* for me. Since this is Purgatory, a telephone with a red light on it is considered advanced technology. This particular line only rings when anything goes wrong at the ghost towers.

I pick up the receiver. "Myla Lewis speaking."

Walker's deep voice reverberates in my ear. "This is an automated recording. There is a crisis at Ghost Tower Nine. Thank you for being the Great Scala." That last bit is Walker being sassy.

I groan, hang up and slide out of bed. My scala robes sit neatly folded on a bedside table. One advantage of being the Great Scala is that all I have to do is touch that fabric. The strands climb up my arm and around my torso. Within seconds, I'm now wearing a fitted white sheath.

Ring, ring...

Someone's calling again. Only this time, it's the phone in the kitchen. I slog off and pick up.

"Myla Lewis speaking."

"Honey, it's Mom."

Let the record show that no good conversations start off with one's mother identifying themselves to their own child. Making matters worse, there's no mistaking the quaver in my mother's voice. She is not in President Lewis mode. Mom's worried.

"What's wrong?"

"Nothing, Myla-la."

I frown. *There's that nickname. Myla-la.* Something is wrong... and it's of the massive variety.

"Mom, something is up."

"There's a minor glitch in ghost tower nine. I thought you might have gotten a call about it on your owl phone."

"It's a bat phone, but yes, I did."

One thing about living in Purgatory: knowledge of human trivia is sparse at best. Compared to most of my fellow citizens, Mom's a pop culture queen.

"There's nothing to worry about, honey."

The background, I hear my father call out. "Did she get a call from the magic rabbit?"

Side note: I have zero idea how my father registered the term 'bat phone' as a supernatural hare. But he's been alive since the dawn of time, so there's that.

"She did, Xav."

"Mom, can you ask Dad who he thinks called me, exactly?"

Mom relays the question. Dad's response sounds in the background. "A phouka, obviously."

That's not a demon, so I have zero idea what Dad is talking about. I make a note to look into it when I have some downtime. Which at this rate, is looking like the next century.

"Repeat back to me what I said," says Mom. "I want to be sure you understand."

"Ghost Tower nine. Minor glitch. Look up the definition of phouka later."

Mom's voice lowers to a hush. "I plan to do that last bit, too."

I smile. *Glad I'm not the only one without a working knowledge of phouka-ness.*

"Thanks for letting me know—I'll go back to sleep now." I yawn. "I was having the best dream."

Mom keeps up her conspiratorial whisper. "I understand, honey. I'm part lust demon, too." And on that note, she hangs up.

Her words seem to hang suspended in the air somewhere above the kitchen stove.

I understand, honey. I'm part lust demon, too.

So, Mom has sexy dreams. I never thought she didn't but… that's a thought to put romantic visions of Castle Xanadu on ice for a while.

Oh, well. There's still a half-box of Crunchy Sugar Bombs with my name on it.

After rummaging through the kitchen cabinets, I discover something truly depressing. There are only five little nuggets of Crunchy Sugar Bomb cereal left in the box. I'd complain about people who put back boxes that are essentially empty, however, I'm the culprit here.

I need to reclaim the mojo of this morning. *Time for coffee.*

"Ooooo!"

A ghostly voice echoes through the kitchen. It's not the first time, either. Most spirits are attracted to a ghost tower in the same way a glutton demon is drawn to an all-you-can-eat shrimp platter. Every once in a while, one gets drawn toward me instead.

I point toward the kitchen window. "Ghost tower four is that way."

"Oooooooooo!"

This time, the ghostly moan is accented by a green face pushing its way through the wall, followed by an equally green body. It's Zelene in her form as an emerald spirit. And if I thought she was a whiner in the past? Let's say she hasn't placed personal growth as a priority over the last one hundred and fifty years.

"I am the Hallowed One!" cries Zelene. "First, I gave my hair. Second, I gave my blood. Third, I gave my word. Now, I'm an emerald ghost. Soon it shall be my turn to rule!"

I scoop some coffee grounds into my favorite machine of the morning. "That's nice for you. Can you keep your voice down while reciting your resume? My husband is trying to sleep."

Lincoln shuffles into the kitchen. "I'm awake." He pauses. "Oh, hey Zelene." He comes over and kisses my cheek. "How's the ghost tower?"

"Mom says she and Dad have it handled. In other news, we're out of Frosted Sugar Bombs and Zelene is celebrating her own little Festivus, complete with a recital of grievances."

Lincoln pulls the muesli box from the cabinet. "Festivus. That's a human pop culture reference."

My heart lightens. "It's so nice to be understood."

None of this conversation puts any hitch in Zelene's giddy-up. "You!" She points to me. "I hid your memory of Cissy as the next emerald spirit. You shouldn't have recalled anything about meeting Lady Reaper."

"Oh, I recalled a little bit." I swap out the coffee decanter for a mug—that way, I can get the freshest brew possible.

Zelene's not letting this drop. "That shouldn't have happened!"

"I know right?" I smack my lips. "I'd say that in terms of your annual performance assessment as a villain, I'd give you a 'meet expectations.'"

If Zelene understands my sarcasm, she doesn't show it. Instead, the emerald ghost rounds on Lincoln. "And you! When Walker took you to the Dark Lands, I erased any recollection you had of the Grim Reaper."

By now, Lincoln is seated at the kitchen table and downing some muesli. "Of this, I am also aware. However, I'm tougher on grading. I'm giving you a 'doesn't meet expectations.' Plus, you're going on a work improvement plan, my dear."

Zelene's demeanor gets creepy-calm. "This is no laughing matter! Soon I'll tear out every soul in the after-realms, starting with you two."

"Unless?" I prompt. "You're not here to just ruin my breakfast. You must want something."

"I've waited too long to become the Hallowed One for everything to be ruined at the last moment. Here are my demands." Zelene looks to me. "Stay away from Cissy." She turns on Lincoln. "Leave Walker alone."

Without missing a beat, Lincoln and I reply in unison. "No."

Zelene starts howling at the top of her lungs. "Then your son will be the first soul I take!"

Don't get me wrong. Zelene in banshee mode is much more impressive than her self-righteous glowering. But things just went from slightly irritating to deadly serious.

This bitch just threatened my kid.

ZELENE

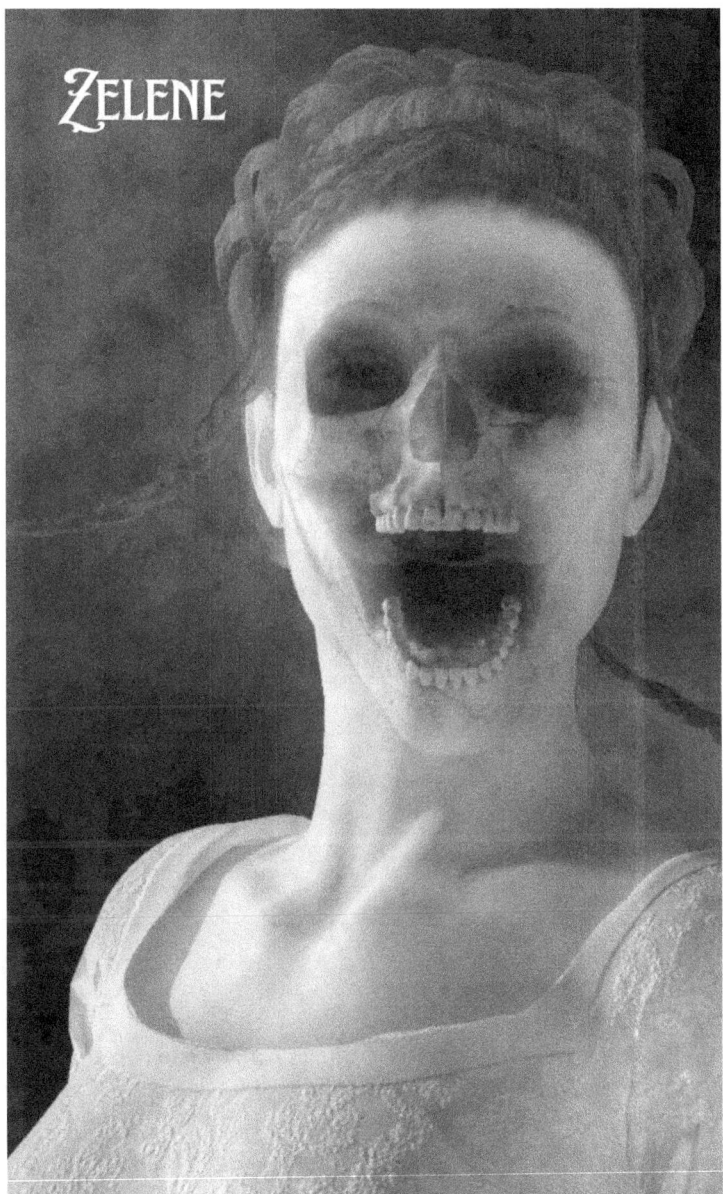
ZELENE

20

MYLA

As the Great Scala, I've had many ghosts insult me. Some even try to bite my neck, vampire-style. Others fight me about going to Heaven. (Yes, Heaven.) And I try to be an understanding demigoddess. After all, it's not easy being dead.

But now?

When it comes to Zelene, pure *momma bear rage* careens through my body. This booger-green blob of nasty is in for a shock. Because there's a big-ass line when it comes to my Great Scala-ness... And it's drawn into a circle around my kid.

I didn't realize Lincoln had walked into the kitchen while being armed. Yet as it turns out, my husband kept his baculum handy. He now ignites the two metal bars as a sword made of angelfire and rounds on Zelene.

"Maxon will be the first soul you take?" asks Lincoln slowly. "Care to elaborate?"

"I've waited too long to claim my rightful place as the Hallowed One! If you two start interfering, it may be years before we find another emerald spirit who's as strong as Cissy. I don't want to wait for Uther to grow up!"

"You know the name of Maxon's best friend?" I ask.

"Of course, I do," says Zelene. "What do you think the necro hunters have been doing all these years? Grim and Lady Reaper know everything that has to do with scalas. But I'm your friend on the inside. Let's create an alliance. Promise to speed my ascent to becoming the Hallowed One, and I'll make sure your son and his friend live."

Lincoln keeps his fire sword pointed at Zelene's heart. Ghosts can die, just like their mortal counterparts. And when you're dead as a ghost, that's the end of the story.

Lincoln glares at Zelene. "Have you been spying on my son?"

"I do what I want. My powers are unusual, and I've had more than a century to hone my skills as an emerald ghost. No one can stop me from doing whatever I want." Zelene reaches forward, setting her hands on the fiery blade.

Huh. At this point, Zelene should be howling in pain. Nothing like that is happening. I think back to the memory blocks that Zelene placed on me and Lincoln. We talked about it being some foreign kind of magic. And clearly, it is. All of which leads to a question.

Who knows what Zelene can do?

"How about we try to kill me, eh?" While still gripping the blade, Zelene steps forward. The tip of the fiery weapon burns just above the emerald ghost's heart.

Zelene inches closer to Lincoln. With each tiny movement, the blade pierces more deeply into her ghostly body. Zelene doesn't scream. And she also shows no sign of pain.

"You can't kill me," says Zelene through a smile. "Only serve me."

"Uh-uh-uh." I tick my pointer finger from side to side. "Someone needs a supernatural time out."

Closing my eyes, I reach out to my igni.

I need you, little ones.

In my mind, I know the world didn't suddenly turn into a black hole. That's certainly how it feels, though. Everything in the room becomes heavy with shadows. There's no sign of Zelene, let alone Lincoln. My igni materialize nearby. Like before, their little bodies appear as tiny black holes. The igni swirl into a column before congealing into the shape of a faceless woman.

A living shadow.

She reaches toward me. "The darkness surrounds me..." The voice is familiar and strange, all at once.

I force my eyes shut once more.

End this, my children.

The igni vanish on my command. Instantly, the room brightens. I look over to see Zelene is still skewered on Lincoln's sword. If my husband is shocked by this turn of events, he doesn't show it.

I blink three times, trying to process what just happened. I summoned my igni... the world stopped... and a living shadow appeared while saying *the darkness surrounds me.*

The happened once before, back when Lincoln and I were in the library. The magic behind Zelene and the Reapers is certainly more powerful than I expected. I've never come across anything like this before. Even worse, it may affect my igni.

Zelene grins. "Think about my offer. Help me or there will be consequences." She walks the full way along Lincoln's sword before stepping right through my husband. After that, she vanishes.

Lincoln extinguishes his baculum. "Not only do I now smell like mothballs, but we have a rogue magic user on our hands."

"You can shower first, no contest."

Lincoln leans against the counter, his eyes unfocused in thought. "Zelene has been planning this for over a century. Clearly, she thinks she can win."

"Zelene's got a plan, that's for certain." I close my eyes and think through everything that just happened. "I don't think she wants to hurt Maxon... at least, not right now. Zelene said it herself—she needs Maxon and Uther to grow up before she can do anything."

Lincoln's mouth thins to a determined line. "I still don't like it."

"Same here. Lady Reaper is scheming with Cissy... Zelene is trying to manipulate us... and who knows what the Grim Reaper is up to?"

Lincoln grips the edge of the counter behind him with such force, the bare muscles on his arms and chest contract. "My heart wants to grab Maxon and find someplace where he'll be safe from everything."

"And my heart..." I try to come up with something heroic to say. *I got nothing.* "Honestly? At this point, I want to find a way to melt Zelene into a big puddle of snot."

"Looks like our work is cut out for us." Lincoln meets my gaze and smiles. "I need to find a certain undead friend. Chances are, I'll find the Grim Reaper wherever I find Walker."

"And while you're at it, I'll protect Cissy while making Lady Reaper's life Hell." I sniff and pat under my eyes. "Torturing ghouls again. It'll just like High School."

"We'll need more supplies," offers Lincoln.

"Plus, we have to activate the tracker we placed on Walker."

"True, and that means a trip to Antrum."

"I've been contemplating travel as well. Did I tell you how Zelene interrupted a pretty good sex dream?"

"Are we back at Castle Xanadu again?"

"We are. It's a little corny, but I think my inner lust demon is going through a sappy phase."

"No matter what the phase, I'm a fan of that particular power." Lincoln steps toward the door and pauses. "I'm assuming our next stop is Antrum, correct?"

"I think so. My parents are playing it down about the ghost towers, but I think they've got a mini-disaster on their hands. Mom's already super anxious. If we tell her about the Hallowed One prophecy, she might be so upset, she could make mistakes while fixing the ghost towers."

Lincoln nods. "Besides, if we brought your parents up to speed, they'd tell us to do what we're already doing. We need to bring Octavia up to speed, grab some new supplies, and get a location on Walker. And of course, we must check on our son. Our dance card is officially rather full."

"One final thing? You really do need to shower. I can smell the mothballs from here."

Lincoln chuckles. "You're just jealous that Zelene likes me better."

"All the more reason for me to crush her like a bug when the time comes."

Lincoln winks. "I only hope I'm there to see it."

I grin. "That makes two of us."

MYLA

A half-hour later, Lincoln and I march toward the Purgatory pulpitum. Usually, this process involves shouldering our way through a crowd of scala fans.

On our last visit, there weren't too many folks here—only a handful of locals living in tents and one little girl.

Which brings us to today. *Yipes.*

This time, the tents are cleared out. The ground's swept clean. Someone even towed away the port-a-potties that had taken up residence on the western side of the courtyard. One quasi woman stands nearby. She sports an A-line dress, short heels and the kind of helmet-style updo that requires at least one can of hairspray.

It's Carol Cheevers, investigative journalist for Purgatory's Channel Two News. Or, as she calls herself, *Carol Cheevers, Private Eye LIVE.* And yes, she says that last word with extra gusto. It's her catch phrase.

Lincoln deftly moves to stand between me and Carol Cheevers. We both pick up the pace. Once we're inside the pulpitum, Zeke's guard buddies will keep Carol out.

Carol does an end-run around Lincoln so she now walks beside me. She holds a small notebook and pen.

In moments like these, I'm super happy that Purgatory has crap for technology. I don't know what I'd do if I were on Earth where everyone has cell phones.

"Carol Cheevers, Private Eye LIVE. May I speak with you, Myla?"

I arch my right brow. This is a singular move that says, *hey now.* I've been working on it in my spare time. "Did you say Myla?"

"Then, Miss Lewis."

"Her name is Mrs The Queen," offers Lincoln.

Carol is totally stumped by this statement. Lincoln rarely talks in Purgatory, so there's that. Also, Mrs the Queen is a bit of an in-joke. It may take a while for her to get it, if at all. And with every passing second, we're closing in on our destination.

Half-way to the pulpitum.

"What do you mean? No wait, I get it." Carol scribbles on her pad. "You two run that secret cabal of demon hunters."

Secret cabal of demon hunters. Technically, that's an accurate description of the thrax. In actual practice, it's the kind of language that makes my people start digging bunkers in their backyards... just in case *Lincoln the Demon Hunter* comes after their family.

Let the record show that Lincoln and I are almost jogging now.

Three-quarters of the way there.

"Do you have any comment about Lady Reaper's announcement?" asks Carol.

I pause. "Announcement?"

"Yes, she's accelerating the timescale for the ghoul carnival. Everything starts tomorrow."

"Um. Oh. That's nice. And it explains where everyone is today. I was starting to wonder." *And at this point, that's really all I've got.*

"Lady Reaper was interviewed last night on my show, Carol Cheevers, Private Eye LIVE."

Lincoln nods toward the pulpitum door. The meaning is clear: *let's keep moving.*

We resume our speed-march to the pulpitum.

"Lady Reaper said and I quote." Carol keeps walking while reading from her notebook. *"Myla Lewis has only been playing at being ill. In truth, the Not-So-Great Scala been spying on me."*

I have to admit, Carol nails Lady Reaper's haughty and high-pitched voice.

Carol continues reading from her notebooks and displaying her skills for a dead-on Lady Reaper impression. *"Last night, I found Myla*

Lewis at a supernatural power pit with her demon-hunting husband. They were trying to ruin the ghoul carnival! To preserve anything of this festival, I had to move the start date up to Wednesday." Carol looks up. "That's tomorrow."

Unholy Hell. Lincoln did see Lady Reaper after the ghost well closed down. Looks like someone's been a busy little bee since then. It can't be easy to move a whole carnival up a month.

Lady Reaper is better than I thought.

While Carol flips through more pages, I keep my gaze locked on the ground. *Don't make eye contact. Pretend you don't hear her.* It's not my best plan, but it's only a few yards to the Pulpitum entrance.

Carol scribbles on her notepad. "Myla Lewis didn't know what to say when confronted with her treachery." Carol refocuses on me once more. "Last question. Are you invited to the wedding Saturday?"

Side note: I always wear little open-toed sandals with my scala robes. These things catch on the street even when I'm not speed-walking over cobblestones.

But after getting the news that Cissy is getting married in four freaking days?

My sandal gets caught and I tumble forward. Thankfully, Lincoln swoops over to grab my waist and prevent a full fall.

Carol returns to writing in her notebook. "Myla Lewis was so shocked to learn she wasn't invited to the upcoming wedding, she almost fell over." She snaps her notebook shut. "Got it!"

With that, Carol Cheevers strolls away. My tail sticks up its arrowhead end. Then it carefully curls the bottom points of the triangle-bottom toward each other. It's my tail's version of a certain nasty hand gesture.

I pat the end. "Good job, boy." I focus on Lincoln. "Cissy didn't call me. Do you think it's true?"

"Look to your right," whispers Lincoln.

I glance in that direction. From the depths of the pulpitum, the infamous Brad-Chad-Tad-Other Tad coalition walk toward us. And the way their eyes are alight? It's the same look I get when I find a half-eaten demon bar under the couch.

As Lincoln and I step into the pulpitum, the guys all start talking at once:

"Is it true you faked being sick?"

"Why would you try to ruin Lady Reaper's carnival?"

"Does Zeke know you aren't going to the wedding?"

"Gentlemen." Lincoln does that thing where he goes right into king-mode. My husband raises his right hand. All the guards go silent. "My wife and I are here to use the pulpitum. That is all."

The guys go silent. Lincoln offers me his arm. Together, we step onto the transfer platform. There's the usual *blah blah blah* about the fact that our destination is Arx Hall in Antrum.

Lincoln does the countdown.

We hurtle through the earth.

And at last, I hit the final page of a virtual book I shall forever call *Myla's No Good Very Bad Trip to the Pulpitum*.

ARX HALL

22

LINCOLN

A short ride later, Myla and I arrive on the pulpitum platform inside Arx Hall.

Mother awaits us. As always, Octavia looks prim and inscrutable in her black velvet gown. Her gray hair is swept back into a beat chignon. "Greetings, children." She focuses on me. "Considering how you're in battle armor, perhaps we should chat in my personal quarters? It's more private there."

"Perfect," I state. "We've much to tell you. It's been a busy few days."

"Isn't it always?" She turns and starts to speed-march toward her personal quarters. Myla and I follow.

"Where's Maxon?" I ask.

"At practice," explains Octavia. "He and his friends don't get breaks simply because there are unexpected guests."

I can't help but grin. "I would expect nothing else."

Mother pauses by a white door. "Ah, here we are."

I do a double-take. "This is new. Why move your quarters?"

"I wanted something out of the hustle and bustle of the main palace."

If Mother thinks that will end the conversation, she's wrong. "And does this change have anything to do with the thrax who's been walking behind us all this time?"

Mother blinks innocently. "I don't know who you mean."

Myla turns around. "Oh, there he is. Hello, guy! You're so stealthy, I didn't know you were there." Myla rounds on Octavia. "I think Lincoln's talking about the warrior in golden armor."

"Ah." Octavia waves her hand dismissively. "That's just my new bodyguard. Children, this is Andalus." In reply, Andalus gives us the barest of nods.

It's not logical, but I instantly hate him.

"Andalus is from the House of Moriaen," continues Mother. "You've heard of them, I assume?"

"They're the house of the Moorish knight from King Arthur's court," I reply. And they're well-respected warriors. A senior member of Moriaen would do an excellent job at protecting Mother. Somehow, I'm not able to verbalize that level of detail right now. My illogical hatred at the idea of Mother dating is still getting in the way.

"King Arthur's not all he's cracked up to be," offers Myla. "Just saying."

"I can assure you," intones Octavia. "Andalus is everything one can expect from a true knight."

These words seem to be some kind of signal between them. Andalus steps up to open the door for us. I catch a distinctive scent from him.

"Honey and cedar," I state. "What a unique cologne you wear, Andalus." I look to Mother. "Isn't that the scent I caught before?"

"I don't know what you're talking about." Octavia turns and marches into the room.

Now that we're close up, I get a better look at Andalus. His golden armor is flawless. He's got dark hair, ebony skin and the determined look of a true knight.

"Although Mother hired you, I remain king," I state. "I'll have your background checked carefully."

"Of course," says Andalus.

With that settled, I should walk into Mother's chambers. For some reason, I'm not going anywhere. Fresh jolts of protective energy course through me, along with many questions.

Who is this fellow?

How did he meet Mother?

What does he want from her?

Myla takes my hand. The warmth of her touch snaps me back to the reason we came here: Maxon, Cissy, and that damnable prophecy. Turning away from Andalus, Myla and I enter Mother's new audience chamber. Andalus closes the door behind us.

Once inside, I find the room to be decorated entirely in white, from the long velvet curtains to the woven rugs and wall tapestries. Octavia sits on the settee. Myla and I take the couch opposite her.

Speaking of Myla, my wife is biting her lips together, which means she wants to say something but is forcibly stopping herself. Octavia has no such restraint.

Mother straightens the folds of her black gown. "I know you have comments, my son."

I nod. "Andalus seems… competent."

"Quite," says Octavia. Myla pretends to cough, but I suspect my wife is hiding laughter.

"How old is he?" I ask.

"Oh, about ninety-seven," replies Mother.

I'm a king. Father. Husband. Warrior. And my father passed away years ago. Now, it appears that Mother may have started dating again. That shouldn't be a big deal. Still, my defensive instincts stay on overdrive.

"Ninety-seven," I repeat. "That seems young."

"Humans wouldn't say so." Mother crosses her ankles and sets her feet under the couch. It's her way of saying, *let's change the subject.* And in this case, Mother's not wrong.

"But you aren't here to chat about my private life," adds Octavia.

Part of me still worries that my mother isn't safe. That said, more of me knows that Octavia's far better able to determine who should serve as her guard. Although, Mother always blindly followed Father, and that didn't turn out too well.

"I can guess what you're thinking," says Mother.

"Can you?" I ask. "Guess away."

"I had a blind spot. That's gone now, at least from a romantic perspective." Octavia's mouth rounds into a gentle smile. She means that she still has a blind spot for her family: me. Myla. Maxon. But not from anyone she might spend time with.

It's still hard to move on, though.

Myla gently rests her hand upon mine. Once again, my wife's touch helps me focus. "Yes, we're here about a number of things," I state.

Myla counts off our troubles. "There are Reapers, Weavers, ghost wells, Cissy, Walker, some ghoul prophecy about a Hallowed One, and this nasty green ghost who threatened Maxon."

"Many things are on the game board," I state. "But only one person is moving the pieces: Regina Reaper. Although I suspect her husband Grim is involved as well."

"Ah," intones Octavia. "Tell me everything."

23

MYLA

*I*t takes a while for Myla and I to explain our recent adventures. Mother asks regular questions and keeps her features level. In my heart, I know she's worried about Maxon... as well as the rest of the after-realms. But you wouldn't know that by looking at her.

After a while, Mother smoothes the folds of her skirt again. "I believe I understand the situation well enough. And based on my own knowledge, I may be able to fill in some gaps. How about I start from the beginning?"

"Please do," I say.

"The Dark Lands were founded by a ghoul named EL1. Everyone calls him Eli."

"Wow, when you start from the beginning, you aren't kidding," says Myla. "Nicely done."

"Thank you." Mother continues. "First and foremost, Eli was an engineer. He founded two laboratories in the Dark Lands, one on top of the other. The rest of the ghoul realm was essentially built up around this lab. And it's rumored that it was during these early days that Eli and the archangel Aquila were married."

"We saw a statue of Eli in Opus X," says Myla. "Normally, ghouls aren't what I'd consider to be attractive. That said, Eli looked to be one *oil-down* short of a body-building competition."

Octavia nods. "Precisely. Anyone would understand why Aquila would have fallen for Eli." Mother shoots a look at the door. I can't help but wonder if she's contemplating Andalus. I don't need to tumble down that *rabbit hole of maternal confusion* again.

"What happened next?" I prompt.

"Ah." Mother straightens her back, which is her way of returning her focus. "Earth was young in those days. Populations were sparse. Ghosts would meander for years before eventually stumbling into Purgatory. And that worked fine for a while. Then, human numbers exploded. Earth became overrun with wandering ghosts."

"I learned about this in school," says Myla. "This is why the first ghost wells were built."

"Yes," confirms Octavia, "Eli took pity on humanity. He was the one who designed the ghost wells. Every so often, the Great Scala would visit Earth and move the souls."

Myla fidgets with one cuff on her scala robes. "I saw a painting in Opus X. It showed Eli holding these golden threads. Strand magic. Those are used for many things."

"Quite." I nod. "By my count, strand magic is used to form the ghost wells, Lady Reaper's scythe, your scala robes, Grim's face, the necro hunters and the Noras. Did I miss anything?"

"Not that I can think of," replies Myla. "That's a lot of stuff, though. How could stand magic stay hidden for so long?"

"It wasn't hidden," I state. "It wasn't given proper attention." A weight of guilt settles onto my shoulders. "There's a difference."

A look flashes across Octavia's face. Could that be regret? It's possible, but the expression is gone too quickly to be certain.

"We'll get to that in a moment," says Mother. "For now, let's circle back to Eli. As I said before, Eli's laboratory grew over the years. The upper part was called the Laboratory of Light. These floors were open to the public. The underground section was the Laboratory of Darkness."

"Darkness," I say, my voice low. "There's that word again."

"What does Myla mean?" asks Octavia.

"Myla's igni have been creating visions of a woman who says, the darkness surrounds me. Do you think it's this lab?"

"Anything is possible," says Octavia. "Although you can't swing an undead cat in ghoul country without hitting something called the darkness."

I lean back on the couch and kick out my feet. "That's exactly what I was saying."

"I'll continue with my tale," states Octavia. "Perhaps that will help narrow down which darkness your igni are talking about. As I stated previously, Eli founded the Laboratory of Light and the Laboratory of Darkness. And the ghouls built up a metal city around him. And then, they added to that metropolis, making it stretch higher and higher. Eli's structures were the only place the ghouls wouldn't build upon. Today, those labs exist at the bottom of a deep pit called the Abyss."

Memories of my vision return. "The darkness surrounds me... maybe were warning me about this secret lab."

"I wouldn't be surprised," says Octavia. "Both the Grim Reaper and Walker worked with Eli. Grim served in the Laboratory of Darkness. Walker took the Laboratory of Light."

Lincoln shakes his head. "Where did you learn all this?"

"It wasn't easy, I'll tell you that," says Octavia. "However good my sources may be, they do have their limits. From this point on, my information becomes rather vague. Sometime after Eli founded his labs, the prophecy of the Hallowed One came into being."

I lean back and try to process this news. It isn't easy. I always realized that Walker had his own secret life as an engineer in the Dark Lands. If anything, I pictured him working alone in a room. But it makes sense that someone like Eli would teach him... or a ghoul such as Grim might befriend him.

Walker, what have you gotten yourself into?

LINCOLN

$\mathcal{M}$y mind sorts through everything I've learned over the last few days. New questions appear. I refocus on Mother. "Does the name Nora mean anything to you?"

Mother shakes her head. "I'm afraid not."

"What about Eli?" asks Myla. "Do you know what happened to him?"

"Most sources say he's dead," answers Octavia. "No one knows his fate for certain. He certainly hasn't been seen in centuries."

"And the laboratories?" I ask.

"That's also rather vague. Both the Laboratories of Light and Darkness are closed down now. Although, even if they were still in operation, we'd have no way of knowing. The Abyss has become a refuge for every dimension-hopping god or goddess who wishes to stay in our reality and cause trouble. The Oligarchy sealed it off years ago."

A chilly sense of foreboding creeps up my back. "Myla and I placed a tracker charm on Walker. We think his location may help us in our fight against the Reapers. We need a reading board."

"I have one." Octavia rises to cross the room. After opening a few drawers, she comes back with what looks like a simple square of pale wood. "Who placed the charm on Walker?"

"I did." Octavia offers me the board. I set the wooden tile onto my lap, then place my palm on top. A small puff of purple smoke erupts from the board. I smile. This is a spell from the house of Striga. They love theatrics.

Tense seconds pass as we wait for the enchanted board to find Walker. At last, a tiny dot appears on the board's surface. It's the same shape and color as the tracker I placed on Walker.

I exhale. *It's working.*

More little spots appear until there are enough to form words. I read the results aloud.

TARGET LOCATIONS
First. Depart Arx Hall sub-basement pulpitum
Second. Arrive in lookout tower by the Abyss
Third. Arrive in Oligarchy dungeons
Current location is Oligarchy dungeons

"If my guess is right," I begin. "Walker wants to reach the old laboratories in the Abyss."

"But…" adds Myla. "My honorary older brother got *stuck* in the dungeons." Myla makes little finger quotes as she says the word *stuck*. And I understand what she means. Walker doesn't go anywhere without a plan. If he's in the dungeons, there's a reason.

"The Abyss can't be accessed directly," says Mother. "Walker must know a back door through those dungeon cells."

"I plan to follow Walker," I state. "MI've never heard of a look-0out tower station in the Dark Lands. Walker must have hard-wired it in."

"And while Lincoln does his thing in the Dark Lands, I'll protect Cissy," adds Myla. "Based on what we saw with Zelene, four ceremonies are coming up." She counts them off on her fingers. "The first ceremony requires some of Cissy's hair. The second ritual needs some of my bestie's blood. On the third day, Cissy must agree to something. And on the fourth?"

I answer my wife's question. "That's when Lady Reaper kills Cissy's physical form with her scythe."

"And on my bestie's wedding day." Myla's eyes flare red with rage. "Not on my watch."

Mother lifts her chin. "It appears that this Lady Reaper person is focused on capturing Cissy's soul. If she's not successful, she may come after Maxon and Uther." Octavia sighs. "Sadly, we don't have any way to stop strand magic. It's a new form that we haven't studied much. Therefore, in this case, the best defense is a good offense." Mother looks to my wife.

"Trust me," says Myla. "Whatever happens, Lady Reaper and Zelene are out of the *scala heir and bestie* business."

"I'll also place extra guards on Maxon and Uther, just in case." Octavia looks to me. "Do you need any help going after Walker?"

"Whatever I need is in the demon patrol prep room," I reply.

"Which reminds me—the latest version of body armor just arrived," says Octavia. "It may be helpful."

"Thank you." Another question appears. I round on Mother. "Strand magic and ghost wells are new to us. Why become an expert?"

Octavia takes in a long and shaky breath. "Weeks ago, Maxon showed me that book about the Earl of Minos. Ever since then, I've been gathering information for this day."

I tilt my head and consider. "Why not tell me as much?"

Octavia grips her hands at her waistline. "You see, you weren't the only one the Earl of Minos approached. He came to me as well. I refused him because I didn't wish to anger Aldred or disappoint your father. I was so blinded..." Octavia pats under her eyes. For Mother, that's a major show of emotion.

"Please," I state. "I could have checked out the ghost well, too."

"You were a child. I was the parent. And sadly, I was also trapped in a cycle of making mistakes with unexpected consequences. Now, my grandson is at risk. My lovely Myla faces a threat to her existence as the Great Scala. And the ghouls may imprison every last soul in existence."

It's a somber moment. And my wife, in classic fashion, chooses this second to pump her fist in the air and break the tension. "That's it! Lady Reaper won't suspect that we know."

Octavia's eyes glisten with held-in tears. "Know what, my dear?"

"As you said, Lady Reaper wants to entrap all souls. That's a whoooole lot of spirits. She'll need a mammoth place to store them...

as in, the mutha of all ghost towers. If we find that, we'll be one step ahead."

"Perhaps Lady Reaper hasn't considered how to store every last ghost in the after-realms," offers Octavia.

"Oh, no-no-no," says Myla. "You haven't met Lady Reaper. She's a scheme-asaurus. And she's been at this for more than one hundred and fifty years. There's no way she'd go through the trouble of tricking Cissy into this spell... then gain the power to imprison every last soul... and not have a place to put those ghosts."

I rub my neck and consider this insight. "I believe I might know where one could find that kind of tower." I shoot Myla a sideways glance. "Do you?"

"Hells, yeah. In Eli's laboratory. After all, that guy built the first ghost wells, for crying out loud."

Octavia smiles, but there's no joy in the expression. "I'm glad I was able to help you, even if this aid is coming a bit late."

"Both of you." Myla points between me and Mother. "This guilt fiesta needs to stop." She sets her palms on either side of her head and makes the kind of motion I've seen humans do when directing planes on a runway. "Focus. The problem is the Reapers. They made this situation. And they will get their asses kicked!"

Mom and I share a smile. This time, it's genuine.

"One last thing," says Octavia. "I'm sure you wish to see your son before leaving. Maxon is in the royal gymnasium, running through battle moves with his friends. I'd appreciate it if you'd observe him from one of the hidden passages. If Maxon figures out you two are on an adventure, he'll find a way to sneak out and help you."

"Agreed," says Lincoln. "And I know just the passage we can use to watch without being detected."

"Thank you." Octavia rises. "It seems we all have our respective tasks. I'll let you take your leave."

Myla's tail swings out to point between Myla, me and Mother. The question is there. *What about my job?*

I address Myla's tail directly. "You have the very important task of protecting Myla."

In reply, Myla's tail bobs happily before going to hang out around her ankle.

"Does that mean we're all ready to go?" asks Octavia smoothly. "I'm still learning to speak tail."

"It does," confirms Myla.

And who are we to disagree with the tail?

25

MYLA

There's something about being with Octavia that makes me feel protected and loved. After a few minutes, I'm ready for a binky and a nap.

Then, our time together is over.

As Octavia steps toward the exit, a pang of sadness moves through me. She reaches the door and pauses. "I'd rather we skipped farewells this time."

"That's fine," I say.

"Understood," adds Lincoln.

She steps out and is gone. Something inside me feels hollow and empty. But that void quickly gets filled up with a heady mixture of rage and adrenaline.

Demon patrol goodies, here we come!

Minutes later, Lincoln and I are in the demon patrol prep chamber, gathering up a selection of the best charms. I set mine into a leather satchel. There's a new design of body armor where Lincoln can store even more stuff in hidden pockets.

And although I realize the world may be about to end and this is all very serious and waah waah waah... I am also part lust demon.

And my husband looks ripped in his new body armor. Wide shoulders. Trim waist. Muscles everywhere. Tasty.

Once we're geared up, Lincoln and I enter one of the many secret passages that wind through Arx Hall. We navigate a labyrinth of narrow wooden hallways.

And we hear Maxon before seeing him.

My son's familiar voice echoes through the dusty passage. "Positions one, four, nine, eight!" A long pause follows. "Come on, Ty. That last pose wasn't anything like position eight."

Excitement churns through me. Up ahead, there's a thin break in the wall. Lincoln and I pause before the hole.

Looking through, I find the familiar view of the royal gymnasium. There's a small practice floor surrounded by levels of balconies. On test days, those viewing seats are all filled with nobles. For now, it's just Maxon along and his friends Ty, Nizam, Raj and Uther. All of them wear black tunics and cotton pants. Each holds a wooden sword in their right hand.

Ty is a bony kid with long braids. As a member of the house of Striga, Ty's much more comfortable casting spells than wielding swords. All of which explains why Ty tosses his practice weapon onto the mat. "How many times do I have to do position eight?"

Uther's a barrel-chested kid with mismatched eyes and yellow hair. "Yeah, we're good enough."

Maxon swings his wooden sword back and forth. He's considering how to handle this next.

Truth is, it may be 'good enough' for Maxon's friends to screw up at the next warrior trials. But this is Maxon's first time showing his leadership skills to the nobles. If it all goes wrong, it won't be the end of the world. But Maxon's eleven. At that age, it can certainly feel that way.

My arms ache to hold my son. A dark thought appears. Grim and Regina Reaper have been stalking us for years. Lincoln and I barely know anything about them. What if we don't succeed?

I shake my head. *Wondering if I can accomplish a mission is a sure path to failure.*

Over in the gymnasium, Maxon narrows his eyes. "G is coming

here in thirty minutes," he announces. "She wants to see this sequence of battle moves. If anyone thinks they've got it down, they can go hang out in the balconies while the rest of us practice."

At these words, all the color fades from Ty's tanned face. "Oh, the Queen Emeritus is stopping by? I can run the moves again, no problem."

I can't help but smile my face off. Maxon isn't berating his friends into doing their exercises, but he's set up Octavia as the baddie. That's pretty darned clever.

I look to Lincoln. Sure enough, my husband is grinning as well. I shoot him a thumbs-up.

Lincoln nods and wraps his arm around my waist. I lean my head against his shoulder. Inside the gymnasium, Maxon and his friends run through the sequence again.

They're getting better.

Lincoln gives my shoulder a squeeze. I know what the movement means, because I'm thinking the same thing.

Time to go.

As we leave Maxon behind, my head gets a little woozy. I love having my guys around. Going away solo feels wrong. There's nothing else for it. Lady Reaper's punched up the timeframe. We must split up to get everything done.

In no time, Lincoln and I reach Arx Hall's main pulpitum station. My trip to Purgatory is official, so this is the go-to platform. By contrast, Lincoln's secret jaunt to the Dark Lands will launch from the sub-basement. No one outside of Octavia and her ally in transfer central will know.

I march on the platform and give my destination to transfer central. Lincoln swoops up to wrap me in a deep embrace. Feeling his touch, my lust demon roars to life.

"This is so embarrassing," I state.

"Really? Why?"

"You look really hot in that new armor and now you have to go hang with ghouls. It isn't fair."

Lincoln pulls me in for a fierce, toe-curling kiss. He steps away and mouths one word. *Soon.*

I wink and give the countdown. The pulpitum kicks to life, sending me hurtling upward.

Back to Purgatory again.

26

LINCOLN

*M*yla may be gone, but my mind replays our last moments together.

My wife stands at the end of the passage. The alcove's curved ceiling frames her like a painting. She could be a version of Botticelli's Birth of Venus, only without a half shell and including both clothing and a tail.

A grid covers Myla's frame. It's one of the last steps before the platform takes my wife away.

Myla gives the countdown. "Three, two, one..."

A flash of light fills the entire hallway with brightness, followed by a flurry of movement as the platform zooms up through the ceiling.

Inhaling deeply, I catch the trace of her scent on the air. *Cinnamon and sunshine.*

I turn away from the pulpitum.

If I head toward the left-hand passage, I can return to the royal gymnasium. Maxon is still in battle practice with his buddies. My heart warms to picture him going through the battle poses with his friends.

However, if I head toward the right-hand hallway, I'll reach a staircase that winds into a sub-basement. The chamber there holds the hidden pulpitum that Walker used to reach the Abyss.

I take the right-hand passage.

One thing about being king—people do tend to track where

you're going. In this case, I need to hide my destination from onlookers, so I take a roundabout route to the sub-basement.

Which brings me to where I am now: in a snug room made of rough-hewn rock. Stacks of wooden chests dot the floor. Cobwebs dangle from the ceiling.

Kneeling, I check the pattern of dust on the floor. Sure enough., it hides the outline of the metal transport disc in the floor. As I step on, a familiar—*if smaller*—grid of light scans me from head to toe.

"Hello, your Majesty." It's a voice that's young, female and serious. This is Sita, one of Octavia's most trusted agents at transfer central.

"Hello, Sita. I assume Octavia informed you of my trip."

"Yes, I'm at a console where no one can hear or see me. Where in the Dark Lands would you like to go?"

"Send me to the Abyss, please."

"Would that be marked in the system as 'Walker's secret place,' by any chance?"

"Yes, that's my destination."

"As you command, your Majesty. On your countdown."

"Three, two, one…"

After a brief ride, the pulpitum comes to a smooth stop. I find myself in the top room of a tall tower made entirely of metal. The structure is hexagon in shape. Eight square windows look out over the Dark Lands.

And I can't believe what I see.

The view is one solid cityscape. Before, I always thought the ghouls liked cramming their population into layered metal buildings. Now, I'm not so sure.

Could the Oligarchy want their ghouls to settle across the after-realms? It's possible.

As I step around the tower, I spy a dramatic change in the landscape below. The sight is so unexpected, it takes my breath away. Far below me, a massive tunnel leads down into darkness.

The Abyss.

A low hum sounds as a ghoul portal opens behind me. Turning around, I find a new trio of bureaucrats waiting. All of them wear long black robes with the hoods pulled low.

"The Oligarchy have decreed that the Abyss is off limits," says one.

"Coming here is forbidden," adds another.

"Per official decree, you must wait in the Oligarchy's dungeons until your crime is reviewed and punished," states a third.

I picture the tracking information we found in Antrum. Walker's in the Oligarchy dungeons. How *perfect*.

"If that's the official decree, then you better take me to the dungeons right away."

And as I say these words, I work very hard not to smile.

THE ABYSS

MYLA

I'm starting to wonder if Brad-Chad-Tad-Other Tad ever go home.

Here's why: All four of them are waiting at the pulpitum when I return to Purgatory. A fresh round of questions hit me as I step off the platform.

"Where's Lincoln?" asks Tad.

"Is he staying with Zeke in the Dark Lands?" That's Chad.

"Why didn't Cissy invite you to her wedding?" Brad.

"Is it true you're jealous of Lady Reaper?" Other Tad.

All of them open their mouths, ready for another round of questions. I raise my hand. "Guys, I have an announcement to make."

In this moment, I could give an eloquent speech about what it means to hold the responsibility for sorting souls. I'd be so eloquent, Brad-Chad-Tad-Other Tad would get all teary-eyed and declare that they were wrong to be distracted by the bright shiny object that is Lady Reaper.

But I suck at speeches. And I knew Brad-Chad-Tad-Other Tad back in high school. If I spend more than two minutes with them, I feel like I'm back at the loser table during lunch.

So, I tell a minor fib.

"Guys, I'm cramping something awful." And I set the back of my hand against my forehead. *Go big or go home.* "Do any of you know where I can find a tampon?"

And does the Brad-Chad-Tad-Other Tad complex run away? *Yes, they do.*

And do I enjoy that sight? *Only a lot.*

In my mind, I have to deal with the cramps, so I should be able to leverage this pain in order to escape awkward situations.

That's my story and I'm sticking to it.

With Lincoln and Maxon gone, I stop by Limbo Pizza and get myself two large meat lover pies. Sadly, it's no fun to eat them without Lincoln to warn me about preservatives. Or Maxon nearby to fight me for the last slice.

I call my parents, but they try so hard to act like they have time to talk to me, I can't keep them on the line. Clearly, Mom and Dad are still dealing some ghost tower problems.

Next stop: the couch.

I fire up the television. Sadly, all the channels drone on about tomorrow's opening ceremonies for the ghoul carnival. There's also a little chatter about Cissy's wedding and tons of praise for Lady Reaper.

And because I'm a glutton for punishment, I watch Carol Cheevers interview my new nemesis. For today's television appearance, Ms Reaper sports a red gown with a super tiny hat.

Carol launches into the interview."Lady Reaper, you helped us the last time the Great Scala fell ill," says Carol.

"Of course."

As I jam another slice of pizza in my head, my thoughts circle back to Lady Reaper's teensy weensy hat. What keeps it in place? Super glue? Evil magic? It's a puzzle.

"Are you here to save the scala again?" asks Carol.

I chuck a greasy napkin at the television screen. "Bite me, Carol!"

Lady Reaper sighs. "I just want to do what's best for Senator Frederickson as well as the quasi people. That said, the ghoul carnival will show everyone what life would be like if I ran soul processing."

Carol looks directly into the camera. "So, there you have it. A new day may be dawning in Purgatory. And I'll see *you* at the ghoul carnival tomorrow. Back to you, Bob."

Wow. Is this ever a shit show.

Bob the newscaster appears on screen. Humans have these cutouts called Flat Stanley. Bob looks like that character, considering how his shoulders appear super-boxy over a concave chest.

Sadly, my pizza box is now empty. I check the wall clock.

9 pm.

Now that Cissy is living with Mrs F, this particular hour takes on a new importance. Mrs F will force Cis to 'go to sleep' at nine o'clock. True story. In reality, Cis uses a flashlight to read books in the dark.

And she turns thirty on Saturday.

Not that I'm in any position to judge. I'm watching the clock so I can drive over to Cissy's, sneak in through her bedroom window, and get the real scoop... all without encountering Mrs F.

I'm not proud about tiptoeing around Mrs F like I'm twelve. But I'll still do it.

Time to drive over to Cissy's place.

My ass is half-way off the couch when Bob the newscaster makes a stunning announcement.

"And now, we have a special interview with Shelton Barnacle, founder of the new Ghoul Rules Rule movement."

My butt parks onto the couch again, fast. *Did he say the Ghoul Rules Rule movement? What the ever loving Hell?*

"Thank you for coming to the studio today, Shelton. Why don't you tell us about Ghoul Rules Rule?"

For someone who's into rules, Shelton is an unreasonably hot guy with dark skin, black hair and twinkly-white teeth. Dollars to donuts, this guy sports a monkey tail.

"It's been a long time since we lost our ghoul rulers," says Shelton. "For a long time, it was fashionable to dislike the undead."

I hop to my feet. "Fashionable?" I yell at the screen. "Fashionable?!" The ghouls brought the King of Hell into our realm to K-I-L-L people like you."

On screen, Shelton keeps going. "These days, my fellow quasis are starting to realize that not everything the ghouls did was terrible.

And with role models like Lady Reaper around, it's easier for those of us who admired ghoul efficiency to come forward. That's why I founded the Ghoul Rules Rule movement."

"How fascinating," says Bob. "Tell me about your work."

"To begin with, we have more than two thousand members, including Lady Regina Reaper herself!"

I narrow my eyes. I wouldn't send a good soul to Hell just because they founded the Ghoul Rules Rule movement. That said, I might be just a little bit tempted.

Bob sets his fist under his chin in that odd way television people sometimes do. "Now, tell us about the ghoul carnival. Any secret insights about the reaper games? Lady Reaper is very tight lipped about it."

"I really shouldn't," says Shelton.

Bob leans forward. "Please, Shelton. All our viewers want to know."

Shelton blushes. "Well, for those of you who are *rule wonks* like me, the reaper games will follow the same regulations as a Class 2 Multi-Day Celebratory Festival in Conjunction With Demonic Exposition Games in the Arena."

A jolt of happy runs through me. "Did you hear that?" My tail arches over my shoulder to point at my nose. "This is huge, right?"

My tail nods.

Those are arena rules. I know them like they're seared into my brain. *This is awesome.*

I hop to my feet and do a happy dance. Things are looking up. I turn off the TV and head for the door.

Cissy, here I come!

CASA DE CISSY

MYLA

I crouch under Cissy's bedroom window. My tail arcs over my shoulder to gently prod the glass to the tune of Jingle Bells.

Tap, tap, tap.

Tap, tap, tap.

Tap, TAP, tap, tap, THUNK.

This isn't working. Maybe I need a new tune. I look to my tail. "What do you think? Change the rhythm to *Shave and a Haircut, two Bits?*"

My tail vigorously wags from side to side. It thinks *Shave and a Haircut, two Bits,* is way too cheeseball. But my dreams are taking me to sexy times in a pink freaking palace. I don't have a lot of pride left.

A shadow moves across the window sill. I punch my fist in the air. *Yes!*

Going on tiptoe, I brace myself for the familiar lines of Cissy's face. That's not what I see. Instead of my best friend, Cissy's incredibly large and mean feline glares back at me. Tiny is fabulously round brown cat with a flat face, long tail and four little nubs for legs. He's mean as Hell and one of my personal heroes.

When I next speak, I use my best *kitty whisperer* voice. "Hey, Tiny. Can you go get Cis?"

In reply, Tiny's little pink tongue flicks out to lick his whiskers.

"Please please pretty pleeeeeease?"

Tiny licks his tongue again and rolls off the ledge. This cat is so mean, it isn't funny.

Mad respect.

I return to my Jingle Bells concerto. I'm on my fifth round when a new shadow moves over the window. Success! It's Cissy.

My bestie rolls up her window an inch. "Myla, is that you?"

"How many people tap Jingle Bells on your window?"

"Oh, I thought you might be Zeke."

"I'm not. Can I come in?"

"Myla, you don't understand. Mom is in a really rough place right now. I don't want to stress her out."

"Please. We both know it's *martini o'clock* in the Frederickson household. Your mom won't notice me unless I sneak out of your room to steal her stash of olives."

Cissy grins. "Okay, fine."

She cranks up the window. I shimmy through and into the inner sanctum that is Cissy's bedroom. Words tumble from my mouth before I have a chance to think about whether or not they're really insulting.

"Wow, this looks just like it did in high school."

"What's wrong with that?"

"Uh, nothing."

Here's what *is* wrong with that. Back in high school, Cissy's decorating taste involved using a retina-searing shade of fuchsia on every surface possible. Plus, the same paintings hang on the walls—all of them acquired by Mr F on Earth (I'm pretty sure one of them's a stolen Jackson Pollock). Her single bed is still adorned with a fluffy pink comforter and matching pillows. And of course, Cissy's cat, Tiny lurks in a corner.

Did I mention Tiny is round, mean and awesome? *All true.*

Cissy wears blue flannel pajamas. Now she pulls at the neckline. "Do you think this room is too immature for a thirty-year old?"

Ruh-roh.

If I answer this question honestly, it will end in a half-hour discussion on the difference between the color fuchsia and petal pink. Trust me, we've had this talk before. So I decide to ignore that question and change the subject.

"Why did you think I was Zeke? I know he's in the Dark Lands."

"Oh, it's part of this ghoul carnival wedding thing. Zeke needs to do some prep stuff in the Dark Lands. Still, I was hoping he'd sneak away."

"Ah." I kick at the pink carpet and debate how to move the conversation forward. After choosing Jingle Bells to knock on Cissy's window, I really didn't plan out the rest of this too well. I decide that it doesn't really matter what I say… as long as I do not speak with a bitter tone.

No bitter tone.

No bitter tone.

No bitter tone.

"So, bestie. I hear you're getting married Saturday."

That sounded bitter as Hell. Oops.

Cissy's eyes get all wide while her mouth rounds to an 'o' shape. "Oh, no! Didn't anybody call you?"

"Ah, nope."

Cissy rushes over to open the top drawer of her dresser. Turns out, it's not stuffed with socks but documents. It strikes me that Mrs F is locking Cissy in at nine o'clock… then my best friend uses bedroom furniture as a filing cabinet.

What's wrong with Mrs F anyway?

Cis rustles through the pages. "It was on my list. I swear, I asked Regina-na to do it. But she's been so busy changing the wedding date because of…" Cissy stops. "Things."

"I know what happened, Cis. Lady Reaper says I've been stalking her or something."

Cis stops fidgeting with the papers and closes her drawer. "I told her that wasn't true. You're not the stalker type. You know, unless it's a demon-killing situation."

I plunk onto the bed and take my regular spot at the foot of the mattress. "Talk to me, Cis. What's going on?"

Cis parks at the tippy edge of the other side of the mattress. "Mom and Regina-na have been, uh, disappointed in some of the things you've done. I try to explain that you're just Myla being Myla."

"Huh. I'm getting the distinct impression that both your Mom and Regina spend a good chunk of their day describing how I suck."

Cissy rolls her eyes. "It's not *all* day."

"Only most of it. Good to know."

And because Cissy is Cissy, she finds my commentary worthy of a chuckle. This is why we get along so well, by the way. Cissy doesn't need me to sugar-coat most truths. All of which is why I now move in for the kill.

"You know I don't blow smoke up your ass."

"And I appreciate that."

"I'll be straight up with you. Lady Reaper wants to kill your body, trap your soul, and wipe out every last spirit in the after-realms... including the ones in Heaven and Hell."

Cis sniffs. She's so *not worried* about that warning, it isn't funny. "Myla, I understand that you have issues with ghouls."

"They killed my whole extended family, so... yeah."

"Regina-na is different. You'll see. By the end of this week, the three of us will be best friends." Cissy raises her pointer finger. "Make that the *four* of us. Mom adores Regina, too."

The whole question of Mrs F is now raising its ugly head again. I scan Cissy's room more carefully. All the pictures of Cis and her parents now have Mr F carefully cut out from the image.

"Wow. I see your mother did some découpage with your family portrait gallery."

Cis nods. "Dad has taken up with a she-ghoul in the human city of New York."

"How can you be so certain? Your dad always disappears for months at a time, am I right?"

"Correct."

"So, how do you know he's run off with a she-ghoul?"

"Regina-na didn't want to share the news, but she felt it was only right for us to know."

There it is. That name again. Regina-na.

"I wasn't kidding before, Cis. Lady Reaper is trying to kill you."

Cissy gives me one of her 'oh you're so funny Myla' smiles. She then points behind me. "Oh, look! Tiny is about to pounce!"

I play along. Turning around, I find that Tiny is indeed crouched down and preparing to level me and Cissy like we're a pair of hapless gazelles in a pink African savanna. Tiny leaps, a motion that's more of a mini-hop than anything else.

Cissy scoops Tiny into her arms. "Did you attack Mommy? Yes, you did. You're the lion of Purgatory."

For a round blob, Tiny can move quickly when motivated. The cat swipes at Cissy's arm. I can't help but notice the scratch marks.

"Those cuts could get infected. You should have Tiny declawed."

"No way! That's cruel." Cissy nuzzles up to Tiny. "Are you the biggest, baddest lion in Purgatory? Yes, you are."

Tiny mewls, which is his way of showing joy. He rolls out of Cissy's grasp and onto the floor. I don't understand their relationship, but there's no doubt that Cissy and Tiny have a bond.

I decide to downshift the conversation before returning to what I call the *Regina kill kill kill* talk. To start with, I catch Cissy up on the latest gossip from Antrum--one of the Acca twins is getting married—and how Maxon is preparing for his battle test. At this point, I consider Cissy to be in the optimal state for a little "come to Myla session."

"So," I begin. "You mentioned Lady Reaper is the reason you're getting married Saturday. We need to talk about that." I point to my mouth. "Read my lips. Lady Reaper wants to chop you up with a scythe until you're turned into a green ghost."

"Don't be silly, Myla"

"It's not silly at all. Emerald ghosts exist."

"Oh, you mean like Zeleney?"

I do a double-take. "Did you say Zeleney?"

"Yup. She's Regina-na's friend."

"Huh." *And that's all I have to say for now.* I was having enough trouble with Regina-na. Zeleney will take far more adjusting.

Cissy hugs her elbows. "This is so awkward."

"Whatever. You have something to share." I fix her with my *I'm totally serious* stare. "I'm here. I'll listen."

"Okay." Cissy slides off the bed to crouch on the floor. After wriggling half-way under the mattress, Cis pulls out a long and flat box that's decorated the words 'Grandpa Ghoul's Big Old Boots.'

"Dang, I forgot all about Grandpa Ghoul!" I smile at the memory. "He had all those commercials on the human channel." I do my best

Grandpa Ghoul impersonation, which involves talking like a super-old guy. "Buy my big old boots, boys and girls. Tell me you saved a some after all these years."

Cissy worries her lower lip with her teeth. "No, I didn't save a pair." She opens the box. It overflows with letters.

My brows lift with surprise. "Wow. You've had a penpal all this time?"

"Yes." Cissy opens one letter and reads aloud.

My Dear Cissy,

Congratulations on becoming Senator of Diplomacy! I have tailored the perfect purple robes for you to wear. Will send them next week. You're doing such a great job!

Cissy shoots me a sideways glance. "That's nice, right? A tailored robe?"

My heart sinks. "May I see that letter?" Cissy hands it over. I scan to the signature. My heart sinks. "This is from Lady Reaper."

"Don't worry, Myla. Regina-na is eccentric but nice. She sends me stuff all the time."

A chill crawls up my spine. "What stuff?" I drag the box over and dig through the envelopes. "These are all from Lady Reaper. Hundreds of them!" I open random envelopes and scan the contents. "This one offers you a magic mirror. Another says she can get you a ghoul portal ring. It goes on for years. Why didn't you tell me?"

"Because you'd be judgy."

"As I should be! Lady Reaper is evil!"

"You are the *only one* who thinks that. To everybody else, Lady Reaper is a heroine."

"Ha. That whole thing about saving souls is B-S. There are millions of missing ghosts from 1857."

"Myla, we weren't there. Who knows what really happened?" She sighs. "Regina-na has been a loyal friend to me for years." Cissy hugs her elbows. "Regina Reaper says there's a prophecy. I'm about to become the Hallowed One. It might be a new era for ghost processing." Cissy shivers. "I could replace you."

My mouth falls open. It's not a pretty look, but it's all I've got. "Wow. I did not see that coming."

So, I kill a little time petting Tiny and trying to find something to say.

Total fail.

Cissy hugs her elbows. "This is what Mom and Regina have been warning me about. You're already jealous of me as a senator. Now, I'm about to replace you in soul processing. You're a warrior. From now on, you'll try to sabotage me every step of the way."

"Ha ha freaking ha ha. That is a joke. I am not Sabotage Girl and you know it." I lean forward. "Tell me. What do you think about becoming the Hallowed one?"

"I'm terrified! Then, I remind myself you were scared at first, too. Maybe I'll adjust the way you did. Zeke and I might end up loving adventures, just like you and Lincoln."

"You and Zeke lost it when his condo board forced you to change curtains."

"Only because the window treatments came in as aubergine blinds instead of terra cotta panels. It throws off the whole design palette for the living room."

I fix Cissy with another one of my most serious stares. "I'm not sure what you said, but I understand it's important to you."

"Well, Zeke and I plan to send a very terse letter to the condo board this year. Very terse indeed."

"And you and Zeke will become adventurers?"

"Sure. Maybe."

"Cis, I ripped out the entrails from an entire pack of colonus demons last week... while laughing."

"My turn." Cissy pats my hand. "I'm not sure what you said, but I understand it's important to you."

We share a long look and a quick laugh. "Oh, Cis. You're the best."

"Back at ya."

"Will you promise me one thing?"

"Sure."

"Tomorrow is the opening ceremony for the Reaper Games."

"Exactly. It's a huge deal. The first time this event has been held in Purgatory. People are so excited!"

"I'm feeling very protective of you. I'd like to meet up before the games and stay near you all day. Not that I'll be your personal body-guard. It's more that I'll just hang within kicking range." I raise my pointer finger. "Oh, and make sure Lady Reaper doesn't get any of your hair tomorrow."

"My... hair?"

"Yes."

"All right. You can be my bodyguard." Cissy sets her hands over her heart and starts to sing. "And IIIIIIIIIIII will always love yooooooou."

"Cis, I'm so serious about keeping you safe, you can sing that song all day and I won't care."

"Wow, you really are worried."

"Told you."

We decide on a time and place to meet. I know how Cissy's mind works. Now that my bestie has agreed, it's best to vamoose. Besides, I've planted a ton of warding charms and alerts in Cissy's bedroom over the years. Combine that with our deal to meet up for the ghoul carnival? Cis will be safe.

With that happy thought in mind, I make a quick excuse and an even faster exit.

LINCOLN

I sit in a dungeon cell that's small, dank and dark. The walls are smooth black stone. No windows or furniture. No one else in here with me, either. There's also a distinct lack of insects or rats, so that's a bonus. As dungeons go, this is one of the cleaner places where I've been locked up.

On the negative side, there are no amenities in here—as in food, water or toilet—because ghouls don't have bodily needs. This dungeon is designed for the dead.

I kick my legs out in front of me and lean my back against the chilly stone wall. There's only one point of light in this cell. It's a small rectangle with a bright screen. Right now, that tiny monitor reads: Oligarchy Dungeon G-8, cell O-457B.

I've ended up in the same general place as Walker. So where is he?

Chances are, he's still trying to figure out how to get to the Abyss. If I find the same back door he's searching for, I'm bound to run across Walker as well.

Suddenly, a low noise sounds. It's the distinct rumble of grinding stones. The chamber around me vibrates slightly. I have the sensation of rising and falling.

My eyes widen. This prison must be formed from thousands of tiny cells like mine. The ghouls shuffle the prison boxes around for their own purposes.

The little monitor shows my cell name. Can I get it to display anything else?

Rising, I cross the tiny room and take a closer look at the small monitor. I tap the screen. Nothing happens. I tap the box, looking for hidden controls. Again, no go. Finally, I grip the small box and pull. It stays stuck to the wall. That part is to be expected.

It's what happens next that's a shock.

While my left hand still grasps the monitor, my right hand now glows with blue light. Threads rise up from my skin. the lines multiply until they congeal into the shape of a gauntlet.

Which means that whatever powers this monitor? It also activates the magic of my gauntlets. All of which adds up to a single conclusion:

This dungeon is built with strand magic.

That opens up all sorts of possibilities.

GHOST TOWER NINE

MYLA

ednesday, 8:07 a.m.
I wait behind a tall rectangle of concrete that looms over an asphalt-covered hill. *Ghost tower nine.* Walker is improving the tech inside this place, so it's all closed up for now. On a side note, it's a short walk from here to the ghoul carnival.

Which makes it a great place to meet Cissy.

I pace a line by the first-floor windows. For purposes of today, I wear ghoul robes with the hood drawn low and a backpack full of demon patrol charms. Taken as a whole, I look like an undead hitch-hiker. And since ghoul robes don't boost my powers, I'm wearing my scala robes underneath.

Yes, it's less than comfortable.

And that's not the only irritant this morning. Cissy was supposed to meet me here over an hour ago. The ghoul carnival starts in twenty-three minutes. I am starting to get concerned.

Also, I'm not the queen of patience.

Clearly, Cissy got derailed. One guess who blew my little train of bestie protection off the tracks: Lady Reaper.

Seventeen minutes to go.

I start the march over to the ghoul carnival. Since this is Purga-tory, the trek involves lots of cracked sidewalks and surprisingly deep puddles. Along the way, I picture the trip Lincoln and I took through time to the ghoul carnival of 1857. There were some games of chance and circus tents. If you were living in an era where a steam engine was the bomb, I'd guess that was pretty cool.

Still, I can't imagine why the whole quasi population is going nuts for what was state-of-the-art over a century ago.

Turns out, I'm way wrong.

First of all, the entrance to the carnival are two arches. Only they aren't just arches, they're massive ghoul heads representing Grim and Lady Reaper. Folks walk under their open mouths in order to enter the event.

I hate to admit this, but that's cool.

Inside, the carnival holds a wide midway flanked by massive pavilions. On the far side of the main aisle, a tall red stage has been erected. The words ghoul carnival are written along the base in bold letters.

I step along the midway and try to look unimpressed. Not happening. There are pavilions for every deadly sin. Along the left-hand side, there's the Carousel of Lust, Envy Mirror Maze, Greed Hot Balloons, and Pride Makeover Palace. On the opposite side, I spot the Cirque du Sloth, Gluttony Food Hall, Tunnel of Wrath, and a cluster of hexagon-shaped kiosks that's called Ghoul Tech Central.

Like every other resident of Purgatory, I'm dying to see what's in each pavilion. The only one I have time to check out is the Cirque du Lust. Inside, a bunch of acrobats dangle from hefty lines of ribbon and just... stay upside down. Assuming they don't have a brain hemorrhage, I bet these folks can stay suspended all week.

Now that I see the vision here, I understand why this place is packed. And it's not just quasis who are roaming the midway. I spy angels, demons and ghouls as well. Every so often, I catch the face of a necro hunter or Nora in the crowd.

Which means those folks are still around. Good to know.

I press my way through the mob until I reach the main stage. It's a long wooden platform that holds four golden thrones and not much else. Cissy sits in the far-left seat. Lady Reaper is parked on the far-right chair. And two unused ones are in the middle.

My heart cracks. I've come to many public events before. It's what happens when your Mom's the President of Purgatory. Those two empty chairs are where my parents would normally sit. A weight of sorrow settles on my shoulders. Mom and Dad live for events like this one. No doubt, they'd be thrilled to sit on stage with Cissy for her big shindig.

Then, I catch her gaze. Lady Reaper.

She wears a white ensemble today, complete with another petite hat. Her all-black eyes sear into mine. If this chick could freeze me with her stare, I'd be an icicle right now. With deliberate purpose, Lady Reaper looks at the two empty chairs and back to me again.

And in this moment, I know what's happened.

It's unclear how this Lady Reaper managed this, but she's been putting our ghost towers on the fritz to keep my parents away. White-hot rage courses through my veins. My tail pokes a hole through my ghoul robe costume to point at Lady Reaper. That's its equivalent of a death glare.

Cissy sits in the far-left chair, wearing a purple shift dress and looking miserable. Lady Reaper rises, blows Cissy a kiss and steps to center stage where a microphone sits on a tall stand. Lady Reaper taps the device. Thuds sound throughout the carnival. I notice Carol Cheevers standing off to stage right. Today, she's brought along a guy who's hoisted a trunk-sized camera on his shoulder. Hefty cords wind out behind him like snakes.

Lady Reaper addresses the crowd. "Good morning, Purgatory!"

Everyone cheers. This midway is packed, so it's an earsplitting noise. Bodies jostle to get closer to the stage, giving the crowd an undulating effect.

Lady Reaper throws her arms up in an excellent impersonation of Eva Perón. "Welcome to the opening ceremonies for the ghoul carnival!"

More cheers. Extra jostling. The scent of perfume and sweat fills the air. Someone's lizard tail jams into my leg. *Ouch.*

Lady Reaper continues. "Tomorrow, we will all share in the reaper games. But today, you will become dazzled by some ghoul entertainments. Once that's over, be sure to check out the pavilions, especially Ghoul Tech Central. You'll see for yourself what a human cell phone looks like. I can bring this wonder to Purgatory."

The crowd screeches their lungs out. I nibble my thumbnail and scheme. *How can I get next to Cissy while ruining Lady Reaper's day?* It's a puzzlement.

Lady Reaper continues. "Today, I have six hours of interesting programming for you to enjoy. I'm happy to introduce one of the greatest speakers of the Dark Lands. I have one fellow, DF-93, who reads the phone book. Trust me, it's a marvel."

Another round of cheers rises up, only this one is far less enthusiastic. The applause dies down as everyone realizes a sad fact: this woman is serious.

Not gonna lie: I'm enjoying the fact that Lady Reaper has made such a catastrophic miscalculation about what qualifies for entertainment in Purgatory.

Which is why what happens next sucks even more.

Little by little, Lady Reaper angles her body to gesture at the empty seats that should hold my parents. "As you can see, your president couldn't be bothered to join us this morning." Lady Reaper stares right at me as she says the next bit. "What a shame."

At last, an idea appears. It's a beauty.

With my plan in place, a preternatural sense of calm rolls over me. I shuck off my backpack and ghoul robes. Accessing my demonic wrath power, I focus extra energy into my limbs. After crouching low, I leap up onstage to land next to Lady Reaper.

Dragging the microphone away, I address the crowd. "Just kidding! Regina-na and I planned that phone book thing as a joke, because we're both such good buddies."

A big cheer follows. *Yay me.*

"And guess what? All those rumors about that I'm sick? It's a total practical joke between me and my new bestie, Regina... na." I look lovingly over to Lady Reaper, who's wearing the fakest smile ever.

I return my focus to the crowd. "Great news, everyone! Now, you can enjoy the carnival check out the pavilions. Oh, and save some food in the Hall of Gluttony for me!"

The loudest cheer of the morning erupts from the crowd. Lady Reaper's false grin melts into a frown.

And I smile.

LADY REAPER

MYLA

*R*uining Lady Reaper's morning? *Done.*
Revenge for whatever fuckery Regina-na is enacting on my parents? *Work in progress.*

Stopping Lady Reaper's entire Hallowed One master plan? *That's up next.*

I scan the scene. Lady Reaper has moved on to chatting up Carol Cheevers. At the same time, ten of her Noras march on stage, creating a semicircle around her. It reminds me a little of the ballet, Swan Lake, only with evil ghouls and random chicks with three eyes.

As for Cissy, my friend still sits alone on stage. And she's trying very hard not to laugh. I saunter over and throw my arms wide. "Great, huh?"

Cis frowns, but it's the kind that still has a smile lurking underneath. "Regina spent months booking today's ghoul speaker. He's number one on the charts in the Dark Lands."

I keep my arms wide, but add *jazz hands* into the mix. "Because they're all dead and don't know any better." I plunk onto the seat beside hers. "How about we check out this carnival? I've just freed up umpteen hours of your day."

Cis nibbles her lower lip. "I promised to go home as soon as I could. Mom found another box of pics with Dad. She's cutting out all the faces now."

"Great, then she's got a project. All the more reason to have fun."

Cis keeps nibbling her lower lip and making zero signs of readiness for leaving her chair. Clearly, more convincing is needed.

"Look," I begin. "Your dad can be a dick."

"Myla!"

"Hear me out. When I talk about dickishness, I mean how your father stole that Jackson Pollock painting in your bedroom. And what your Mom calls the *cute etching* on your bathroom wall? I'm pretty sure it's a stolen Rembrandt."

"I don't see where you're going with this."

"Your dad's a thief, but I don't think he's a cheat. Just be open to the idea that you deserve a little fun today."

Cis shoots me a sideways grin. "I'm thinking."

I grip her wrist and haul. "And I'm taking that as *yes.*"

Lady Regina and her unholy *swan lake crew* still linger at the other side of the stage with Carol. By this point, Lady Regina has taken to flicking her gaze in my direction. I'm sure she'd love to give me the ice-stare again, but she'd have to do so in front of the cameras. Instead, all she can do is cut a glance or two in my direction.

And do I stick out my tongue ever so slightly when she gazes my way? You bet, I do.

My bestie and I leave the stage to saunter along the midway. Tons of people congratulate Cissy on her big day. Every so often, I catch Lady Reaper lurking from some shadowy corner. She's like a whack-a-mole, only I can't hit her yet.

Meh. There are other things to focus on.

Turns out, the pavilions are really well done. Mostly because my bestie did all the hard work. Cis explains the negotiations that went on behind the scenes.

"The envy pavilion was the worst," exclaims Cis. "Whenever another deadly sin came up with a design, envy HAD to have it. Finally, I told them we were living with a mirror maze or nothing."

"Tell me your irises glowed red when you put the hammer down."

"That they did."

I sigh. "I would've liked to see that."

We check out each pavilion in turn. Hands down, my favorite is the Tunnel of Wrath. You ride around in a little car inside a dark box of a building. Every so often, demons pop out at you. Because I love my bestie so much, I took the time to explain in detail how to kill every one of them.

Cis said I was ruining the ride. I reminded her she could be listening to a phone book.

The one pavilion I didn't like is the Pride Makeover Palace. It's nice and all, but everything was focused on hair. I'm talking updo stations, a section dedicated to the history of blow dryers, and even a wall of brushes. This was way over the top.

"Don't you think it's weird?" I ask Cissy.

"What? Pride and makeovers… that's a natural combination."

"But all they do is hair. And like I've been telling you, the first spell Lady Reaper wants to cast involves your hair. She needs some so she can turn you into a green ghost and eventually chop you with her scythe."

Cissy hums a little tune to herself as she walks along.

I clear my throat. "Cissy."

"What?"

"Did you hear anything I said about Lady Reaper and the hair spell?"

"Not really. Whenever you start talking about Lady Reaper, I start thinking about how Tiny would love this carnival."

I do a double-take. "Tiny? As in your cat?"

"Lady Reaper thinks it would be great for him. Lots of exercise."

I open my mouth, ready to complain about Lady Reaper. Then, I close my yap just as quickly. Lady Reaper wants Tiny to slim down. There's really nothing bad about that. Two things can be true at the same time: Lady Reaper is balls-out evil and she also has a soft spot for cats.

Eventually, the day winds down and the sky darkens. Cis and I are hanging out on the Carousel of Lust. We're both sitting in a sled that's pulled by life-size plastic centaurs. The carousel itself was turned off an hour ago. No one's nearby.

And there's something I've been wanting to do all day.

"Cis, may I ask you a question… and you don't have to answer if you don't want to?"

"Oooh." Cissy mock-shivers. "Nothing fun ever follows that lead-in from you."

I slap on a look of mock-surprise. "Is that a *no?*"

"No, it's a yes. I mean, go on."

"Let's say that you could pick your own wedding. There's no one else to worry about. What would you and Zeke do?"

"We actually talked about that." Cis blushes. "You'll think this is dumb."

"Nah. Remember when you tried to save a wasps' nest by hiding it in your closet? That was dumb."

"Hey, I was nine at the time. And you helped me. Plus, I only ended up in the hospital for two days."

"Who knew you were allergic to wasps?" I smile.

Cis giggles. "Nobody."

At this point, I'm feeling pretty good about my bad self. Cis and I are in a solid place here. All I need to do now is point out how completely twisted it is for Cis to abandon her dream wedding for some dried-up old ghoul.

I can do this.

"Come on, I know you have a plan. What is it?"

Cis blushes. "Do you remember the night Zeke and I became a couple?"

"Sure, it was at Zeke's parent's place. The Ryder mansion. They were having a diplomatic thing. I wore an orange gown."

"Right. We'd do that again. A small group of folks would come over from across the after-realms. You'd be my bridesmaid and wear any color you want. And we'd have Octavia plan it all."

"As in, Lincoln's Mom?"

"Sure, she's really good at this stuff, so everything will be perfect. Also, let's just say there are a lot of big personalities in both my family and Zeke's. Octavia is a total battle axe, and I mean that in the nicest way."

"Good thinking. Bring in Octavia, and there will be a whole level of hassle you won't have to deal with. I like that plan."

I have her now. Time to go for the close.

"You know what that's different from?" I ask. "A multi-day carnival."

Cis sighs. "I realize that, but the carnival can heal the divide between Purgatory and the Dark Lands. I'm a Senator now. I can't pass up this chance."

I bob my head and consider. *Dang, she has a point.*

"I get that. You wouldn't be *you* otherwise."

"Thanks. Now, it's your turn. What's your ideal wedding?"

"Oh, the one I had was perfect. Are you kidding? I rode around on a supernatural bug with my bridal gown covered in demon goo. I wouldn't change a thing about that, but…"

Cissy does that *thing* where her eyes get super-wide. "But, what?"

"I'd change the honeymoon. Lincoln getting kidnapped was bad enough. Then, it turned out the kidnapper was Ethan, Lincoln's supposed friend from growing up. Blech."

"So, if you had it to do all over again, where would you go?"

I mock-groan. "Ugh. This is so dumb."

"Hey, talking me into building a trebuchet in my backyard was dumb. I can still remember it now." Cissy clears her throat and does an impression of me when I'm really excited about something. It involves lots of hand motions (and she's not wrong). *"It'll be awesome, Cissy! In the middle ages, humans used these trebuchet-lever-things to chuck severed heads over castle walls! How great is that?"*

"In *my* defense, I was twelve. And it only took three months for your parents to rebuild the living room wall."

Cissy winks. "The same point applies, though. Unless you want to spend your honeymoon tossing human heads around, I promise not to be judgy."

"Fine." I take a deep breath. "I sometimes dream about Lincoln and I spending our honeymoon at…" I wince, waiting for the laughter. "Castle Xanadu."

"Oooh, the one with the perma-pink skies and fluffy beds?

I nod. "That's the one."

"The guys have to wear fuchsia tuxedos and the girls sport puffy gowns."

"Only if you leave your bedroom," I state. "And I happen to know their delivery menu includes both demon bars and quinoa, so there's something for both me and Lincoln."

"Wow, you've really thought this out."

"Hey, we all have down time."

"True." Cis leans over so her shoulder bumps mine. "I'm glad we talked."

"Me, too. And I understand why you still want to do the carnival, but can you promise me one eenty beentsy thing?"

"Sure."

"Let's meet before everything starts tomorrow and walk over together. Ghost Tower Nine."

"I'm so sorry I ghosted you this morning. Mom was having an episode."

I twist my invisible mustache and speak in a mock-evil voice. "But I can be even nastier than your mother."

"And you really want to do this because...?"

"I want to be your bodyguard. I don't ask you to understand it, just accept this is one of those me-things, like how I keep an alphabetized list of my favorite demons."

"And that's all you're asking?"

"It's the whole magilla. Oh, and go straight home from here. Your room is well warded against danger."

"In that case, it's a deal."

Cissy and I share a smile. And all is right in the world.

I walk Cis to the parking lot and watch my bestie get into her car and drive away. Maybe we didn't meet up in the morning, but I was able to keep my friend safe from Lady Reaper.

Today was a good day.

But the night? Not as great. After the ghoul carnival, I make a beeline for Scala Central. But the moment I step into my house, I know something is wrong. The shadows lengthen. Lights sputter and die out.

My igni materialize.

Like before, they aren't tiny bolts of lightning, but oblong black holes that pull in life. I feel energy seep from my pores. The igni congeal into a single figure. My body chills over with foreboding.

Her voice sounds again. "The darkness surrounds me..."

I stand in place, transfixed. I can only manage one word. "No."

The igni vanish. My home turns bright and welcoming once more. I decide that I am clearly overwrought and in need of sleep. All of which is why I make an extra-large Pillow Lincoln to cuddle with in bed. Even then, it takes me a long time before I can fall asleep. That sense of doom seeps into my soul.

Today was good.

Tomorrow is anyone's guess.

THE DARKNESS

LINCOLN

*A*mazing how much progress one can make on a project... when there's nothing else to do.

Which is the case for my situation in the Oligarchy dungeons. I've spent hours in the dark, charting the movement of the prison blocks around me. At the same time, I've been tinkering with my gauntlet. Myla's shared how she makes her scala robes take different shapes. I can't do that with my gauntlet, but I can make the thing appear and vanish at will. It's a start.

And I've formed a plan as well.

This dungeon may be made of blocks, but there are lots of blank spaces. *Holes in the mega structure.* Ghouls manipulate the missing parts in order to move prisoners around. And it all runs on strand magic.

Here's my plan: use my own strand magic to realign the blocks and create a single square passageway that leads out of this dungeon. And if my guess is right, that escape tunnel will take me directly to the Abyss.

My big question is how to access the strand magic all around me. I played around with the little monitor that shows the name of my cell. That's not working. I need a new plan of attack.

Creeeeak.

A low grinding noise sounds as my prison cell door opens. It's the first time I've seen any brightness in days. On reflex, I shield my eyes. At the same time, I focus on my gauntlet and make it disappear.

A figure walks into the room. As my vision adjusts, I make out ghoul robes and a familiar face.

Walker.

He steps over and grins. "Hello, friend! How are you today? I hope this place isn't too cold for you. Do you need a glass of water?"

Oh, no.

In all the years I've known Walker, he's never one for small talk. In fact, Walker used to show up in Myla's room and say, "Good morning, you are called to serve," as a way of instructing her to fight in the arena.

The man offers me his hand. I take it and rise. In the light, my mystery guest certainly looks like Walker. That said, I've spent too long in a cell by myself. Now that I see another face, I realize how hungry I am for company.

I must be sure this is Walker.

After all, I saw the Grim Reaper change his face before. Back at the ghost well, Grim transformed his features from bone and decaying flesh into a perfect imitation of Walker. I need to know if this is really my friend.

Fortunately, there's an easy way to test this. Walker and I are descendants of the archangel Aquila. Our group shares a secret greeting.

I rest the back of my fist against my forehead. "Welcome, brother Aquilinean."

This is far from the proper greeting. A long moment of silence hangs between us. A thread of worry twists inside me. Perhaps setting my fist on my forehead was too obvious as a fake.

At last, the man repeats the gesture and sets his fist to his forehead. "Welcome, brother Aquilinean."

With that, I'm certain of one thing.

This isn't Walker. It's the Grim Reaper.

Grim-Walker gestures toward the door. "I'm so sorry you've been treated this way, brother. But you must understand how odd it is that we both chose to enter the Dark Lands through an unregistered portal. And into the lookout tower for the Abyss, no less! I'm a ghoul, so I didn't get locked up. But you? It's taken me all this time to secure your release."

"Thank you. What happens next?"

"I've gotten you an audience at the Red Court," replies Grim-Walker. "They have a few questions for you." Grim-Walker tilts his head. "Have you ever met the Oligarchy before?"

In truth, the real Walker and I were one locked into a bunker with the Oligarchy... a fact that this fake Walker doesn't know.

"I have met them."

"In that case, this will be easier. Allow me to give you a tour of our capital city."

After leaving the dungeon cell, Grim-Walker and I and step through a series of glass tunnels overlooking a city made of metal skyscrapers.

"These passages are lovely, aren't they?" Grim-Walker keeps talking without waiting for a reply. It's yet another thing the real Walker would never do. "This is the fastest route to the Red Court. Only the most important ghouls get to use these tunnels."

I examine the glass tube around us. "Is this more strand magic?"

"Where did you hear about that?"

Which isn't the same thing as saying no.

"As king, I pick things up. What do you know about it?"

"No idea," says Grim-Walker quickly. "I know I seem like a good engineer, but strand technology? Wow. That's above my pay grade."

"Then, how did you design the ghost towers in Purgatory? Those are lined with strands."

"I did tell you that, didn't I? The truth is, I'm part of a laboratory of ghoul engineers. A brilliant ghoul named Grim did all the strand calculations for me."

Grim did the calcs. Sure.

"Ah, how very interesting." *And a total lie.* The real Walker needs no one to help him with math. "Speaking of Grim, where is he?"

"I'm afraid Grim is off at a memorial service for his late, beloved wife, Nora."

There's the barest hitch in my step as Grim-Walker shares this news. I recall the Noras that Lady Reaper conjured back in 1857.

Beyond them being reproductions of the same statue, I hadn't given them much thought. Until now.

"I thought Grim was married to Lady Regina."

"Ah, for some men, there is only one woman," says Grim-Walker. "I'm sure that you—of all people—understand this. Who would have thought a part-angel demon hunter would fall for his prey?"

Protective energy burns up my spine. "You see my wife as prey?"

"Of course, not! I refer to what the *rest of the world* thinks. Most folks simply don't understand love."

"I suppose not."

"But most folks understand hate. Do *you*, Lincoln? Do you ever suspect someone carries enough loathing for you in their heart, that they've been stalking you for years, causing every last problem in your life, and serving as the darkness to your light?"

I hear speeches like this one all the time, mostly from lower nobles who are trying to seem far more badass than they really are. It's best to shut down these conversations early.

"No, Walker. I do not wonder about that."

"Pity."

We pause along the elevated walkway. Grim-Walker points to a particular spot up ahead. "There. That's the Red Court. It's a great honor to be asked into the Oligarchy's inner sanctum."

I look out through the glass wall. A round red building is perched over the city. Clear access tunnels—just like the one we're in now—criss cross over the metal buildings below. Many end in this massive sphere.

The Red Court.

"Indeed, it is impressive," I state. "I've never visited before. Are there any etiquette rules that I need to be aware of?"

"For other people, perhaps, but not for folks like you and me." Grim-Walker chucks me on the shoulder, something no one's done to me since I was eight years old. "*We'd* have to do something pretty extreme to offend them."

"But if I did anger the Oligarchy, what would happen?"

Before, Grim-Walker exuded an easy charm. Now, his entire demeanor turns so cold, it's as if the temperature in the passageway has dropped twenty degrees. "I've worked too hard to get you out of that dungeon to have you get chucked back in there. Do we understand each other?"

"Perfectly."

And since Grim-Walker wants me out of the dungeons so badly, I know one thing for certain.

I need to get back to prison, fast.

Because if my guess is right? Grim-Walker knows the dungeons are a back channel to the Abyss, the same as I do.

RED COURT

33

LINCOLN

Grim-Walker and I step into a great glass sphere that's divided in half by a clear floor. *The Red Court.* Essentially, it's a domed room that's part of a larger sphere. The bottom half of the circle—meaning the bowl-shaped part under the floor—is filled with a dozen ghouls in dark robes. All are crouched down with their arms splayed out before them. It's the classic pose of worship.

Somehow, I doubt the folks below me are bowing out of reverence.

The top half of the room serves as the audience chamber. A semicircle of red glass arches above my head. On one side of the room, the Oligarchy sit atop four glass thrones. They wear identical crimson robes with the hoods pulled low.

Memories appear. These are the four ghouls who rule the Dark Lands... as in, the same ones who tried to sacrifice Myla to the King of Hell on the day my wife first gained her scala powers. My muscles tighten with held-in rage.

If these four would risk Myla, then what else are they capable of? All this while, I believed Walker knew the Dark Lands well enough to be safe. Now, I'm not so certain.

Grim-Walker takes the same forehead-to-the-floor pose as the ghouls below my feet. "Greetings, Oligarchy."

All four hoods angle in my direction. "Finally, you deign to join us."

I shoot a downward glance at Grim-Walker, who still has his forehead stuck to the floor. "I didn't realize there was an open invitation."

"Do not bother lying," hiss the Oligarchy in unison. "We trust..." Here they leave a dramatic pause in the air. "Walker."

The Oligarchy speak Walker's name in a tone that says, *we know something you don't.* And that's how it is with these four. They are so convinced of their own magnificence, it doesn't occur to them that I already figured out this is really Walker-Grim.

The Oligarchy continue. "We wish to make a bargain."

That grabs my attention. "I'm listening."

"You see the city below the Red Court. It is a beautiful realm, yet overcrowded. In Purgatory, souls move in and out. The population there stays stable. Heaven and Hell have more space than they can manage. Earth is overrun with humans. And Antrum's numbers remain low because so many foolishly lose their lives on demon patrol."

My inner anger flares hotter. It's becoming hard to keep a calm demeanor. "Antrum's warriors sacrifice much to keep Earth safe. They deserve respect."

The Oligarchy keep speaking as if I hadn't said a word. "A new era is about to begin. Are you aware of the Hallowed One prophecy?"

"I am."

The Oligarchy repeat it aloud:

When there are two reapers, two scythes and two emerald ghosts, then the Hallowed One shall appear, ignite the great tower and imprison all souls.

"We have two reapers. The first scythe was made long ago. The second is about to be finished. All we need is the second emerald ghost. We believe you know who that is: Senator Cissy Frederickson."

"I thought you also needed a place to imprison all souls. Is that ready as well?"

"A ghost tower is not necessary," hiss the Oligarchy in unison.

These four ghouls can be thick. But they aren't that short-sighted that they can't see the need for a ghost tower. Not for the first time, I wonder at the Oligarchy's motivation. They never talked about taking over all the after-realms before. *What's the real plan here?*

"We shall not discuss the tower," declare the Oligarchy. "You're in our reception chamber. Answer our question. Will you go to Purgatory and procure the Senator?"

Grim-Walker looks up from his prostate pose. "But Lady Reaper has everything in hand. There's no need for this."

The Oligarchy hiss in unison. "Do not play games. *You* don't trust Lady Reaper any more than *we* do. The Oligarchy succeed because we weave plans within plans. If Lady Reaper should fail, then King Lincoln could deliver Senator Frederickson to us. And another ghoul could finish out the ritual."

Grim-Walker sets his forehead against the floor again. "Yes, oh Oligarchy."

"Your dear friend *Walker* will accompany you to Purgatory," adds the Oligarchy. "You will be placed somewhere that's quiet, secure and secret. If and when we need your services, you will be called upon."

"And what will my payment be?" I ask.

"You get to stay out of the dungeons," replies the Oligarchy. "We know you keep magical trinkets in your pockets. These help you with food and drink, but how long can that continue? If you wish to live, then agree to our terms. Only know this—we will hold you to the agreement with a blood oath that's sealed by magic."

I set my pointer finger against my chin in a way that's meant to look as if I'm really considering this. In reality, the Oligarchy's offer is ridiculous. I'd never trade Cissy just to save my own skin. And the fact that they'd even offer this? It says more about the Oligarchy than it does about me.

These four rulers lack the capacity to imagine someone doing anything that isn't in their own direct self-interest.

Still, they did drop a good tidbit of information. The new scythe for the Grim Reaper—as in the version made with strand magic—isn't finished yet. That work must be going on in Eli's laboratories at the Abyss right now.

"Well?" prompt the Oligarchy.

I raise my hand. "Still thinking."

"Convince him, *Walker.*"

Grim-Walker hops to his feet. "The prophecy of the Hallowed One is inevitable. We must refuge in the shadows of greatness." He offers me his hand. "Come with me. We'll find a nice place in Purgatory to lay low for a while. Perhaps we'll both celebrate with a few glasses of mead, just like old times!"

"I have made my decision." I turn to Grim-Walker. "You don't drink mead. Never have." Next, I focus on the Oligarchy. "My wife isn't here to verbally torture you properly. Still, I shall try my best in her absence." I clear my throat. "Fuck you, you fucking fucks."

"Back to the dungeons," say the Oligarchy. "Some more time in the dark should help you focus."

Underneath the glass floor, I see one of the tube passageways curl up through the half-bowl of space below us.

Grim-Walker grabs my arm. "Watch out! That tube will drag you back into the dungeons."

What I want to say is this: You mean the dungeons which serve as the only way into the Abyss? Those dungeons?

But it isn't time yet for Grim-Walker to know that I'm onto him.

"Oh no," I say blandly. "Not the dungeons."

The floor below me opens up. I fall into the glass tube and tumble through the city. The tunnel drops me off into a new dungeon cell. As in, I literally fall through the ceiling and onto the floor. It's a reflex to check the cell name.

Oligarchy Dungeon G-1, cell A-4A.

So they've set me someplace that's new to me, but rather old in terms of their naming conventions. Above me, the circular portal grows smaller as the connection to the glass transport tube closes down. Even so, the opening gives enough light for me to quickly scan my surroundings.

Cracks line the walls and floor. I step over to one of the fracture lines and prod at it with my thumb. A chunk of what looks like black stone falls off, revealing a network of golden threads underneath.

Excitement charges through my nervous system. I can access the strands here!

The portal overhead fully closes. I summon the strand gauntlet to appear on my left hand.

Then, I enact my plan.

34

MYLA

rue fact: Pillow Lincoln isn't as good as the real thing.

Long story short, I have a crap night's sleep. I keep dreaming that I'm in a wheat field, loving the feel of sun on my skin. The wind rustles my hair. Birds tweet nearby. I'm two squirrels and one cheery song short of a Disney movie.

It doesn't last.

Shadows creep across the ground. Dark clouds roll in, blotting out the blue sky. A voice sounds.

"The darkness surrounds me..."

Dream Me gasps. There's no question who's the speaker here: it's the same shadowy figure I've been seeing for days. Her voice echoes louder and louder. *She's getting closer.* I take off and haul ass until I find another sunny field. A chipper little fox frolics nearby with some bunnies.

And since this is a dream, I get all happy about the scene until, sure enough, the darkness rolls in again.

When I eventually leave dreamland behind, my entire body feels drained instead of refreshed. It's an effort to open my eyes just a sliver.

My head is still trying to process my nightmares, so it takes me a few seconds to realize that my ceiling holds an emerald hue. Only one person pops in here who's both uninvited and green. Lady Reaper's little helper, Zelene.

Which means I'm about to have Zelene Encounter 2.0. It doesn't have to be too bad. Maybe I can experiment with skewering her with other things than a baculum.

When you have green ghosts in your life, one must be open to unconventional ways of having a good time.

Rolling onto my back, I open my eyes fully.

There is a green ghost on my ceiling.

It is not Zelene.

All the blood seems to drop from my body. "Cissy?"

"Yes, I'm totally stuck to your ceiling as a ghost." Cissy accents this point with a scream.

"Stay calm. I'm the Great Scala. Ghosts are what I do."

After jumping out of bed, I crane my neck for a closer look. Cissy wears her classic flannel pajamas. Her back, palms and feet rest flush against the ceiling. Taken as a whole, she has a distinctively insect-like appearance.

I check out my own flannel PJ set. "We're wearing the same outfit," I say lamely. "So, there's that."

"Be serious, Myla. What should I do?"

"I don't know yet. I need more information about—" I gesture broadly across Cissy "—this situation."

"Sure." Cissy nods so quickly, the movement makes her semi-transparent curls bob below her. "What do you need to know?"

"Well, um…"

Turns out, it's a little odd to have a conversation with someone who's stuck to your ceiling, but I can roll with it for now.

"Last thing I knew, you were driving home. What happened?"

"It's like this," Cissy winces. "Oh, you're going to be so angry."

I raise my pointer finger. "Before we get too deep into this, can you please float down here?"

"Why?" asks Ghost Cissy.

Cissy is always a sensitive soul. *Best to be careful here.*

"So," I begin. "You know how you always say that I don't spray paint turds?"

"Of course. I like that you're honest."

"Cool. Here's the problem. From my point of view, you're totally..." I try to think of a better verbal image and get nothing. "You're stuck to my ceiling like a bug."

"Eew." Cissy scans the floor. "I need to get down, but I'm not sure how."

"How did you direct yourself to float here?"

"I do have some mass, but not anything like I used to. Oh, and I can do this." Cissy closes her eyes. A look of calm washes over her features. Cissy's green body flares more brightly.

"Day-um!" I exclaim.

"Right?" Cissy opens her eyes again. "I have some brightness in me." And because Cissy is Cissy, she starts to hum *This Little Light Of Mine.*

This is one of those quintessential Cissy moments. She's stuck to my ceiling as a ghost, and yet, happy enough to hum. Even so, the tricky part is this: Cis is calm because she trusts I can get her ghostly ass out of this situation.

And I can.

Maybe.

I'm so distracted, I don't notice that Cissy has stopped humming. I do perk up when she asks me a direct question. "Did you know ghosts could control their brightness?"

"As a matter of fact, no. Most of the ghosts I see have only been that way for a short time. If you were really dead, you'd be drawn to the towers. " I tap my lips. "Which still leaves the problem of how you're stuck to my ceiling."

"Only now, I feel really gross and bug-like."

"My scala robes change when I picture them taking a certain shape," I state. "Maybe ghost stuff works the same way. How about imagining yourself floating down?"

Cissy squeezes her eyes shut. "Okay, I'm picturing it. How's it working?"

"Give it a sec."

Cissy opens her eyes. "Anything?"

"Nope."

Next, I try shooing Cis off with a broom. That doesn't work, either. After that, I stand on the bed and try to grab her hand. Also not successful. My other big brainstorm is to wave my scala robes at her, thinking that the strand technology may act like a ghost tower and bring Cissy down. Total fail.

"This is surprisingly tough." I lace my fingers behind my neck and ponder. "Hey, how did you get yourself to light up?"

"I pictured the sun."

I swing my torso from side to side. As a warrior, movement always helps me think. An idea appears. "Okay, how about imagining that your body is super heavy?"

"Oooh, that's a good one." Cissy closes her eyes and—*joy of joys*— she starts to lower until she lands on my mattress. From there, she sits cross-legged on my comforter and grins. "Wow! I did it!"

I sit up across from her. My tail rises with the arrowhead end facing up and facing Cis. It's a clear request for a high five, which Cissy provides. And even though my friend's ghostly hand goes through the arrowhead end, my tail doesn't seem to mind. It bobs in place, which is its way of saying, *happy times.*

Cissy and I try to share a hug, which goes just about as well as the high five. Still, a victory is a victory. We're taking it.

I rub my palms together. "Now, let's figure out how to fix this."

"I *knew* you'd say that."

Suddenly, a children's choir starts up in my head. It's my light igni. Seconds later, they materialize in the air nearby. Which is both good and bad. The good part is that my igni aren't turning into black holes and a mystery predator. The not-so-nice bit is how they probably want to send my best friend to Heaven when she's not technically dead.

The igni swirl around Cissy in a column of light. "Uh, Myla? What are they doing?"

I swat at my igni. "Guys, get out of here. She's not dead."

It takes a few rounds of shooing, but my igni finally disappear.

"Okay, then," I declare. "Back to our previously scheduled conversation. What happened after I left you in the car?"

"I was ready to drive away, just like you told me to. But then, Lady Reaper rushed up to my car at the first light. She knocked on my passenger-side window." Cissy winces. "Her hairdo was ruined."

"You didn't."

"Lady Reaper said she got caught in the rain and it torched her updo. She asked me if I would join her in the Makeover Palace. You know the one?"

"I know it."

"Lady Reaper asked if I would hang out with her while she got cleaned up. And I knew what you told me—how Lady Reaper wanted my hair—but I wouldn't be getting anything done to me. I'd just be keeping Lady Reaper company while she got cleaned up. People were honking for me to drive on. I panicked and agreed." Cissy looks at me sideways, as if I'll explode and release a torrent of rage in her direction. I don't.

Not that I'm happy about this situation. That said, the person who deserves the anger tsunami is Lady Reaper, the nasty ghoul who's manipulating Cissy's sweet side.

Oh, you're going down, Lady.

While looking at Cis, I make a circular gesture with my right hand. "Keep going."

"I went into the makeover palace. It was technically closed. Only those pretty Noras around. I thought that was a good sign. But then, all the Noras pounced on me and held me down. Everyone began chanting some nonsense song. After that, Lady Reaper snuck up and yanked out a handful of my hair."

"Ow!"

"It really sucked. And you know that walking stick Lady Reaper carries around?"

"I do."

"Next, she slammed it on the floor and the thing turned into a scythe. Then, she totally chopped me with it."

I wince. "Did she hurt you?"

"It didn't hurt so much as knock me out. The next thing I knew, I was back home. My body was sleeping on my bed. And Ghost Me was floating by the ceiling. It took some doing, but I figured out how to haunt you. Now, I have a big question."

"Ask away."

"Am I dead?"

"Not yet. Lady Reaper plans to murder you on your wedding day."

"Wow. Talk about not sugar-coating things."

"Sorry if that was harsh. You know me."

"The real trouble isn't you. It's Lady Reaper. Her letters were sooooo nice. Now, I think that if someone's perfect-perfect, then they're hiding something. I feel more comfortable with you. I know where the turds and spray paint are, if you get what I mean." Cis lifts her chin until she's looking right at me. "I'm ready to listen now."

"Let's go to the kitchen," I state. "I'll tell you everything over a cup of coffee." I pop my hands over my mouth. "Oops. You can't drink coffee."

"I like this idea. Just pour me a cup and put it by my regular place at the table. It will help to have everything seem as normal as possible, even if I am a green ghost."

I shoot her thumbs-up. "You got it, girlfriend."

35

MYLA

$\mathcal{A}$s we chat about Lady Reaper, Cissy has lots of questions. I explain in detail about the House of Minos, crop circles and how I came by my Reaper intel. Next, I explain the dreaded ceremony that will entrap Cissy's emerald spirit.

"I need to be sure you understand this because with any luck, you'll remember everything when you're awake."

"Okay."

"Lay it on me. Tell me Lady Reaper's evil plan."

"She wants to turn me into an emerald spirit."

"Correction," I state. "You already *have* an emerald spirit. Lady Reaper wants to control that part of you."

Cissy nods quickly. "Right, right. I'll try again. Lady Reaper wants to make my emerald spirit serve her forever."

"That's right. Keep going."

"There are three parts to the spell. The first bit needed my hair. That's done. For the second part, Lady Reaper needs my blood. The third day, I agree to something." Cissy leans over and pretends to blow at her coffee. "I don't know how much I can control my Physical Me now that there's Ghost Me, but I'll do everything I can to stop Lady Reaper."

"That's it! And remember, blood is trickier to get from you, especially since it seems like Lady Reaper needs to have her Noras chanting around her while she does it. Now, what happens on the fourth day?"

Cis fidgets in her chair. "I can't believe I'm saying this, but the last of the ritual takes place on my wedding day. Lady Reaper totally plans to chop Physical Me with a scythe while I'm wearing my freaking wedding gown. That way, Ghost Me will be stuck serving her forever." Cissy shivers. "Poor Zelene."

"Come again?" We haven't had a chance to cover Zelene yet.

"Zelene's been tortured by Lady Reaper all this time."

"Yeah. About her... No blowing smoke up your butt, right?

"Right."

"Here's the truth. Zelene is evil as Hell and wants to become the next Hallowed One herself. She killed her own brother, the scala heir, just because she was jealous of him."

"Zelene wants to become the Hallowed One? You're sure?"

"Not everyone has a best friend who got forced into being a demigoddess. Most people think this kind of gig is a lot of fun."

Cissy gasps. "I can't believe I forgot. We have to find Zeke! He's in the Dark Lands at a day spa or something. Do you think I can float there and warn him?"

"This is another bit of info we haven't covered yet." I glance out the window. It's getting close to dawn. "Long story short, Lincoln is in the Dark Lands right now, looking for Walker."

"Why?"

"The prophecy of Hallowed One requires two scythes and, long story short, Grim's scythe is in a secret laboratory under the Abyss."

Cis does a double-take. "Not the Abyss."

Now, it's my turn to look twice. "What's wrong with it?"

"You don't want me to put lipstick on this pig, right?"

"Never."

"The Abyss is the most dangerous place in the after-realms. Old gods and goddesses hang out there. Those folks are more powerful than any demon and twice as easy to tick off. I mean, if you said I could go to Hell or the Abyss? Hell, please. Plus, I don't know how Lincoln will even get in there. It's locked down tight."

I lean back in my chair and try not to freak out. "You know what?

I'll put that information in the tippy back of my mind and just focus on the fact that my best friend is a ghost. If Zeke is getting his toes painted and scalp massaged somewhere, then there's nothing to worry about."

"And if not?"

"Walker can tap into the ghoul hive mind with Group Think. He'll know if anything is wrong with Zeke. Then Walker and Lincoln will fix it."

"Okay, if you're sure."

I'm anything but sure. Still, there's nothing we can do about it if I'm wrong, so I lie my ass off. There are limits to every rule, including the one to always tell the ugly truth. "Positive."

I glance at the clock. 5:03 am. My parents will be awake. As an archangel, Dad doesn't need to sleep much. And Mom can't snooze without him. That runs in the family.

"Do you think Physical You will keep sleeping for a while?"

"Maybe."

"My parents are up. I want to call and see how they're doing. They've been fixing the old ghost towers."

"What? I didn't hear anything about that."

"I think Lady Reaper is putting the towers on the fritz just to take my parents off the playing board."

I pick up the wall phone and dial. Mom picks up on the first ring.

"Myla?"

"Yes, it's me. Is everything okay?"

"I'll be honest, honey. The ghost towers are unstable."

"Are there too many spirits? I can go over and move some souls. Give things more breathing room."

Years ago, we had a situation where I couldn't move souls and the ghost towers almost blew. If that had happened, there would have been blood thirsty ghosts roaming Purgatory. Walker fixed up the towers, but no system is perfect.

"That's not the problem, honey."

"What do you mean?"

"There aren't too many ghosts. There are too few."

I can't believe what I'm hearing. "Did you say... too few?"

"I'm afraid so. The towers use powerful magic to contain the ghosts. Without enough spirits, the magic tries to contain itself. Unless your father and I step in, the tower could explode."

"How big of a boom are we talking about?"

"One that would wipe out most of Purgatory."

Alarm rattles down my spine. "Maybe I can help."

"No, this is a job only Xavier and I can do. Our demonic and angelic energy perfectly balances the towers for short periods of time. It's an amazing coincidence."

"Yeah. Coincidence." *My ass.* Lady Reaper had more than one hundred and fifty years to figure out how to sideline my parents.

Mom yawns. "Only it does make us both very sleepy."

"There might be another reason."

"I'm all ears."

"What if I told you the Oligarchy wanted to empty out the after-realms and populate every land with ghouls?"

"I'd be skeptical. All they care about is themselves and Purgatory."

Mom's words echo throug my mind. Part of me says this is important. More of me is very concerned about Lady Reaper.

"Let me try another hypothetical. What if I told you that Lady Regina has been scheming for years to imprison every last soul in the after-realms and she needs Cissy's ghost to get the job done. Oh, and Lady Reaper's also siphoning off spirits from the ghost towers in order to distract you and Dad from her evil master plan?"

A long pause follows. Then Mom starts laughing her ass off. "Oh, honey. I needed that smile. Now, we're trusting you to ensure Cissy's wedding is as lovely as possible. If we aren't there, please take some pictures." Mom's voice cracks as she says that last bit.

A mixture of sorrow and rage fight it out in my nervous system. "Mom, you need to understand—"

"Not now," she interrupts. "Your father says another ghost tower is at risk. Give our love to Cissy!"

With that, Mom hangs up.

I look over to Ghost Cissy. "Did you catch our conversation?"

"Most of it."

"I know I'm the President of the No BS Club, but my parents are wiping themselves out with the ghost towers. Does it serve any purpose to tell them about Lady Reaper?"

"None. It will just distract them from what they have to do. And from what I overheard, that's some tricky stuff. I'm—" Cissy gasps. "I think my physical body is waking up. I've got to go!"

A moment later, Cissy is gone, too.

MYLA

*G*host *Tower Nine*
Thursday, 8:18 am.
I wait for Cissy at Ghost Tower Nine. Why? If Ghost Cissy remembered our conversation, then Robot Cissy would be here.

Sadly, both of them are a no show.

Not that I'm shocked. Even when her soul is intact, my friend has trouble with Momular management. I can only imagine the havoc Mrs F causes now that she thinks Mr F is off with a ghoulette.

Still, I stall bit more before heading off to the carnival. Unlike yesterday, I don't bother concealing my identity under ghoul robes. Some folks give me a wave. Others say they're glad I'm such great friends with Lady Reaper. Most ignore me.

To be honest, I like it. It's been years since I've been able to just mosey around without causing a scene. This is me in my natural state.

Eventually, I make my way into the carnival. Unlike yesterday, I don't lurk in the crowd this time. Instead, I march right on stage and plunk my ass down beside Cissy. For her part, Lady Reaper is off getting interviewed by Carol Cheevers again. All of which means this is the perfect opportunity for me to find out how my friend is doing now that her body and soul are back together.

"Good morning, Cis."

My friend stares off into space. Cis reminds me of that documentary on the Human Channel about trench fighters from World War One.

"Cissy, did you hear me? I said, *good morning.*"

She slowly turns her head. "Oh, hi."

"How are you feeling today?"

She goes back to staring into space. "Fine."

"Do you remember our last discussion?"

"No."

I lean forward so she has to make eye contact. "You really don't remember?"

"No."

At last, Cissy's face lights up. "There you are, Tiny!"

Sure enough, the fattest, meanest and bestest cat in Purgatory waddles over to Cissy. Tiny swats Cis' ankle and hisses.

Cis scoops her feline into her lap. Tiny swats her arm. "Did you attack Mommy? Yes, you did. You're the lion of Purgatory."

I pinch the bridge of my nose. *This is a disaster.* Sure, Ghost Cissy knows the deal. But Robot Cissy is worse than before. The only thing she cares about is Tiny. *Don't get me wrong,* I'm glad Cis has a project, but… how am I going to stop Lady Reaper now?

Speaking of my new nemesis, Lady Reaper saunters up to the microphone at center stage. Like yesterday, she taps the mic. The crowd quiets.

"Hello, citizens of Purgatory!" Lady Reaper goes back into *Eva Perón mode* and raises her arms.

The crowd loves it.

From the right side of the stage, Carol and her camera guy capture every moment.

"As promised, today we shall hold some reaper games!"

More cheering.

"Since this is an official ghoul event, we do have some rules. The first game will be a dart toss. We've set up dart boards all around the midway. Whoever gets the most bullseyes wins. Only be careful, you wouldn't want to jab yourself with these darts!"

My skin chills over. This is the second day of the ritual to transform Cissy into Lady Reaper's eternal toady. And that part of the spell requires Cissy's blood.

While the audience applauds, Lady Reaper does a golfer's clap by the microphone. When things get silent again, Lady Reaper addresses the crowd once more. "And to make the games even more fun, my devoted servants have volunteered to sing for us."

Lady Reaper claps. About fifty Noras march onstage and stand in neat rows. They begin to sing.

This is not a tune I'm familiar with. The language is also foreign. I glance over to Cissy. All the blood has drained from her face. She points to the Noras. "Don't let them hold me down!"

I'd had my suspicions before, but Cissy's exclamation confirms my worst fears. This isn't the reaper games—it's day two of the Kill Cissy Spell.

I grasp Cis' hand. "Let's get you out of here." I yank on her arm, but Cissy doesn't move.

Lady Reaper strides over. Bending at the waist, she looks directly into Cis' eyes as she speaks: "Why don't you pet Tiny? After that, we can play a game of darts."

"As you command." Cissy scoops up Tiny.

Lady Reaper turns to me and smirks. Not gonna lie. I want to punch her in the boob right now. Instead, my gaze lands on Carol Cheevers.

What was that interview I saw the other night? I saw something about ghoul rules. *Now, I remember.* A wicked smile rounds my lips.

I know just what to do.

Rising, I march over to center stage and grab the microphone. It's an oddly satisfying thing to do. "In a spirit of friendship, I hereby challenge Lady Reaper to a classic ghoul duel."

Lady Reaper arches her right brow. "Ghoul duel?"

"Here's the situation. When I fought in the arena, there were demon exhibition days where warriors like me could take on decent battles.... but the emcee Sharkie hated my guts and kept me on the sidelines. So, I learned every ghoul rule there is when it comes to games."

And I don't even finish that out by adding *nyah.*

Lady Reaper folds her arms across her chest. "Is that so?"

"This event is subject to Dark Lands Schedule Five Regulations. Section 18-S, article 24. Anyone may challenge a ghoul to a duel of their choice as part of an open festival game. And so, I challenge you to a formal challenge of obscure administrivia. The winner gets to name today's reaper game. And I should warn you, I hate darts."

"A ghoul administrivia challenge? You can't be serious. Besides, I've already chosen today's game. You can't do this." Lady Reaper accents this last point with the angriest smile I've ever seen. It's a great look on her.

"Nuh uh. According to the Great Ghoul Conclave of the Harmonic Convergence, Special Rule Section AD-6, Subsection D-98 says that I can challenge you to a duel to determine anything. In this case, if I win, I'll name the game for today."

"The great ghoul constitution says the senior ghoul runs every event."

"Only, we're in Purgatory, not the Dark Lands. Therefore, Subsection D-98 is the ruling principle and it says that the indigenous challenger claims precedence. Boom."

Regina purses her lips. "How do you know all this?"

"I'll take that as an agreement to the duel. Best of three questions."

Lady Reaper's nostrils flare as if I just pooped on the stage. "Make it quick."

"First one. Per regulations, this question must pertain to this very event—" here I gesture across the midway "—in order to win the chance to decide today's game. In the great ghoul agreement called Magna Wormenda, the second section refers to events like the one being held today. What does that paragraph refer to? Bonus points if you can name which ghoul administrator penned the section."

Lady Regina's mean smile deepens. "No need for more administrivia. I'm happy for you to name today's game."

"How nice." I lean over and make a fake drumroll on my thighs. "Today's game is... a three-legged race down the midway!"

The crowd cheers.

Robot Cissy stares off into space.

Lady Reaper scowls.

I'm really getting into this now. I take the microphone and tilt it a little sideways in the classic move of Elvis impersonators every-where. "And for this game, I name my partner…. Lady Reaper!"

More cheers.

More staring.

More scowls from Lady Reaper.

Boom!

Thunder sounds, followed by sheets of heavy rain. Since this is Purgatory, that won't slow anything down, but it does mean the three-legged race will be taking place in a whole lotta mud.

"Are you sure about this?" asks Lady Reaper slowly.

"So sure," I reply.

Lady Reaper stares at me with such rage, it's a wonder I don't burst into a puff of smoke. Still, she's scheming to lock up every last soul into an eternal jail. Lady Reaper has this and a whole lot more coming.

I scan Lady Reaper from head to toe. "Nice white dress. See you in front of the stage for the start of the race." And as I walk away, I twiddle my fingers at her.

Sometimes, it's great to be me.

MYLA

I stand in front of the main stage for the ghoul carnival. Cissy is parked on a nearby chair. She's still petting Tiny and staring off into nothing.

At this point, I wonder if Lady Reaper's magic requires Cissy to have the equivalent of a *supernatural lovey* in order to keep her happy, body and soul.

Note to self: If I get out of this, learn more about strand magic. Threaten Walker if necessary.

Lady Reaper stands to my right. She wears her white outfit, complete with hat. I've got on my scala robes and a shit-eating grin.

This will be so awesome, I can't wait.

Beside me, Carol narrates the scene for television viewers across Purgatory. Although, we aren't a huge realm—and a ton of people are here—so I'm not sure how many are watching. Still, I appreciate the support.

"This is Carol Cheevers, Private Eye... LIVE. It's 11:42 am. And this is the first ghoul carnival in Purgatory. Before me are two supernatural women. One is a ghoul with a prophecy to perhaps take over our realm one day. The other is a quasi who's moved souls for a decade. Now, they're almost ready to race, side by side."

Rain keeps coming down in sheets. Thunder rolls.

Carol continues. "Yes, the first reaper game will be a three-legged race. In this competition, two contestants stand in a row. Then, their ankles are tied together. The two runners must speed forward as one. Whoever crosses the finish line first, wins. "

Carol's right about some stuff. Indeed, Lady Regina and I now stand side-by-side in that arm-bendy pose favored by sprinters. Regina volunteered to tie our ankles together with the equivalent of toilet paper.

I agreed.

Then, I silently commanded by scala robes to slide under her super-sketchy tie and create an unbreakable rope to connect our ankles.

Heh heh heh. Lady Reaper may *think* she's running away from me. That is not happening.

"Wait, everyone!" Carol's voice goes up an octave. "New players are entering the field, Yes, ladies and gentlemen, it's true. Actual necro hunters are here. These are elite guards for the Reapers and they appear to be joining the race. Over to you in the studio, Bob."

This gets my attention and how. Straightening from my sprinter pose, I crane my neck back to see what Carol's up to. She nods and stares into the camera while touching her earpiece.

"Thank you, Sheldon, for that important commentary," says Carol. "Folks, that was Sheldon of Ghoul Rules Rule. Apparently, since the necro guards are in Lady Reaper's retinue, they can legally join the race. What an unexpected twist! First, the dart games are canceled. Now, the three-legged race expands."

"You can still back out," whispers Lady Reaper. "My necro guards won't go easy on you."

"Eh, kiss my tail." I look up and feel the rain. Yes!

Side note: I already know the Noras and necro hunters are both formed by strand magic. And I'm pretty sure that they're both extensions of Lady Reaper's will. Specifically, I'm guessing she needs to see them in order to puppeteer them around. A three-legged race is a great place to test this theory.

This just keeps getting better.

Lady Reaper thinks she's about to ruin my day. In truth, she's giving me a chance to perform a fun little experiment. And if all goes well, it will also be a painful one... for her.

Carol keeps on announcing. "Now, Senator Frederickson is stepping up to the microphone. She's wearing the same dress that she did yesterday. Not that everyone has to dress up, but we do have a fashion watch when it comes to the senator."

I purse my lips. There are actual people who watch Cissy's fashions and comment about them on the news. *That settles it.* I need to catch up on my television watching.

Carol lowers her voice. "There's Senator Frederickson stepping up to the microphone... staring out into space... not saying anything... still not speaking a word... Ah, here she goes."

Cissy's monotone echoes through the carnival. "The three-legged race starts in three, two, one."

Boom! Someone shoots off a flare gun, which I totally appreciate.

Regina and I rush forward.

What happens next is a flurry of awesomeness. More thunder rolls. Extra rain pours. I tap into my demonic energy and haul ass at double speed. Lady Reaper tries to keep up. That's not easy.

Then, Lady Reaper tries to shake her leg loose. That's not possible.

By the time we're half way down the midway, Lady Reaper and I are far ahead of the necro hunters. I shoot a quick look over my shoulder. As I suspected, all the necro hunters have stopped running. Some even slip and land face-down in the mud.

I shouldn't enjoy that sight, but I do.

By the time we near the finish line, Lady Reaper is panting for breath. Ghouls really aren't big into cardio. We're only inches from the end when Lady Reaper falls over back-first into the mud.

I could stop, there are two big reasons not to. One, the crowd is cheering their guts out. And two, I really hate Lady Reaper.

Tapping into my inner demon strength, I run faster than ever before.

"Dragging... your... fat... ass... to... the... win!"

I cross the finish line first. Carol's voice sounds over the loudspeakers. "It's Myla Lewis for the win!"

While Lady Reaper is stuck in the mud, I command scala robes to untie us. The crowd keeps cheering. My tail pops up to wave and grab attention because... what else would it do?

After hauling her ass out of the mud, Lady Reaper comes over to stand beside me. She's a single sheet of gooey dirt. Like me, she smiles and waves to the crowd.

"I hate you," says Lady Reaper.

"Yeah?" I counter. "Neener neener neener."

"You're so immature. It's unbecoming to a grown woman."

"Hey, you don't hear me needling you for being such a stuck-up bitch, do you? Mind your own business." I blow the crowd one last kiss. "Now, if you'll excuse me, I'll sit by Cissy until she exchanges wedding vows with Zeke."

"There's no need for that. I give you my solemn oath that nothing more will happen to Cissy."

"And you expect me to believe that."

Lady Reaper takes out what looks like a penny from her pocket, only the item is purple and engraved with the Letter L.

"I believe your own Lucas, Earl of Striga, cast this truth charm." Lady Reaper raises the coin. "I, Lady Reaper, shall not cast any spell on Cissy Frederickson for the duration of the reaper games." She sets the coin under her tongue. Purple light flashes in her mouth.

The spell is set.

"Good afternoon, Myla." Lady Reaper saunters away.

Rest of the reaper games, my ass. When exactly does that mean? Five minutes from now? Ten?

I slog my way back to the stage and sit by Robot Cissy for the rest of the day. Then, I make sure she gets home and even double check all the protective charms and portal alerts in her room.

Once I'm confident Cis is safe, I go home, shower and cuddle up to my Pillow Lincoln.

And hope the real one is safe as well.

38

LINCOLN

For hours, I've been digging out a big stretch of the wall in my new prison cell. Now, about a third of one panel is nothing but an exposed patchwork of golden strands. I stand before the filaments and test out placing my hands at different spots. As long as my gauntlet is visible, my fingertips can tap into different powers. It's a bit like playing the guitar.

I try a new configuration. For the umpteenth time, Group Think streams through my head. This is a constant stream of ghoul hive mind chatter. It takes some practice to pick out different voices. Soon, different internal monologues sound in my head.

I want worm soufflé for dinner.

That's an elder man's voice. Next, a young woman speaks.

Fill out form 67-D8 and return it tomorrow.

Next, I hear the clipped tones of someone with military training.

On my mark, reconfigure Oligarchy Dungeon G-1, cellblock A.

A jolt of excitement moves through me. This last thought is what I've been looking for—internal chatter about my prison. Closing my eyes, I focus on that last data stream.

Configure in three, two, one.

Lights flash in my mind's eye. A master view of the prison appears in my head. I see my dungeon and sense the ghoul's commands as the messages move through different strands. Instructions come through for my cell block.

Rumbling sounds. My entire cell vibrates as it moves within the greater structure. My pulse speeds. *This is it. My chance to try and move the system on my own.*

I sense the command for where my cell block should end up. I picture it moving to a different spot.

The strands do as I tell them.

It's almost beyond belief. In my mind, I see the prison blocks shift around in the greater cube. My cell starts off in one direction but comes to rest in a different place.

I did it. I manipulated the dungeon.

Excitement zings through my nervous system. Now, all I need to do is tap into a map of the greater area. From there, I can command the prison to build me an escape tunnel.

"Walker," I whisper. "I knew you'd have a way out of here."

A barrage of new voices sound in my head. As part of their punishment, our prison cells are cut off from Group Think. Still, the guards monitor prison cell audio. Now, a surveillance feed runs through my mind.

Three days until I'm up for parole.

I don't belong here.

Let me out! I'll miss my wedding!

That last speaker makes my body turn cold. That sounds like Zeke. I recall the guards saying he was heading to the Dark Lands. Did he ever get back?

Another voice sounds in my mind.

Finally. I'm on my way.

I smile so hard, my face hurts. That last speaker would be Walker.

My cell spins about in a new direction. The action is too fast for me to track the motion using the strands in my wall.

Slam!

My cell block has hit something, hard. Bit by bit, one wall of my little prison crumbles. There, on the other side, is the real Walker.

"You're here at last!" He looks at my gauntlet. "Good, you found some strand magic. That'll be useful."

"Hello, Walker. How are things? Anything you wish to share?"

Walker strides into my cell. His ghoul robes shift and billow behind him. "We both know I"m here to break into the Abyss... Oh, look at this wall. You've exposed a lot of strands. This is a much better control panel than the one I was able to make. You are a marvel, Lincoln."

"I got lucky. Check the monitor."

Walker scans the tiny screen above my cell door. "Of course. An older cell would have more imperfections and chances to access the underlying strand technology. Serves me right for choosing a newer part of the dungeon."

I cross my arms. "I'm still waiting for my update." Over the years, I've learned that if you don't push Walker to share, he forgets to outline basic risks.

"Ah, yes. I am here about the Hallowed One prophecy, the same as you are. It requires a second scythe. Grim and I plan to fabricate said item once I reach Eli's old lab."

"I don't think that's a good idea, Walker."

"I know Grim. Trust me, this is best." Walker turns his attention back to the exposed wall of strands. "How's Myla?"

"The prophecy also requires a second emerald spirit. That's Cissy. Myla's back in Purgatory, making sure her friend is safe."

"Understood," says Walker. "The sooner I have the second scythe, the faster we can both get to Purgatory and help. I've been trying to break into the Abyss for days."

"The prophecy also talks about a tower," I state. "What about that? It seems for this scheme to work, there will need to be the mother of all ghost towers."

"Nothing exists as far as I know," says Walker. "That said, if anyone could design the prophecy's tower, it's Eli. Once we get to the laboratory, we'll check for information on that as well. I guess that catches us up."

"Not yet." I narrow my eyes. "You *knew* I'd show up here."

"What makes you say that?"

"When you greeted me by saying, *You're here at last!* It was a bit of a giveaway."

"Honestly, I thought Grim and I would break into the Abyss earlier. We've been a bit stuck. The longer I stayed in the dungeons, the higher the probability that you'd join me. As of today, there's an eighty-seven per cent chance." Walker's all-black eyes widen. It's the face he makes when being playful. "I always work the odds."

"And what about the Grim Reaper? He came by my cell disguised as you. I got the distinct impression he was trying to shoo me out of the Dark Lands so he could get the scythe and tower for himself."

"Grim has a good heart, Lincoln. He means well, trust me. As I told you, I've known him for hundreds of years. Allow me to manage that part of this mission."

Walker sets his palms onto the wall of exposed golden filaments. What happens next takes place so quickly, I can barely keep track. Walker's fingertips fly across the strands. While I felt like I was playing the guitar, what Walker is doing is something I've never seen before.

The cell rumbles and shifts. Only this time, my cell and Walker's move as a unit. When we come to a halt, a scraping reverberates from Walker's side of the joint cell. I walk up to the threshold between my block and his. Walker's floor is gone. In its place, a long tunnel now opens into the depths.

"There you have it," announces Walker. "A back door into the Abyss."

Here we go.

ESCAPE TUNNEL

39

LINCOLN

*S*oon, Walker and I will enter the Abyss. *At last.*

I kneel by the tunnel's edge and scan below. "The fastest way down would be to repel." I take out my baculum. "I can ignite these as ropes."

Walker winces. "Not sure that's a good idea. There's one *additional factor* to consider."

The prison cell around us shimmies. The system is realigning. That much is to be expected. I look down the tunnel. Huge blocks speed across the shaft as the system reconfigures.

I round on Walker. "When you say *additional factor,* do you mean that at any moment, cell blocks can speed across the tunnel and crush one like a bug?"

"Correct."

"In that case, my rope idea won't work." I take a closer look. "This tunnel is lined with uneven grooves. Do you know what those are?"

"Every prison cube has exterior grooves to help them change locations. They're like train tracks... very stable."

Tilting my head, I make silent calculations. "Those grooves look at least an inch deep. I've descended cliff faces that are far smoother. The *not getting crushed* part will keep me on my toes, but I can handle it." I look to Walker. "You?"

"I'll be fine." He pulls his ghoul robes off over his head, revealing that he wears thrax body armor as well. "Mine are the old model. How are the new ones working out?"

"Good so far. Let's see how the armor works while climbing."

Suddenly, the cube around us shivers more violently than before. Bits of stone cascade from the ceiling. Long metallic groans rend the air. Little by little, the ceiling panel slides away. A new figure drops onto the floor beside me.

The Grim Reaper.

Unlike last time, Grim isn't pretending to be Walker. Instead, he sports his traditional skull-head look.

All this while, I've been keeping my gauntlet visible. Now, I command the armor to retreat into my skin again. With any luck, Grim didn't notice that particular bit of magic. But it might help to distract him to another topic.

"I see you're wearing your own face," I state.

Walker shakes his head. "Grim, you didn't take Lincoln to the Red Court, did you?"

"Hey, I was only trying to help." Grim steps up and sets his hand on my shoulder. "No hard feelings, right? Walker and I are working on breaking into the Abyss. We have a plan. I didn't want a child getting in the way."

"Meaning I'm not hundreds of years old."

"Of course," says Grim. "Age brings wisdom."

I stare pointedly at his hand. "Not in the realm of respecting personal space, it seems."

Moments pass. Eventually, Grim realizes what I mean and ceases to grab my person. "Ah. Was I making you uncomfortable, secretly enabling every last problem in your life, and serving as the darkness to your light?"

I eye Grim carefully. This isn't the first time Grim has said something like this to me. During our trip to the Red Court, he gave a similar speech.

But most folks understand hate. Do you, Lincoln? Do you ever suspect someone carries enough hate for you in their heart, that they've been stalking you for years, causing every last problem in your life, and serving as the darkness to your light?

I didn't take this speech seriously before, and I won't start now.

Without another word, I step over to the tunnel and look to Walker. "I'll see you at the bottom."

"Not so fast, friend," says Grim. "When I first dropped in, I thought I saw something on your arm. Do you mind telling me what it is?"

"Yes, as a matter of fact, I do."

Without another comment, I slip into the tunnel and begin my descent. One thing about growing up in an underground realm—I spent much of my childhood climbing rock walls. Muscle memory kicks in.

Every so often, the tunnel rumbles. The section that's about to break loose shimmies with the most force. Sometimes things get dicey, but I'm able to move out of the way. Walker and I move down in tandem. Grim speeds up and gets below us, which is fine with me. The farther I am from the Grim Reaper, the better.

About half-way down the tunnel, I hear rhythmic tapping against the wall. I pause and look to Walker. "That's an SOS."

An expression shifts across Walker's face, only it's gone too quickly to be sure. Only, I'm almost certain about what I saw.

Walker looks guilty.

"We should keep moving," offers my friend.

I pound on the wall with my fist. "Hello?"

A familiar voice echoes into the tunnel. "Yes, I'm here! They have me locked up. Help!"

I refocus on Walker. "That's Zeke."

"Yes."

"You knew he was here?"

"I had my suspicions. The identity of prisoners is secret. But I caught his voice on some of the surveillance feeds."

"If you thought Zeke was here, why not help him?"

"Because Grim's not wrong. This is a tough mission. Zeke is safest in his cell."

I can't believe what I'm hearing. "Zeke is a trained warrior. We're foolish if we leave him behind."

Walker checks the tunnel below me. Grim is now three-quarters of the way down. "I have to keep moving."

My eyes widen with a realization. "You don't think you can leave Grim alone, do you? You don't trust him."

"If Grim is unpredictable sometimes, he has his reasons."

"So you've said. Let's set Grim aside. We have to help Zeke. "

"I know you, Lincoln. You won't leave until Zeke's free, so I'll speed the process along."

Walker grasps a different ridge. A flash of golden thread appears on his palm. That settles it. Walker is sporting some thread technology, same as I am. No wonder he wasn't surprised to see my gauntlet when he entered the cell.

Walker grips the ridge with suck force, he pulls it out. The panel across from us rumbles and slides down, revealing the interior of a cell. And Zeke.

"The wardens will notice that broken ridge," says Walker. "It won't take long for them to check it out. You better go fast. And don't break anything else or they'll send the guards."

With that, Walker starts descending at double speed.

Zeke steps to the edge of the cell. "Lincoln, is that really you? They said I was supposed to come to the Dark Lands for some spa day or something. Then, they locked me up. I have to get out of here or I'll miss the wedding!"

"I can get you out, but you need to climb down this tunnel. Can you make it?"

Zele scopes out the pit below us. "Sure."

"Let's get climbing. I'll bring you up to speed along the way. Oh, and stay alert. The walls can move and crush you, if you aren't careful."

"Understood." Zeke slides out onto the tunnel wall and begins his own descent. "But before you start the mission brief, tell me one thing. Does this have anything to do with how Lady Reaper is a fiend?"

"As a matter of fact, it does."

"And Cissy's not the real Hallowed One."

"Correct again."

"If you told me that a week ago, I could have laughed. But I've had a lot of quality time in the cell to realize that things have been wrong for a while now."

With that out of the way, we begin our descent.
And I tell Zeke everything.

40

MYLA

What a crap night's sleep.

Every time I almost fall a-snooze, my brain wakes me up in a big way. My mind sends image after image of Lady Reaper with her little white hat. She rubs her hands together while crying *mwah hah hah.*

Because, honestly... *What is that ghoul up to?*

Around 2 am., I decide it's a good idea to check through our stores of truth charms and see if the one Lady Reaper used today was legit. If it's fake, then she's just playing mind games.

But it turns out, that charm was the real thing.

Which means she's *still* playing mind games, only she's reeeeeeeeeally good at it.

That is concerning.

I go back to bed, I lace my fingers behind my neck and stare at the ceiling. Lady Reaper must be trying to lull me into a false sense of security with that charm. Her goal is that I never guess when she's really about to strike.

A glimmer of green light appears on the ceiling. Suddenly, I'm wide awake again, only with a happy sense of anticipation.

"Cissy? Is that you?"

When a disaster approacheth, it's great to commiserate with your best friend. Cis may not have any answers, but together? We'll know if we've missed any questions.

The emerald glow shines more brightly. Then, it congeals into a female shape that descends from the ceiling to sit at the base of my bed. As more of the ghost comes into focus, one thing is clear.

This is most definitely not Cissy. I stifle a groan.

"Hi, Zelene."

"Is that any way to greet the future Hallowed One? Show me some respect."

This time, I straight-out groan. "Why couldn't you be Cissy?"

Zelene lifts her chin. "Because I am the future Hallowed One."

I roll my eyes. "Did you really float over here just to tell me that?"

"As the Hallowed One, I can save you and your family. However, you must help Cissy finish her transformation. Will you do this?"

I tap my chin. "Let me guess. The person who told you to ask me this was maybe…. Lady Reaper?"

"I don't see what that has to do with anything."

"Did it ever occur to you that maybe Lady Reaper thinks *she'll* be the Hallowed One? That perhaps she's been playing *you* this whole time?"

Zelene gasps. "You don't know the great gift Lady Reaper once awarded me."

"You mean, how she helped you poison your brother, the scala heir? Yeah, that's one sweet present."

"The Great Scala is already an empty title," declares Zelene. "The time of the Hallowed One is nigh and you are worthless!"

I sit up and stretch. "Well, my worthless ass needs some coffee. If you want to keep screeching at me, I'll be in near the fridge."

I slide out of bed and shuffle my sweet self into the kitchen. A glorious sight awaits me. Ghost Cissy sits at her favorite spot on the kitchen table.

I grin. "Am I glad to see you!"

Zelene floats into the kitchen behind me. When she spies Cissy, Zelene pauses and bows her head. "Greetings, Senator Frederickson."

"Don't you Senator Frederickson me. I heard what you said to my friend." Cissy wags her finger at Zelene. "You leave Myla alone!"

"I was only acting under orders from Lady Reaper," says Zelene. "And your so-called friend addressed me in a way that was most undignifi—"

At this point, Cissy goes ballistic, ghost style. The last time I saw Cissy, she made herself glow slightly. Now she becomes searingly bright as she rises up from the kitchen table and screeches. As an extra level of scary, Cissy's bones turn even brighter than her skin.

Zelene flies her ass out of my kitchen at double speed.

Once it's just me and Cissy, I slow clap for my friend. "That was amazing."

"I have literally nothing else to do all day but practice how to haunt people. Besides, you know I was always a natural in theater class."

I rustle through the cabinets in search of caffeine. "You're doing a great job."

"It takes my mind off, you know. Being a soul sucks. I can't stop physical me from sitting around like a zombie."

"I think of 'physical you' more as a very stylish robot, if that's any help."

"Thank you. That does make me feel better." The light in her body dims. "Although this is really tough. Lady Reaper sent me all those letters. She lied to me for years! And now, she's using the nicest parts of me to hurt everyone."

I take my regular seat at he table. "I'm so sorry, Cis."

"Where's Zeke? Where are Cam and Xav? And once I'm back in my so-called body, what if I stay stuck inside, watching myself be a zombie forever."

"Cool robot forever," I correct.

Cissy sniffle-smiles. "Now, you're making me laugh. Not fair."

"Did Lady Reaper get any blood from your yesterday?"

"No. And those Nora people didn't chant at me, either."

"So that's good."

Cissy holds up her hand. "This doesn't look good. How can I get married if no one can put a ring on my finger?"

I lean forward. "Look, we talked before about adventures. You know Lincoln and I enjoy them, right?"

Cissy dabs under her eyes. "Yeah."

"I'll show you how it works. Follow me."

I lead Cissy into our garage, which is home to the most fantastic car in the after-realms: a green station wagon with wood paneling and lots of rust. This vehicle is so incredibly uncool, it's sublime.

"That's really her?"

"Yes, that's Betsy, the same freaking station wagon that I drove in high school."

"I don't think you washed it since then, either."

"Sarcasm, yes!" I pump my fist in the air. "That's the spirit!"

I get in behind the steering wheel and start searching for the keys. There's nothing under the visor or front seat, which means I'm out of ideas. I look to my tail. "Do you remember where I put them?"

Betsy has what I call, *benchy front seats*. Over the years, my tail has jabbed this area so many times, the springs are exposed. Now, my tail dives into the exposed fluff. It comes out a moment later with my keys dangling from the arrowhead-shaped end.

"Thank you."

My tail rubs against my cheek, which is a rare sign of affection. I lean forward and call to Ghost Cissy through the window. "Are you coming?"

"Do you really think it will help?"

"It's already an improvement from crying at the kitchen table."

"True." Cissy floats through the passenger door to sit in the front seat. "Ready."

I rev the engine and hit the button for our newfangled electric garage door opener. Only I hit the button a dozen times since this is Purgatory and nothing mechanical works on the first try.

With the door open, I pull out into the street. "Now," I tell Cissy. "For the best part!" I turn on the radio.

The announcer's voice echoes on Betsy's tinny speakers. "Thank you for listening WPLK, Purgatory's All-Polka channel!"

"Are you kidding? Betsy's radio is still stuck on the polka channel?

"You know it. And guess what? It's impossible to be grumpy while listening to polka music."

"Up next," continues the announcer. "A special polka for Laureen in Lower Purgatory. This one's for you!"

The music starts and I screech with delight. "I love this polka!" I turn up the volume and sing along with gusto.

I don't want her you can have her she's too fat for me.
She's too fat for me. Hey!
She's too fat for me. Hey!

Now, I'm having a dandy time but Cis still looks little mopey. But then, the powers of the universe step in. For the next tune, an absolute classic starts up.

Na na na na na na na
Na na na na na na na
Na na na na na na na
Clap clap clap clap

"It's the chicken dance!" I cry. "No one can be unhappy during this song."

As the name suggests, this tune includes some minor interpretive dance moves. I keep my hands on the wheel, but my tail does the motions of pretending to quack, flap, and lay an egg. At least, I'm pretty sure that's what it's doing.

This time, Ghost Cissy joins right in. It's a blast.

One the song is over, Ghost Cissy kicks her feet onto the dashboard, just like old times. "I think I get it now. Even when life is crappy, it's awesome. You just have to live it."

"You got it, girlfriend."

Ghost Cissy sits upright. "Uh oh. My body is waking up. See you later!"

Little by little, my friend vanishes. I turn back, park the car, and get ready.

Time to live the adventure.

MYLA

*A*n hour later, I'm still humming the chicken dance as I step onto the midway of the ghoul carnival. The place is packed again. Everyone looks happy. I come to a big decision.

Even if I do end up killing Regina Reaper, I'll encourage Mom to hold the ghoul carnival every year. Lady Reaper may be evil as fuck, but she throws a good party.

I saunter past the pavilions. It's part of my ritual to check on the Cirque du Sloth. And it's the same acrobats, hanging upside down, all day, every day. It's some kind of miracle of science.

I switch to humming the *Too Fat Polka* as I watch the greed pavilion's hot air balloons rise and circle the midway. As I pass the Tunnel of Wrath, I wonder what reaper game I should choose for today. Yesterday's three-legged race was superb. That will be hard to top. I have a trio of alternatives in mind: tiddledy winks, water balloons or dodge ball. Tough call, really.

As I march toward the stage, I'm feeling pretty good about my bad self.

That's when everything goes to Hell.

Lady Reaper is already on stage. Her Noras are arrayed behind her with their white cloaks and creepy masks. Robot Cissy sits in her regular chair with Tiny on her lap and a dazed look in her eyes. And there's a tea table between them.

A tea table.

What kind of Hell is this?

I stroll onto the stage and pause by Lady Reaper and her dreaded table. "Hey."

"And good morning to you, Myla Lewis."

"What's with the tea?"

"Today's game is a little something called 'let's get to know each other and drink tea.'"

"No, it's not."

"Yes, it is. I got special permission from the Oligarchy."

Crud. I should have figured that Lady Reaper would out-rule me once she had a little time to work the system.

I plunk down on my regular chair beside Robot Cissy. "Good morning, Senator Frederickson." I lean in and whisper in a low voice. "Don't worry, I know you're in there."

One of the Noras sets a tea cup before me. Another fills it with very stinky yellow tea. I remember the trip to the past where Lady Reaper gave Zelene a special tea to kill her brother.

Lady Reaper sips her own cup. "Why don't you give it a try?"

"Maybe later."

Carol Cheevers steps up. A bright light shines in my face. The camera guy hoists up his mega machine... and the real torture of the day begins.

"This is Carol Cheevers, Private Eye LIVE. And we're covering today's small-talkathon with Lady Reaper and the Great Scala. They're going to make interesting—*yet not in any way offensive*—chatter for the next six hours straight."

I raise my hand, ready to announce my departure.

"And don't forget, this is a fundraiser for Senator Frederickson's Charity, Orphans Without Boundaries. All donations go to helping quasi orphans on Earth find a more accepting home here in Purgatory."

Aaaaaand I lower my arm. *Orphans without Boundaries?* I can't walk off the stage when I could raise money for those kids. It honestly is Cissy's charity.

Truth time: I've never wanted laser beams to shoot out of my eyeballs... until now. After catching Lady Reaper's gaze, I mouth two words at her: *you're diabolical.*

She grins and offers her own soundless reply. *Thank you.*

Thus begins eight hours of talking about the weather. Carol Cheevers covers the whole thing live. We raise a ton of money for Cissy's charity. More than once, I debate about performing an appendectomy on myself with a fork, just to have an excuse to leave.

At no point do I drink Lady Reaper's tea. Nor do I eat any of the cookies. I'm not proud of this, but I do split a few demon bars from my secret stash with Tiny. The poor cat looks really hungry. With Cissy so out of it, I don't know who's filling his bowl back at Casa de Cissy.

At last, the marathon is over. I drive Robot Cissy home and make sure she gets to her bedroom safely. The process involves interacting with Mrs F who's already well into martini time. All images of Mr F have been cut out of the family photo wall in the living room. Someone's been busy.

I go home and worry.

Tomorrow's the big day. Cissy's wedding. I'm supposed to show up at the stage, wear my scala robes and do very little. Lady Reaper is playing mind games with the eight-hour tea-athon, but other than that? She's really keeping to her word not to do anything else to Cissy.

Maybe I misjudged her.

Perhaps Lady Reaper really doesn't care about the Hallowed One prophecy.

Or maybe there's a master plan here and I just don't see it.

In the end, I decide to think about something else for a while by catching up on my television watching. And I hope Lincoln is having better luck, wherever he is.

LINCOLN

Zeke's a good climber, but he hasn't spent days memorizing the tell-tale signs that a massive block of stone is about to smash you into a pancake. So we go more slowly. And I explain to him everything that's happened, from Lady Reaper and Grim to the prophecy's missing scythe and mysterious tower.

For his part, Zeke talks about what's been happening with him and Cissy. It's the first time we've really discussed important stuff. For some reason, I think it helps that we're sharing while trying not to get squashed. There's no extra mental energy to conceal things, even from yourself.

"I didn't notice Cis for a long time," says Zeke. "But once I did, there was no one else for me. I wanted to get hitched right away."

I find a new foothold that allows me to slide down a few extra inches. "I remember that night. You two were dancing at the Ryder mansion."

Zeke inches down as well. "I proposed the next month. She said no. And I've proposed once a month since then."

I'm so surprised, I forget to keep moving for a few seconds. "Wow, I didn't know that."

"No one does. I thought it was the change of Cissy becoming a Senator. Maybe she needed some time to adjust to her new job. She needed room to be herself before we started our lives together."

I recover enough to resume my descent. "Was that why she wanted to wait?"

"I honestly don't know. About a month ago, I asked Cissy to marry me. At last, she said yes. I asked what changed her mind. Cis said it just felt right. And I agree. It was only afterward that Lady Reaper got involved."

I climb down a bit more and realize a key fact: I've run out of tunnel. "I think we've reached the end."

Zeke scales down so we're side by side. "It looks to be a seven-foot drop into an alley."

I scan the ground below. After years of hunting demons, I can sense when others are near. "This place is deserted. Let's do it."

Both Zeke and I drop to the ground. The zone looks like a typical alley in any city on Earth. There's no sign of Walker or Grim.

Somehow, I'm not surprised.

Lights and sounds come from the alley's mouth. We slip along the wall to check out the street beyond. It looks like something out of a human science fiction movie. Hover cars speed through the air. Run-down metal buildings are covered in elaborate webs of neon light.

And a steady stream of ghouls stride along the dark asphalt. But there are more than ghouls here. I count demons, quasis and angels in the mix.

"How does it look?" asks Zeke.

"We should be able to blend in with the crowd. The question is, where do we want to go?"

"Didn't Walker tell you?"

"We didn't have enough time to discuss the topography of the Abyss." I rub my neck. "By now, Walker would already have opened a portal to the labs."

"Are you worried?"

"Not yet. I trust Walker. If he's not here, then there's a reason. Besides, I'm a hunter and tracker. Finding a particular place? That's what I do."

Zeke nods. "Let's get started."

I step out onto the street. The sight that greets me takes my breath away. The Abyss is a deep well cut into the ground. A wide street winds around the interior of the pit. Zeke and I came out about half-way down.

"What do you think?" asks Zeke.

"Eli's lab should be the lowest spot in the city. If we follow this street, it should take us there. "

Zeke shrugs. "Let's go."

As we march lower in the Abyss, the crowd gets more sparse and strange. There are beings with extra eyes and arms. I'd heard the Abyss was a dumping ground for ancient and lost deities. Clearly, those beings hide out on lower levels.

Eventually, Zeke and I come to the base of the Abyss. It holds the burned out ruin of a building… and nothing else. I do a double-take. I knew Eli's laboratory was divided into two parts. The upper part was called the Light. The lower levels were named the Darkness.

Zeke steps closer to the building. He pushes some trash aside, revealing a sign. "This is it," says Zeke. "The Laboratory of the Light." He looks toward me. "Were you aware the place was lost in a fire?"

I shake my head. "I know Walker and Grim used to work here, but I assumed the place was still standing. Maybe closed up, but not burned out."

"You didn't expect this," says Zeke.

"I don't know anything about Walker's life as an engineer in the Dark Lands. Walker and me? That, I understand. But Walker and Grim? I'm starting to wonder."

We step under the threshold. A flight of stairs leads down to the lab's main level. We reach a large room that's littered with burned and rusted out parts of machines. Cracked windows send beams of moonlight onto the ground. The scent of charcoal still fills the air.

I step on some glass. A chorus of cracking noises fill the air. I lift my foot and find I've stepped on the remnants of an old drawing in a glass frame. My friend Walker is a talented artist. I know his style, and this is definitely one of his pieces. It shows the image of a woman.

I've seen her before, back when Myla and I visited the ghost well in England. Lady Reaper had summoned up women who she described as moving statues. They were all identical. She called them the Noras.

And this picture? It's of that woman. *Nora.*

The Grim Reaper himself told me about Nora, saying she was his first wife and true love… just like me and Myla. A creeping sense of dread moves over me. Questions ricochet through my mind.

When did Walker draw Nora? How did the real version of Grim's first wife turn into a moving statue made of strand magic? And why would so many duplicated Noras serve Lady Reaper?

The longer I search, the more questions I find.

LABORATORY OF THE LIGHT

43

LINCOLN

I slip the drawing of Nora into a pocket on my body armor and return to the challenge at hand: finding the laboratory under this one.

Zeke and I split up. We start with the basics: looking for exits and doors. Other than the flight of stairs that lead back the street, there's nothing.

Which isn't too surprising. Octavia said the Laboratory of Darkness did questionable things. It makes sense that the entrance to such a place would be hidden. We scan the tiled floor for signs of a hidden exit... press on wall panels to see if anything opens... and search for any signs of keyholes or codes.

Still nothing.

Frustration tightens up my back and shoulders. Zeke and I stand in the burned-out remains of the Laboratory of Light. Chances are, Walker and Grim are below us right now in the Laboratory of Darkness. They probably know we're here. So why haven't we seen or heard them?

I don't know whether to be worried or angry. As a warrior, I know the entire question is becoming something worse than rage or frustration—it's turning into a distraction. Myla, Maxon and all the after-realms are at risk. Nothing else matters.

A memory appears. It's Octavia back at the pulpitum in Antrum, twisting the pulpitum ring on her thumb.

"I bet there's a portal between here and the lower lab," I state.

"Wouldn't we have seen it?" asks Zeke. "We couldn't have missed a huge black door in here."

"True." I rub my neck and think this through. "Unless the portal was an unusual size."

"Right," adds Zeke. "And maybe it was placed somewhere no one would expect. That way, you wouldn't even need to bother with a ring key. The fact that you hid the portal would be enough."

I step around in a slow circle. "Where would I hide a portal in here?"My gaze locks onto a tall section of pipe that's propped up in a corner. I point to that spot. "How about the top of that tube?"

"It's crazy enough to be brilliant."

"Let's check it out." As I get closer, my hunter's sense kicks in. I point to the stack of melted steel containers by the tube. "See those places where there isn't any dust? That's where someone has been stepping."

I follow the path to the top of the trash pile. From here, I have the perfect view into the top of that metal tube. Sure enough, a round ghoul portal sits at the top of the pipe. "It's here."

Zeke climbs up and checks out the spot as well. "Clever."

I grip the edge of the tube and leap in. There's the weightless feeling that happens with every ghoul portal, followed by the pressure of landing on solid ground.

What I see is both dark and beautiful.

Where the last laboratory was a charred mess, this place is pristine. Metal rows of workstations stretch off into the distance. Each one stands about waist-high and is topped with a large glass sphere.

I scan the chamber. The place is too dark to know if anyone lurks nearby. Still, the air smells stale. Plus, there's no subtle vibration to tell me that anyone else is stepping around.

All of which means there's still no sign of Walker and Grim.

Where are they?

The Laboratory
of Darkness

44

LINCOLN

J step closer to a workstation. The lower part is a modified desk with built-in buttons and keys. A glass orb sits atop the metal base. I lean for a closer look. Within the depths, I find a three-dimensional representation of one of the prison cells from the Oligarchy's dungeons.

Zeke lands behind me and steps up to my side. "What's in the glass?"

"These machines are three-dimensional design stations." I gesture toward the sphere before me. "And this one was used to design the cells that held us in the Oligarchy dungeons."

Zeke leans. "That's them, alright." He scans the buttons on the console. "I've seen some of these before. This one shows you a summary." He clicks a console button.

Inside the sphere, the 3D image of the prison cell is replaced by a list of information. Zeke scans the text. "This cell was designed here and fabricated in someplace called sub-basement level 42-J." Zeke shakes his head. "Wow, forty-two sub-basement levels! This laboratory goes deep."

Closing my eyes, I think through the implications of this discovery. A jolt of excitement streams through my limbs. *We're close to finding the scythe... and maybe even plans for the tower!*

I focus on Zeke. "If my guess is right, then the scythe was designed at one of these stations and then fabricated somewhere below us. Grim and Walker told me the second scythe wasn't complete. Once we find the design station for the scythe, it will tell us everything we need to know."

Zeke grins. "I'll start on the end of this row and work toward the center."

"And I'll work from the opposite direction."

The first station I check is for fabricating masks like the ones on necro hunters. The second holds a model for the odd headgear the Noras wear.

And the third workstation stops me cold.

I wad kidnapped on my honeymoon. This design station is for one of the glass confinement cases where I was trapped. I click on the button for more information. It shows the item was fabricated in sub-basement 110-Q. And it was delivered to Ethan, the same thrax who kidnapped me all those years ago.

A realization moves toward me, but I push it aside. Plenty of organizations use strand technology. Ethan was a smart fellow. That has to be a coincidence.

I move onto the next workstation. This one shows a mallet and chisel made from strand technology. A sinking feeling settles into my bones. I fought a villain who used a supernatural mallet and chisel to cause trouble. I click the information button again.

Sure enough, this particular mallet and chisel were fabricated for the Tithe.

That realization I'd been pressing aside now returns with a vengeance. I recall what the Grim Reaper had said before.

But most folks understand hate. Do you, Lincoln? Do you ever suspect someone carries enough hate for you in their heart, that they've been stalking you for years, causing every last problem in your life, and serving as the darkness to your light?

For hundreds of years, the Grim Reaper has been working to become the Hallowed One. Once Myla and I became a couple, he had to know that I'd protect her and Cissy. All this time, has he been working from this lab in order to strengthen my enemies?

"Over here," says Zeke. "I found it. The was fabricated a few minutes ago. Sub-basement 1. There's even a map." Zeke leans in to check something inside the glass sphere. "It's through that back door."

Zeke takes off at a run.

I follow him for a few paces and stop. My mind sorts through every fact about the Hallowed One prophecy. I analyze Grim and Lady Reaper… strand technology… the missing tower to store all the spirits… and the news about the Tithe, Ethan, and Grim's scythe.

Information aligns. Realizations form. I fabricate my own model of this prophecy. My work isn't done yet, but I'm close enough to know one thing.

"Zeke, stop! We can't go into that room."

"Why? It's everything we've been looking for."

"No, it's a trap. This whole place is one. It's all designed to set us off on a meaningless side mission."

"But we need the scythe."

"You saw the facts yourself. The scythe was made minutes ago and there are directions to the fabrication site? That's too easy. Which means Grim *wants* us to go after the scythe. But that's only to get us out of the way."

"But if they don't want the scythe, what is Grim after?"

"A way to store every last soul in the after-realms." I gesture around the room. "Somewhere in this building, there must be a plan for building the mother of all ghost towers." After taking a deep breath, I add six final words.

"And we must find it, fast."

MYLA

That night, I dream I'm back at the ghoul carnival. Only, it's not the one that's being celebrated in Purgatory. Instead, it's the event that Lincoln and visited in the past, back at the ghost well in England.

This time, I'm not just visiting the event as a recording. I'm living it. The lanterns shine more brightly. The carousel music sounds louder. Barkers call out for games and shows. I step past them all and make my way to that ragged structure at the back of the carnival grounds.

Lady Reaper's tent.

Before, the Grim Reaper stood outside the place, along with the human version of Zelene. There's no one here now. As I step closer, the air turns cold. My skin prickles over with gooseflesh. The noise of the carnival fades away.

I pull back the entrance flap and step inside. The place is inky black. A sliver of light cuts through the entrance flap, highlighting a woman inside. She sits at the same table where Lady Reaper prepared her poisons. I feel drawn to move closer.

"Lady Reaper, is that you?"

The woman looks up. She wears a white dress that oozes across her face and body. It strikes me that scala robes are white. Bridal gowns are, too. She reaches for me.

"The darkness surrounds me…"

At those words, the woman reaches for my throat. Fear spirals through my soul. Gasping, I run off into the darkness. And no matter what I do, I can't stop racing into the void throughout the night.

THE DARKNESS

MYLA

It's Cissy's wedding day. I'm a wreck… And not in the *oh, I'm so excited* kind of way. It's more of a *damn, we're all gonna die* type thing.

Moving on.

I wait on the main stage at the ghoul carnival. Fifty Noras stand behind me. Lady Reaper is holding court at stage right, where she's being interviewed by Carol Cheevers and her long-suffering cameraman. Everyone onstage is wearing white except for the camera guy.

I feel a little sorry for him.

In classic Purgatory style, the skies are overcast. The carnival pavilions are all done up with holiday lights, which is a nice touch. The midway's crammed with what can only be called a hyperactive mob. Case in point: Although the Cirque du Sloth folks are blasting classical music, the crowd jumps up and down as if they're in a mosh pit.

Beyond the crowd, Cissy stands by the carnival entrance. Somewhere. It's hard to tell. A pack of necro hunter guards surround her —as Lady Reaper puts it, "for her own safety."

Have I mentioned that Lady Reaper is a lying liar? She is. The issue is that she's also a Class A schemer, and I have no idea what to expect today.

All in all, the most unsettling part is how everything seems relatively normal.

A man in ghoul robes lumbers onto the stage. He pulls the hood back and it looks like Zeke. Lady Reaper comes over and greets this person as Zeke. She then introduces the guy to Carol Cheevers as Zeke. They do a quick interview and everyone seems totally convinced that this is Cissy's future husband.

Except me. This guy is not Zeke.

To begin with, Zeke is not seven feet tall. Second, Zeke has a full command of the English language. Therefore, he is capable of saying more than the words *yes, no* and *Cissy*. However in his interview with Carol Cheevers, those are the only three words that *this Zeke* speaks.

Back when Lincoln and I visited the ghost well, I saw some strand magic turn into a necro hunter. How hard would it be to switch out that ghoul's face for Zeke's? Not hard at all.

Necro Zeke finishes his interview and lumbers over to stand beside me. "Hello, Zeke."

"Yes." Not only is this the wrong comeback, Zeke speaks the word in a voice that is about three octaves lower than Cissy's actual fiancé.

"I know you're a fraud who's made of strand magic."

"Cissy."

I roll my eyes. As fake-n-magical fiancees go, Necro Zeke is one of the worst.

Lady Regina finishes her interview and marches to center stage. She taps the microphone to get the crowd's attention. They calm down surprisingly well.

Over on stage right, Carol Cheevers goes into announcer mode. "As you can see, Lady Reaper is kicking off today's ceremony. Let's listen in."

"Good morning everyone," announces Lady Reaper. "As you know, I am Lady Regina Reaper. Today, it's my honor to serve as Minister of Ceremonies for the union of Senator Cissy Frederickson and Captain Zeke Ryder."

The crowd cheers. Some throw rice.

Lady Reaper gestures in my direction. "As you can see, we have Myla Lewis here today as a witness. Sadly, her parents are unable to join as they remain busy elsewhere."

Which is both true and a pack of lies. My parents would love to be here, but Lady Reaper is still somehow making the ghost towers melt down on a regular basis.

Lady Reaper gestures across the audience. "I'd like to ask everyone to please step back from the center aisle of the midway. My guards will help guide you in place."

A hundred necro guards march out from behind the pavilions to muscle everyone away from the center line of the midway. At the same time, the Cirque du Sloth folks blast more classical music from the brand-spanking new wall of speakers by their tent. Not sure who made these folks deejays, but they are remarkably competent.

Overall, things are relatively normal. Lady Reaper launches into a speech about how wonderful Cissy is, which is all true. The crowd has stopped slam-dancing into each other. I cut a sideways glance at Necro Zeke. Perhaps I was too quick to judge before. This could be Zeke, only he's wearing platform boots under those long ghoul robes; that might explain the extra height. And on their wedding day, I'm sure a lot of guys sometimes talk like Lurch from the Addams Family.

The music swells and Cissy begins her long march down the midway aisle. She looks lovely in a pale purple gown (Purgatory's theme color, natch.) Her expression is a little blank, but she could perk up as she gets closer.

Maybe, just this once, everything will work out alright.

I no sooner embrace this thought than I notice something terrible. The Noras aren't just standing behind me and looking creepy with their extra eyes. They're also singing in low voices.

Leaning back on my heels, I focus on the lyrics. It's hard to catch much of what they're saying, but the words 'eternal subjugation' come up quite a lot. I inch forward to scope out Lady Reaper.

Dang, she's whisper-singing too. And with the same nasty lyrics, no less. It's just that the Cirque du Sloth sound system is drowning them out.

Things aren't going to work out on their own.

Some big-ass trouble is coming.

Fuuuuuuuuuuuuck.

CISSY

MYLA

*J*olts of worry move down my spine. Lady Regina and the Noras are definitely whisper-singing some witchy stuff. Clearly, they want to move Cissy forward on her ritual journey.

But the only rite Cissy finished was the one where Lady Reaper took my bestie's hair. There are still more separate spells to go. Cis gives her blood. And in another rite, she must agree to something. And that's all before the final act in the Killy Cissy Show.

Based on what we saw with Zelene, those other rituals should take place over a number of days. They can't smush them together into one spell, right?

I focus more on the Noras' singing. And now that I'm paying really close attention? They are definitely crooning out stuff like *blood sacrifice* and *forever oath*.

Clearly, they can do all the rites in one day. Damn.

Plus, the whole *oath agreement* will be easy-peasy for Lady Reaper to get. In her current state, Robot Cissy into saying *yes* to just about anything. But giving blood? That is not a simple thing to do, especially with Cissy in a wedding dress.

Lady Reaper may be a diabolical genius, but she's not a *super* diabolical genius.

Meow!

Over on the midway, Tiny waddles onto Cissy's oath. Every nerve ending in my body goes on alert. Suddenly, the risk becomes clear: Tiny's whole raison d'être is to draw blood from Cissy. That takes care of the second ritual. Blood. And what does my bestie always say afterward?

Did you attack Mommy? Yes, you did.

The Noras are singing some incantation about both blood and oaths. With Tiny in the mix, Regina can get a *twofer ritual* out of Cissy before my friend is anywhere near the stage.

Oh, no.

This whole time, I thought Tiny was allowed to run around the carnival in order to keep Cissy happy. After all, the only time my robot friend perked up was when her beloved cat came around.

Now, I see the truth. Tiny didn't wander over here to serve as a comfort animal. Lady Reaper planted that feline on site so he could lull me into a sense of relaxation and then un-lull me during the ceremony. And Lady Reaper did make a magical vow not to hurt Cissy during the reaper games, but all that is over. Cissy's getting married now.

I take it back. Lady Reaper *is* a super-diabolical genius.

What happens next is total instinct. I leap off the stage. Tapping into my inner demonic energy, I run toward Cissy so quickly, my movements blur.

"Cissy!" I cry. "Noooo!"

As I get closer, it's clear that Robot Cissy doesn't even notice me. Sadly, she perks up at the sight of her beloved Tiny. Leaning over, Cis scoops her kitty into her arms. Like always, Tiny scratches the Hell out of my friend's forearm. A single drop of blood falls to the ground. When it hits the earth, a small puff of golden magic erupts from the spot.

That's the blood ritual. It's over. Damn.

Cissy cuddles Tiny. "Did you attack Mommy? Yes, you did. You're the lion of Purgatory."

The classic music stops. The choir does the same. A charged sense of power moves up the midway. The energy is so potent, even the crowd feels it and goes silent.

The sound of Cissy saying 'yes' echoes in odd ways around the carnival.

And when I say *odd*, you think: *magic.*

A cloud of green smoke swirls around Cissy. When the haze fades, there are now two brides on the midway. And one of them is semi-transparent and green.

A heavy silence descends. Most of the crowd stands with lifted brows and half smiles, a combination that says they're waiting for someone to say this is all a joke. Not that I blame them for being oblivious. I already knew the prophecy of the Hallowed One and I thought everything might work out fine today.

I come to a skidding halt beside the two Cissies. Robot Cissy stares off into space. Ghost Cissy sighs. "At least, after everything that happened this morning, my mother was too upset to come here today."

Oh, right. I forgot all about Mrs F.

Hold on. Mrs F isn't here because something *more* upsetting has come up? What could be worse than Mr F and his supposed New York ghoul girlfriend? Awful as it is, a small part of me is tempted to ask.

Note to self: If you live through this, be sure to grill Cissy about her mom.

On the other side of the midway, Lady Reaper slams her walking stick against the stage. A fresh puff of green smoke erupts from the spot. When the haze clears, Lady Reaper is back to her black and red ensemble... and it comes complete with a matching scythe.

Lady Reaper approaches the microphone again. "For too long, ghouls like me were stuck with physical bodies but no souls. Meanwhile, other beings have both bodies *and* spirits. It isn't fair, especially since the realms you currently occupy could be put to better use. All I need to do is put your souls in storage." She raises her scythe. "And I have just the tool to do so."

At these words, screams echo through the air. Everyone runs for the exits. Lady Reaper speaks into the microphone once more. "I'm the Hallowed One, the force foretold in prophecy. I'm here to send every soul into a ghost tower. I shall empty out Heaven and Hell."

Ghost Cissy grabs my arm, but her semi-transparent hands go

right through me. "Wait, she can't have everything she needs for the prophecy. There are supposed to be two reapers, two scythes and two emerald ghosts. Grim Reaper doesn't have a scythe, does he?"

"I'm guessing he's figured that out, Cis."

"After that, the prophecy specifically states that the Hallowed One will appear." Ghost Cissy dramatically scans from side to side. "I don't see any Hallowed One."

"She's not wearing the name tag, but I'm pretty sure think Lady Reaper thinks the Hallowed One is her."

"But there's another part—" Ghost Cissy taps her forehead "—wait, I've got it. The prophecy says the Hallowed One shall ignite the great tower and imprison all souls. That's a deal breaker! Lady Reaper can't really send everyone's souls into storage, right? There aren't enough ghost towers in the after-realms to contain every last soul."

"Do you want the truth... or should I blow smoke up your ass?"

"The second thing."

"Everything's going to be fine, Cis. Lady Reaper has been scheming about this for over a hundred years and she totally spaced on key parts of a two-line prophecy."

Ghost Cissy rolls her eyes. "You're a crap liar."

I quirk a smile. "I only said I'd blow smoke up your butt. I didn't say you'd enjoy it."

48

LINCOLN

I comb my fingers through my hair and focus on what to do next. "You're right that this place is too big. If we're going to find the tower from the prophecy, then we need to locate some kind of directory."

Zeke lists out different places we might begin our search, but I only half-hear his words. My hunter's sense has kicked in. The scent of sour mint is in the air. The barest vibration moves across the floor. It all adds up to one conclusion.

Someone is in the chamber with us now.

"I say we check the workstations on the other side of the room," says Zeke. "What do you think?"

I fix Zeke with a warning look. "I'd like to hear what the Grim Reaper thinks of our plan."

Sure enough, Grim steps out from the shadows. And he holds a red scythe with a black stone. It's the opposite of Lady Reaper's weapon. And even from a distance, I can see Walker's mark on the gem.

My heart sinks. *Walker, what have you done?*

"Nora was my true love," he begins. "But Regina and I do agree on some important things. Like the fact that some of us only have bodies while others get to enjoy both bodies and souls. That's not fair."

"You're still immortal," I state. "You just exist on another plane."

"And you have a soul," adds Zeke.

"True." Although looking at Grim, I wonder if it might be better if he did have a soul of his own. That way, Myla could sort him to where he belongs.

"It's so much worse for us ghouls," counters Grim. "You see, if Nora had a soul, she'd still exist somewhere. As it is, I've lost her forever. That's an injustice. I want to balance the spiritual ledger. And because I'm a fair man, I'll only take your physical form, not your ghosts."

I shake my head. "You're talking about billions of people, Grim."

"And Nora was worth more than all of them combined!" Grim's voice shakes as he speaks. "Do you know why she made her head-dress? Because she didn't think it was fair that ghouls only had one pair of all-black eyes. So she made a mask that gave her three blue ones." He shakes his scythe. "This prophecy… it's the kind of thing Nora would have understood."

"Did she know you couldn't finish what you started?" asks Zeke. "You've no way to store all those souls."

I shoot Zeke and approving glance. It's a clever move to dare Grim to show us the prophecy tower. If Grim takes the bait, it will save us a lot of time.

"Ha!" Grim grips his scythe and swipes it over the floor. Wherever his blade touches, the stone glows with green light. The tiles slide away, revealing a staircase that goes downward. "This way."

Zeke and I follow Grim down a corkscrew staircase that ends on a long platform. Grim steps out on what turns out to be a wide steel gangway. It's a viewing spot for a massive landscape below. Looking down, we see a sprawling city made of red and pink glass.

It's beautiful, pristine and made entirely from strand magic. Unbelievable.

Grim gestures toward the tallest skyscraper. Its peak reaches just above our gangway. "This is the Technocore."

I scan the tall building. The structure is so tall, I can't even see the bottom. "This whole building stores ghosts?"

"No," corrects Grim. "This whole *city* stores ghosts. The skyscraper is the only part that's tall enough to break through into Purgatory."

I scan the urban skyline that stretches off into the distance. "How big is it?"

"Not sure. Eli had been working on this in secret for twenty thousand years. I found it after Nora died. That's when I knew... even Eli saw this as the future of ghoul kind. We will take out rightful place in the realms. And the soul beings will exist in the Technocore."

"You've never tested this?" asks Zeke. "How do you know it works?"

"Oh, we're testing it. Today."

My heart sinks. Grim is deadly serious.

I look out once more over the cityscape. It's easy enough to destroy a single tower. But what would happen if I wipe out this entire Technocore? Who knows how far this landscape stretches?

My options just became a lot more complicated. The way it looks now, I might be able to save the rest of the after-realms, but I could easily end up destroying the Dark Lands.

49

LINCOLN

*A*t this point, I don't see any good choices. I could step aside and allow Grim to kill all those who live in the after-realms. Afterward, he'll imprison all their souls.

Or I could find a way to destroy the Technocore. Trouble is, this mega city is far too large. Who knows what would happen if it's destroyed? *I can't risk it.*

Which leaves a final option. *Kill Grim.*

I pull my baculum from their holder at the base of my spine. "I challenge you to a duel, Grim. If you kill me, you can continue with your plan. If I take you down, you destroy your scythe and the remaining laboratory. We'll seal off the Technocore."

Grim's tilts his skull-like head. "Why not simply attack me?"

"I'm thrax. We have rules of battle. Honor dictates I fight back or offer a challenge. Sneak attacks are not our way."

"They are mine."

The ghoul grasps his scythe and swings the magical blade across the floor. I saw this move before when we were in the laboratory. This is Grim's way of casting a spell…. and playing dirty.

I leap forward while igniting my baculum into a longsword made from white flame. I swing the blade toward Grim's scythe.

Our weapons never cross.

Walker steps between us. Both Grim and I freeze in place before lowering our blades. Neither one of us wishes to hurt our mutual friend.

"I cannot allow you two to do this," says Walker in his low voice.

"You gave me your word," snarls Grim.

"Yes, I did." Walker looks to me. "When Nora died, I told Grim I would grant him one boon. That means he could make a single wish that I would help come to pass, no matter the cost. And he asked for my assistance with the prophecy of the Hallowed One."

My mind blanks with shock. Walker is such a careful and kind person. Grim is clearly deranged. *This arrangement between them makes no sense.* "Why would you do that?"

"I owed Grim this boon because..." Walker takes in a deep breath. "The fire in the Laboratory of Light was my fault. I was excited about a new discovery and working too quickly. The place became engulfed in flame. No one escaped... including *Nora*."

Walker's voice trembles as he says the name Nora. My friend's entire body seems to exude pain and longing. I don't understand why.

Zeke takes a step closer to Walker and pauses. This is another unexpected turn of events. If I didn't know better, I might think Zeke was about to embrace Walker.

Confusion and grief battle it out inside me. I feel sorry for Grim. Losing a spouse? I can't imagine the agony. Yet, Walker went too far in offering a boon to someone who's so unstable.

I round on Walker. "What choices are we left with now?" There's no mistaking the menace in my tone. "You're asking me to decide between you and Grim... versus every soul in the after-realms, including my wife and son. Don't make me choose."

"That won't be necessary." Walker turns to Grim. "My friend here is overcome with grief. Yet, now that we're in the moment, I'm sure that he'll see the truth. Wiping out so many of the living won't bring the dead back. Or lessen your pain."

Grim grips his scythe and stares out over the Technocore, but he doesn't reply.

"Tell me my faith in you is justified," adds Walker. "Give me your scythe. I'll destroy the rest of the lab and seal off the Technocore myself. What do you say?"

Grim keeps staring out over the cityscape. Long minutes tick by. Most times, I have a pretty good idea what will happen in any battle, whether it's with swords or personalities.

But in this fight between Walker and Grim? *I haven't a clue.*

50

LINCOLN

The moment sears into my memory. An underground city stretches out before me. I stand on a long and thin gangway. The streets below are so far away, I can't detect them at all. And in a city of tall glass buildings, the largest one stands close to this gangway. If I step to the end of this bridge and reach forward, I would touch one of the many stacked glass rectangles that make up the skyscraper's exterior.

And I'm not alone.

Walker, Grim and Zeke stand beside me. None of us move. The city is an empty shell. We're the only living beings down here... perhaps the only ones who know this place even exists. Chill air makes my skin prickle over with gooseflesh. The place is so quiet, I can hear all our breathing.

It's Walker who breaks the stillness. Reaching forward, Walker sets his hand on his friends' shoulder. The movement is a simple one with a strong message: *Stay here.*

Grim's response is swift. He shrugs off Walker's touch. With his scythe still in hand, Grim leaps off the gangway and lands on one of the many glass rectangles that stick out from the building's exterior like geometric spikes. Grim remains standing with his back to me, Walker and Zeke.

My heat cracks. I sense the friendship between Walker and Grim. Hurt and sorrow seem to roll off Walker in waves. A long moment passes while Grim stands on the building's top level, his scythe gripped in his right hand. He hasn't moved yet.

As king, I've taken part in my share of negotiations. Without saying many words, Walker and Grim are trying to find an agreement between them as to what happens next.

Grim isn't wielding his scythe. He might still give up on the prophecy.

"Please," calls Walker. "Won't you turn back?"

Walker's words hit me with force. In all the years I've known my friend, I've never heard him more desperate.

Although I can't see Grim's face, there's no missing how he straightens his stance and tightens his grip on the scythe. I sense his answer before Grim even gives it.

"No." Grim twists around to face us. Lifting his scythe high, he brings the weapon down in a single smooth motion. The blade scrapes across the red glass by Grim's feet. Wherever the scythe touches the building, the glass erupts in shimmering lines of crimson light. *More strand magic.* Grim leans into the new column of brightness. The colored beams cast odd shadows on his skull-like face.

I move to stand by Walker. "What's Grim doing?"

Walker's reply sounds low and mournful. "What he thinks is best."

Grim arches his gaze upward. "I summon the power of strand magic. Make this structure touch the rain."

Before, crimson light shone out from the place where Grim's scythe had scraped across the building. Now, red mist billows within the skyscraper itself. Flares of green light spark within this dense cloud.

An electric charge fills the air. *Fresh magic.* A spell is being cast, and if my guess is right, it's a strong one.

Long fracture lines appear in the nearby buildings. The air fills with the sound of a thousand sheets of glass breaking at once. Although the entire cityscape vibrates with hidden power, the skyscraper before us trembles with such force, I worry that it will burst. Adrenaline and worry charge through my system.

I think back to what Grim said before. *Make this structure touch the rain.* The Dark Lands are known for clear and moonlit nights. Only one realm is known for rain.

Purgatory.

The skyscraper starts to rise.

Bits of metal and stone cascade around me, Walker and Zeke. Some part of my soul yells that I should run. It's all I can do to stand in place.

This cannot be happening.

From our perch on the gangway, it appears as if a world of red glass rises before us. Although I stand in place, my stomach has the odd and weightless sensation of falling through space.

Beside me, Walker's body tenses. "I have to go."

Sorrow sears into my chest. I never thought I'd have to choose between Walker and the rest of my family. I firm up my grip on the baculum and prepare to leap onto the skyscraper.

Zeke grabs my arm. "Before you face Walker again, there's something you need to know."

I shake my head. "You heard Grim. This skyscraper is heading for Purgatory."

"Lincoln, I know what happened between Grim and Walker."

I keep my gaze locked on the skyscraper. As the structure moves, the misty shapes inside become more visible. I point toward them. "Do you know what those are? Ghosts. Grim must have activated the Technocore weeks ago. It's already pulled some spirits inside." My mind races through everything that's happened the last few days. I recall the talk with Cam and Xav when we first returned to Purgatory.

"That's why the ghost towers are glitching," I murmur.

Zeke steps closer. "What did you say?"

"The Technocore skyscraper has been siphoning off souls from the ghost towers in Purgatory. Don't you understand? Grim and Regina are making Purgatory's ghost towers glitch in a way that only Cam and Xav can fix. Myla and Cissy are even more vulnerable than we thought."

I try to step away again. Zeke holds me firmly. "If you go into battle without knowing what I have to say, you'll be at a disadvantage."

"There's no way to improve the odds here. Walker's not the person I thought he was."

Zeke's voice takes on a deep and urgent tone. "Yes, he is. The last time Walker spoke the name Nora, I recognized the expression on his face. Because I've felt that agony myself."

A prickle of awareness moves up my neck. For a while, I've sensed something strange in my friend. "What do you mean?"

"All those years when Cissy refused me... I thought she loved someone else. She didn't. But Walker? He loved Nora. I know it. And she didn't feel the same way. Nora loved Grim. That's why Walker offered the boon after her death. It wasn't for Grim. It was for *her*."

I close my eyes and take in the news. Walker's strange actions around Grim take on new significance. Nora's portrait still sits in my pocket. Walker drew that with adoration. As I reopen my eyes, a new realization appears. Perhaps I can use this knowledge about Nora to persuade Walker to break his vow. If nothing else, it's worth a try.

"Thank you, Zeke. That does help. Maybe I can convince Walker to do the right thing." I fix my gaze on the rising skyscraper. "But it doesn't change what happens next. I must protect my family."

With my baculum in hand, I leap onto the rising skyscraper.

This time, Zeke doesn't hold me back. He jumps onto a level right beside me.

MYLA

*L*ady Reaper is having the time of her undead life. The carnival is total pandemonium. People scream, run and trip over each other's tails. The Cirque du Sloth tent falls over.

Someone tramples Necro Zeke. When he falls on the ground, his body transforms from a guy in a ghoul robes into a knot of golden strands. Then, he oozes into the earth.

Buh bye, Necro Zeke.

While the rest of the carnival goes berserk, Lady Reaper stands with her scythe pointed at Robot Cissy. And I stand between Robot Cissy and Lady Reaper.

Technically, the scythe is pointed at me.

Ghost Cissy tries to help by setting her semi-transparent form between Lady Reaper and Robot Cissy as well. However, Ghost Cissy doesn't really have good spatial control yet, so half the time we're occupying the same spot. I try not to think about it too much.

Mostly, I focus on Lady Reaper. After all, she's the one with the scythe.

As minutes pass, the crowd clears out. I can't help but notice that while Lady Reaper talks a good game about being the Hallowed One, she's not wielding her scythe or causing much trouble.

I get the feeling she's waiting for something.

Turns out, I'm right.

The ground everywhere shimmies, but the area behind the stage hits a nine-point-five on the Richter scale. An ear-piercing hum echoes around us. My stomach drops to my toes. There's no mistaking that noise.

Someone's opening a ghoul portal behind the stage.

And either that mystery someone is a ghoul Kaiju, or the undead have a new weapon that I'm about to hate.

Little by little, a glass structure rises from behind the stage.

And rises.

And rises.

Turns out, it's not some lump of glass. This thing is a freaking skyscraper. As the building rises higher, I spot some ghosts floating around inside.

Aaaaaaaaand it's a facepalm moment for yours truly.

I was so mopey about how my parents weren't around. All I focused on was the ongoing trouble at the ghost towers. It didn't occur to me that there might an already-functioning mega-tower somewhere… and that such a building was ruining my parents' lives. If anything, I figured Lady Reaper had placed a magical block on the towers, like the ghouls did back when they stole Lucifer's orb.

Turns out, Lady Reaper is not only torturing my parents, she's scheming for their souls to go into this massive pink huge tower… along with everyone else's. The idea makes my inner wrath demon roar with fury.

Before, I wanted to hurt Lady Reaper. Now, killing her is becoming a life goal.

And all this while, the skyscraper keeps moving higher. A memory appears. Years ago, I watched this TV show on the human channel which said how one day, Earth would build super-tall towers from the ground into space.

Looks like the ghouls might have beat them to it.

I shake my head in awe. *Wow.*

Lady Reaper notices my reaction and laps up every bit. No wonder she's been standing with a scythe in my face the whole time. This is what she's wanted to see.

I shoot her the side eye. "Enjoying yourself? I can play it up." I kick my voice an octave higher and blink to excess. "Oooh. Ahhh.

Pinky-pink skyscraper." I look over my shoulder. "What do you say, Robot Cissy?"

Let the record show that Robot Cissy has been staring into space this whole time. She does say two words, though: "Almond paste."

"Ooooooookay." I try to think of something encouraging to add. "That's not part of the conversation, Robot Cissy. But points for trying."

Ghost Cissy frowns. "I'm getting worse."

"No, that reply included a two-syllable word. That might mean you're getting better."

"You really think so?"

"No. Sorry."

Lady Reaper tilts back her head and lets out a maniacal laugh.

"Uh-oh, she's going into full baddie mode," says Ghost Cissy. "I don't think the pink skyscraper is all she has up her sleeve."

Lady Reaper keeps on cackling.

Ghost Cissy may be right.

"Psst." That's Ghost Cissy. "Quick question for you."

"Shoot."

"Does all the sarcasm really help you cope, or do feel like you might puke and-or scream at any moment?"

"Uh, it really helps. But if you're feeling barfy, I wouldn't worry. You have to give it more time."

Ghost Cissy forces a smile. "Okay."

For her part, Lady Reaper takes a break from laughing her tits off to raise her scythe high. In a move that's not unlike Arnold Palmer going for a hole in one, Lady Reaper swipes at the ground with her blade.

"Strand magic," she intones. "Bring me my servant."

The place where Lady Reaper's scythe touched the ground now glows with emerald magic and light. A moment later, Zelene rises up from the spot.

Zelene doesn't look too happy, but her default expression is pretty much bitch face. It's hard to tell if anything extra-angry is churning through her ghostly system.

"Now, we're ready!" Lady Reaper does another golfer impression and brings down her scythe again. The ground starts to glow green once more.

My heart beats at double speed. You don't spend years as a warrior and not know when something super-awful is about to hit.

"Scythe magic," calls out Lady Reaper. "I summon the power of the Great Scala."

I raise my hand. "I'm right here, you know."

Lady Reaper totally ignores me. *Rude.*

"I shall use the scala energy in these emerald ghosts to move every last spirit in the after-realms to my new tower." Lady Reaper gestures toward the pink skyscraper in a way that vaguely reminds me of a game show hostess. All of which settles a particular point of fact in my mind.

Lady Reaper is deeply weird.

And as it turns out, she's also frighteningly powerful. "Let the prophecy of the Hallowed One be realized today! All souls become my prisoners!"

Don't say it.

Don't say it.

Crap, I have to say it.

"I'm still right here, you know. I can move those souls out when you're done."

Lady Reaper's mouth curls into an evil smile. "Notice anything odd about your igni lately? Have they been showing you strange visions? Perhaps they appear to you as covered in darkness?"

Crap. She totally has me there. "Yeah."

"That's my strand magic. I've been casting spells on you and your igni. Listen to me carefully, girl. You'll never move another soul again."

I'm tempted to say something snarky, but in this case? Lady Reaper has a point. And she's also on a roll. I didn't see the Tiny cat scheme coming... or the fact that she'd been using a working ghost tower... or how Lady Reaper has been dipping my igni in supernatural black goop.

I may be Sassy Girl, but even I know when to keep my mouth shut. Besides, this fight isn't over.

"Understood." I give Lady Reaper a little wave. It's not my best move, but under the circumstances, I'm giving myself an *A for effort.*

Lady Reaper lifts her scythe until the blade arcs above her head. Energy and magic fill the air. Darkness gathers over Lady Reaper. Thunder rolls. Emerald lighting bolts churn inside the black clouds.

"Now!" cries Lady Reaper.

Everything goes berserk.

A pair of green lighting bolts reach out from Lady Reaper's scythe. The first one goes into Zelene's chest, lifting her off the ground. She aches her back and lets her arms fall loose beside her.

The second green bolt zaps Ghost Cissy in the same spot. My friend also rises from the earth. Like Zelene, Ghost Cissy arches her back but otherwise goes limp as a rag doll. I scan my friend's face. She doesn't seem in pain. Still, this can't be good. Frustration and fear tighten through my limbs. I'm a warrior. Everything in me wants to fight.

Yet how do you battle something like this?

Zelene and Cissy's bodies glow bright green. Waves of emerald power move out from their chests, flow along lightning bolts, and end up inside Lady Reaper's scythe. As the blade glows more brightly, Zelene and Cissy's bodies become dimmer.

I twist my hands. Should I grab Ghost Cissy? Would that help or make things worse? I figure it's best to wait. This is my scala power, after all. And igni get destructive when interrupted.

Lady Reaper's blade glows more brightly than ever. Then the lightning bolt connection to Zelene and Ghost Cissy turns dark. Both of them float to the ground. I rush over to Ghost Cissy.

"Are you okay?"

Ghost Cissy opens her eyes a crack. "Am I alive?"

"You're still a ghost, if that's what you mean."

"Then I'm okay."

For her part, Zelene glares at Lady Reaper before vanishing into the ground. *Huh. What's up with that?*

For a hot second, I debate about grabbing all the Cissies and running. After all, Zelene just took off. *What does she know that we don't?*

As soon as the idea hits me, I set it aside. Sure, we could run—or in the case of Robot Cissy, get dragged. But what's the point? There are still a ton of Noras and necro hunters around. And even if we get past those nasties, Lady Reaper will only zap us back here. Best to hang out and wait for Lady Reaper to make a mistake.

Which brings me to my big point (because I do have one.)

When it comes to Lady Reaper, I bet that a stupendous error is coming and soon. Why? Any villain who gestures at evil towers in *game show hostess style* has serious limitations. I just need to be patient enough to find them.

Plus, Lady Reaper is now the top name on my Bucket List Of Kills. So there's that.

Lady Reaper swipes her scythe once more, golfer-style. The green lightning bolts from Cissy and Zelene now burst from the scythe's blade in an explosion of thin green lines.

Some emerald bolts zing up into Heaven. Others dig down toward Hell. A webwork of them stretches out across Purgatory. More twist through the cloud portals overhead. No doubt, those are heading to Earth.

A breathless pause hangs in the air. Lady Reaper just announced that she would move every last soul to her fancypants new ghost tower. Some scala-like energy went *from* Cissy and Zelene and *into* Lady Reaper's scythe, just as the prophecy foretold. But after that? It's been a big nothing.

Maybe this is all that'll happen. I cross my fingers and hope for the best. Even my tail gets into the act by looping on itself, which is a tail-version of crossing fingers.

One moment passes.

Two.

Then ten.

I exhale. This isn't happening. *Whew.*

BOOM!

Fresh rolls of thunder sound. Green lightning bolts return from Heaven, Hell, Purgatory and Earth. If I wasn't the great Scala, I might think this is ordinary lightning, even if it is emerald colored. Only I *am* the Great Scala. I hear the voices of all the souls trapped inside those bolts. Angels. Demons. Humans, Quasis. Thrax.

They're frightened and calling for me. *Great Scala! Help us!*

On reflex, I try summoning my igni. Just as before, my friends materialize, but they appear as small voids... Black spaces in an otherwise-colorful world.

Lady Reaper is right. My igni are doused on strand magic. I'd been so focused on all the other things that had been taking place, I wasn't asking why my powers were changing.

As the lightning bolts enter the new ghost skyscraper, the structure glows more brightly. In my mind, millions of souls reach out to me. I can do nothing to help them.

More green lines stretch out from Lady Reaper's scythe. The bright bolts crackle off in every direction. There's so much light and smoke, it's hard to see what's happening.

And by this I mean, it's tough. But not impossible.

Under the frantic light and screaming souls, I catch the deep hum of an oversized ghoul portal opening. A dark shape appears behind Lady Reaper.

For her part, Lady Reaper lowers her scythe. The lighting vanishes. There's nothing but an empty landscape with me, the Cissies, a very smug Lady Reaper... and whoever is behind her.

I push my mind to figure out who the newcomer might be. Everything that's happened over the last days spins through my consciousness. I see the Reapers and Carnival... Opus X and the glitchy ghost towers... a missing Walker and my poor Ghost Cissy. And more than that, I see the power behind everything.

And in this moment, I finally catch up with what's happening. I know who's really behind this whole thing.

Pro tip: it's not Lady Reaper.

Another hum sounds as the portal vanishes. The grin fades from Lady Reaper's face. Her gaze locks with mine. "Is someone behind me?"

"Actually," I say slowly. "There are four someones behind you."

The Oligarchy have arrived.

For a bunch of old ghouls, the Oligarchy can hustle when motivated. There's a flurry of movement. One second, Lady Reaper stands before me with her scythe in her grasp. The next second, she's empty-handed and toppling forward.

Lady Reaper face-plants into the dirt. One of the Oligarchy

stabbed her in the back. Now, the blade of her own scythe is embedded through her rib cage. For a moment, I wonder if Lady Reaper's truly dead. Then, all the nearby Noras and necro hunters turn into blobs of golden strands before melting away.

Which means Lady Reaper's dead, alright.

And while I should be thankful to the Oligarchy for killing Lady Reaper, I can't help but feel a wee bit disappointed. After all, that she-ghoul just made it to the top of my bucket list.

The Oligarchy turn toward me. Per usual, they all wear long red robes with the hoods drawn low. The only way I know where they're looking is that their hoods shift direction.

"We rule the Dark Lands," they say in a rough whisper. "Our will decides who becomes the Hallowed One. And it has always been you, Myla Lewis."

I do a double-take. *What?*

"Grim and Lady Reaper were only puppets in our master play," continue the Oligarchy. "For years, we've been planning this moment. We inspired everything that Grim and Lady Reaper have done. Many think we are weak-willed. That is all a ruse. We are the true masters of the after-realms."

I point toward the glowing skyscraper filled with unwilling ghosts. "Is this your idea of mastery? Wiping out all life and bottling up every soul?"

"Of course, not," retort the Oligarchy.

That makes me do a double-take. "Say what?"

"The prophecy was created to lure in Grim and Regina Reaper. We've played along, pretending that we share their dream of clearing out the after-realms for ghoul kind. But that is all a lie. What we want is what we had in years past: the Dark Lands ruling over Purgatory."

My stomach tumbles. Isn't that what Mom said before? The only thing the Oligarchy care about is Purgatory.

The four ghouls continue. "We worked for years to position Armageddon to do our dirty work and invade your land. You sent him away."

"I got you four kicked out, too. Don't forget that."

"Now Grim and Lady Reaper are our pawns. Your many battles

with Armageddon were for nothing. In the end, nothing will change when it comes to the Great Scala. You will serve us."

"And if I say no?"

"Then Grim and Lady Reaper will get their wish. The prophecy will come to pass. And you'll be the only one alive in a desolate world without living beings… all while knowing you imprisoned those you love."

My gaze locks on the new tower. Would the ghouls really leave me to roam the after-realms alone… but keep those I loved imprisoned in that thing?

Sadly, yes.

"You realize the truth," declare the Oligarchy. "For years, the darkness of our strand magic has been closing in around you. Every time you almost lost a loved one, that was our power going in for another kill. Now, our work has finally come full circle. The darkness surrounds you. There is no way to break free."

One ghoul steps forward and raises his hands. A pair of golden manacles are gripped in his fists. The metal shimmers with underlying filaments. A jolt of awareness moves through my soul.

Those handcuffs are made with strand magic.

Once those are clasped on my wrists, I'll never get them off. And I'll be forced to serve the Oligarchy forever. My skin chills over with shock. *This can't be happening.*

"Put these on," say the Oligarchy in unison. "Accept your fate."

And I may be someone who has a quick comeback for every situation. At last, I may have reached the end of myself.

Because I don't know what to say, let alone do.

LINCOLN

*T*he Technocore rises.

As the building stretches toward Purgatory, the many glass blocks that make it up divide and stretch, enabling the tower to rise ever faster.

Zeke and I keep climbing toward Walker and Grim. However, each time we get close, the building extends again.

Suddenly, the interior of the Technocore fills with green lightning. Ghosts materialize inside. Every cell in my body goes on alert.

It's happening. The prophecy is coming true.

Like we're trapped in some kind of nightmare, Zeke and I keep climbing. Yet Walker and Grim stay out of reach.

Slam!

The Technocore skyscraper comes to a sharp halt. Zeke and I pause to see where we've stopped. Far above us, the tower emerges into Purgatory. A thin sliver of room separates the glass building from the muddy earth of Myla's home realm.

Shadowy figures move above us. Based on the angles of movement, there are two men on the upper reaches of the skyscraper. That must be Grim and Walker. If my calculations are correct, the two now fight it out at the realm's ground-level.

Inside the skyscraper, ghosts fly and howl. Some pound on the glass. Others call for the Great Scala. My heart sinks. Myla must hear those cries. What is she doing right now?

Focus, Lincoln. Grim, first. Then, Myla.

Zeke and I resume our climb. Finally, we're able to close in on Walker and Grim. The pair are still battling it out. Although, to be accurate, Grim is fighting while Walker attempts to wrench the scythe from his friend's grasp. Both are bruised and bleeding. Neither seem ready to give in.

Zeke and I speed to where the two fight. Grim is a tough opponent. We'll need the element of surprise.

I hoist myself onto the glass platform where Grim faces off against Walker. Continuing my momentum, I leap through the air and slam my shoulder against Grim's thigh. He loses balance and drops the scythe.

Zeke leaps up to finish Grim off from a different angle. Now, the Reaper is aware of our presence. Grim kicks Zeke in the chest and sends my friend falling down the skyscraper.

Sadly, there's no time to check if Zeke is safe. *I must stop the Grim Reaper.* Fortunately, Zeke's attack distracted Grim from retrieving his blade. Rushing forward, I scoop the scythe from the ground. The weapon feels light in my hands. Turning, I face Grim and Walker.

Only now, they both wear the same face. Even worse, their injuries are similar. I look between the two men.

Who do I save?

Who do I fight?

Which one is really my friend?

Walker on the left reaches toward me. "Help me, brother!"

The one on the right scowls at me. "Run."

I stalk over to the left-hand Walker. He exhales a long breath. "Thank you."

"You're welcome." I raise the scythe and bring it down. The blade pierces right through the man's chest. I lean in closer. "Walker would never ask for help when someone else is in danger."

The man's skin melts away, revealing the skull-like face of the Grim Reaper. Black blood trickles from the side of his mouth. "Liar! You said your people never attack without warning. It's your tradition to challenge foes to a duel."

"One nice thing about being king," I retort. "You get to change the rules."

Grim opens his mouth, ready to say something else. No words come. His head lolls back as his eyes close. Grim's body goes limp. He's dead.

Although wincing with pain, Walker forces himself into a sitting position. "Thank you. I couldn't have done that myself. It's... complicated. This didn't have to happen. I know I've failed you."

I move to sit beside him. "You haven't failed me. We all have our blind spots. I could have prevented this as well. Only, I allowed my own limitations with my father to stop me. I could have discovered what Grim and Regina Reaper were doing years ago."

Walker nods. "I suppose we all have blind spots."

"True. But if we're lucky, we have people who love us and can help."

"Noooo!" A woman's scream sounds behind me. "You killed my Grim! He promised to make the Hallowed One!"

Turning, I find none other than Zelene running toward me. Her open mouth is lined with fangs. I've seen this effect before. When ghosts turn bloodthirsty, they can tear your throat out before you have a chance to scream.

Normally, my reflexes are faster. Unfortunately, that's the risk of being a warrior. Leave your guard down for one moment... and that might be a second too much.

Zelene is almost on me when she freezes in place. Looking down, she sees a small dagger implanted in her chest. The blade shines with golden strands of magic. A gem gleams on the handle. Walker's maker's mark sits on the stone.

For a few seconds, Zelene stares at the blade. Whatever she expected to happen, it wasn't this. Her body fades, along with the dagger. Soon, no sign of her remains. After living with Myla, I know one thing.

That's how a ghost dies.

Shifting my gaze, I find Walker is still seated across from me. He holds another one of those gold daggers. "You were saying something about blind spots, I believe?"

"That I was. Thank you."

"If you ever need specialty daggers for killing unusual ghosts, I have a wide collection."

"Good to know."

A voice calls down to us from above. "Lincoln!"

I look up. Zeke now stands at the lip of where the Technocore skyscraper meets Purgatory. I smile. I should have known he'd be fine… and use the opportunity to check on his fiancé.

I cup my hand by my mouth. "Is Cissy alright?"

"You must come quickly. It's Myla. The Oligarchy are here. They're after her."

Adrenaline spikes through my system. There's no need for Zeke to say anything more. I scale my way onto Purgatory and take off at top speed.

I must find Myla.

MYLA

*M*y mind turns hazy from adrenaline and shock. A moment ago, wasn't I protecting Cissy? All around me, the midway was in chaos. Now the Oligarchy are here and insisting I wear enchanted manacles that will force me to serve them forever.

"What do you say?" ask the Oligarchy in unison.

"I don't know."

"Let's clear up your mind, shall we?" ask the Oligarchy. "Lady Reaper was acting on our orders. We asked her to darken your igni. You've spent too long with this baseless belief in your own strength. It's time you learned what every other being in the after-realms seems to know."

"And what's that?"

"The darkness surrounds you."

My heart sinks. *It's true. They've been behind everything.*

The Oligarchy take up Lady Reaper's scythe and point it at me. My igni materialize as so many swirling brushstrokes of ink. The many points of darkness spin around me, becoming larger and more dense by the second.

It all happens so fast, I don't have time to process the spell, let alone scream.

The next thing I know, I stand in a limitless black void. The silence is so extreme, my ears ring from the lack of noise. I sense the vastness of this space and my insignificance within it. I am alone.

If I accept the Oligarchy's offer, everyone I love will be safe. *What else can I do?*

My legs turn wobbly. While flailing around, I stumble about in the perfect emptiness and whisper my fate.

"The darkness surrounds me."

I think of the old Myla—the person I was before all this. That version was someone of light. Now that's all gone. This time, I speak with a louder voice.

"The darkness surrounds me."

I freeze in place. Images flash through my mind. I recall all the times I'd seen some shadowy figure reaching toward me through magic and igni. That was me, now. And I was reaching back to me, then.

I'm not alone.

"The darkness surrounds me."

I recall what Ghost Cissy did in the kitchen—how she made her own light.

I asked her: *How did you do that?*

And her reply refills my heart: *I picture myself as the sun.*

Closing my eyes, I picture the brightness within me. How it twists along my fingertips and swirls about my legs. The way its warmth seeps into my bones. How the eternal darkness may be vast and empty, yet it only has form when I shine my light.

"The darkness surrounds me," I say again.

I open my eyes to find my own soul shining in the dark. Tiny beams of light emanate from every pore. This inner sun melts dark strand magic from my exterior world.

"The darkness surrounds me," I call. "But it does not become me!"

With a burst of light, all my igni return to their normal state. They swirl around me in a great bright column. My heart soars. A sense of rightness moves through the deepest parts of my soul.

My igni vanish. Blinking, I adjust to a different kind of brightness. It takes a few moments for me to realize that I'm back at the ghoul carnival in Purgatory. The Oligarchy stare at me, open-mouthed with shock.

I bob my brows. "Hello, boys." Striding forward, I grab Regina's scythe and point it in their general direction. "Do not move."

In my soul, I call out to my igni.

I need you, little ones.

With a blinding flare, my igni materialize. Millions of tiny lightning bolts fill the air. With my heart, I reach out to every entrapped spirit. Faces flicker through my mind. There are demons and quasis. Angels and thrax. Newborn humans and ancient souls. I hold them all in my mind and spirit.

Find them, little ones.

Igni congeal into massive columns that bore into the Technocore skyscraper. I picture each bolt of light locating one of the many spirits I'd found before. Each soul merges with a single igni.

Take them home.

Thunder booms. Purgatory's skies light up as igni lead souls back to Heaven. Other igni dig into the ground, creating pin pricks of brightness in the dirt as they transport spirits back to Hell. Even more igni disappear through clouds as they conduct ghosts back to Earth. Those who had bodies before now become alive and whole once more.

I sense my loved ones as they return to health as well. And I ensure Cissy's emerald ghost merges back with her physical form, too.

As the work winds down, my igni flare more brightly than before. Then, they all vanish. Once again, I become trapped in some kind of black cloud. This feels like a different version of Oligarchy's spell. Soon, the four ghouls appear before me.

My inner wrath demon awakens. Rage and power stream through every muscle in my body. *Guess who just got kicked to the top of my bucket list?*

Still, there are good and bad ways of fighting. I take a deep breath, ready to give my standard speech. It goes something like, *you four don't have to die if you walk away.* But I've really had it with these clowns. Long story short, when all four of them rush at me, I could not be happier.

I suck at names even when I give a crap about someone. And I loathe the Oligarchy. In my mind, I decide to call them One, Two, Three and Four.

One comes at me first.

I wait until One is within a few inches. Then, I leap up and wrap my ankles around his throat. Twisting my hips, I slam One's skull against the noggin of Two. The distinct sound of bone crushing fills the air. One and Two lay on the ground, immobile. And let's just say their skulls have looked better.

Those two aren't getting up.

Number Three rushes me from behind. My tail stabs him through the heart.

Which only leaves Four. It's almost a shame that this fight won't last too much longer. Sure, the Oligarchy can move fast when they want to, but when it comes to one-and-one battle *strategery*?

Two words: total suck.

Four brandishes a dagger with the pointy bit facing upward. Major rookie mistake. As he closes in, I leap high while slamming my knee against Four's wrist. After doing a backwards somersault, I land facing my opponent.

And as I'd planned, Four has stabbed himself in the face. He slumps over, dead.

With the Oligarchy extinguished, their final spell fades. The heavy shadows around me lighten again. I squint, trying to see where I am. There are tents nearby. Everything is all squishy and strange. My legs turn watery beneath me.

And somehow, Lincoln is here. He's scooped me into his arms and has me cradled against his chest.

I blink up at him. "Am I dead?"

"No, you're safe now."

"Are the ghosts alright?"

"They're fine. You did it, Myla. Everyone's safe now."

I smile, close my eyes and lean my cheek against Lincoln's chest.

Oblivion descends around me again. And since I feel safe and loved, I give into the darkness.

And this time, it is beautiful.

—The End—

The Angelbound Abyss Saga continues!
Cissy, Zeke, Myla and Lincoln return in Angry Gods

ALSO BY CHRISTINA BAUER

ANGRY GODS

ANGELBOUND ORIGINS BOOK 12

The adventure continues in ANGRY GODS!

LINCOLN

Enjoy Lincoln's perspective with the Angelbound LINCOLN series!
Read on for a sample chapter...

OFFSPRING

The next generation takes on Heaven, Hell, and everything in between with MAXON!

FAIRY TALES OF THE MAGICORUM

A modern fairy tale that *USA Today* calls a 'must-read!' Check out WOLVES AND ROSES!

DIMENSION DRIFT

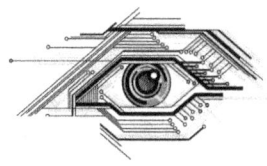

A kick-ass heroine + a swoon-worthy prince + an all-girl heist = the DIMENSION DRIFT series!

BEHOLDER

Medieval mages … Slow-burn love … And heart-pounding action!
Check out the BEHOLDER series!

PIXIELAND DIARIES

PIXIELAND DIARIES tells the story of sassy pixie Calla and 'her' elf prince, Dare.

*B*efore me looms a dissolus demon. Think about a waist-high glob of mayo—only both alive and deadly—and that's the general idea.

No face.

No limbs.

Just mega-bacteria with attitude.

For hours, I hunted this creature through the forests of Purgatory. Why? I'm both part angel and a demon hunter. *One of the thrax.* Killing monsters is what my people do. Now I've cornered this slime ball (as in a ball literally made of slime) against the back wall of the royal stables.

All that remains is the kill.

This won't be easy.

Little by little, I pin the dissolus against the wall with my body. The white goo of the demon's exterior smears across the legs of my Kevlar armor. The creature's round form pulses, heartbeat style. Reaching forward, I slip my hands through the monster's outer layer, careful to keep my palms tipped at precisely forty degrees. Unless I use that exact angle combined with slow speed, the demon's interior will transform from ugly slop into deadly acid.

Then I'll be dissolved in seconds. Painfully.

Sweat beads down my spine as I search inside the monster. My goal is to find the creature's nucleus—the equivalent of its heart—

which is solid, transparent and egg-shaped. I shift my arms inside the demon's gooey interior. Slurping sounds ricochet through the air. Across the stables, a horse whinnies. Adrenaline spikes through my system. There's a time limit here. If I don't grab the nucleus fast enough, then the demon's insides will turn acidic anyway.

Again, death. Not a fan.

It's an effort, but I somehow keep my motions slow and steady. All thoughts collapse into a single goal: Grasp the nucleus.

A familiar voice breaks up the quiet. "Interesting monster, eh?"

Seriously?

That's Aldred, the Earl of Acca and an extraordinary scumbag. At this point, he and I are the only people in the stables, if you don't count the demon. Aldred's a portly fellow, middle aged with thinning hair and long jowls. His clan, the House of Acca, is a perennial pain in my royal backside. While I spent hours hunting the dissolus, Aldred followed behind at a safe distance. All the while, he released a steady stream of chatter.

"I said," Aldred really drags out the word *said*. "Interesting monster, right?"

"*Interesting* isn't the word I'd use," I reply.

"What can I say?" Aldred steps beside me, scanning the scene. "I'm an earl, not a walking thesaurus."

For a moment, I see myself in Aldred's eyes. I'm Lincoln Vidar Osric Aquilus, High Prince of the Thrax. My family rules the land of Antrum, which is hidden far below Earth's surface. The rest of the After-Realms consist of the angels in Heaven, demons of Hell, quasi-demons in Purgatory, and the ghouls of the Dark Lands. At eighteen, I'm tall and broad-shouldered with brown hair and mismatched irises. I also happen to be leaning over a possessed blob of white goo the size of an engorged Hippity Hop. Being a demon hunter is rarely glamorous. Neither is being royal, for that matter.

"This is taking too long," declares Aldred. With mincing steps, the earl creeps up beside me.

"Stay back," I warn. "That's for your own safety."

"No, I shall kick it for you."

"Absolutely not," I counter. "You'll end up losing your leg, and that's if you're lucky."

Aldred holds his hands palms forward, in the universal motion for, *it's not my fault.* "No need to get testy."

Frustration sends my thoughts reeling. How did I end up here anyway? The answer flickers through my mind like images on a carousel. On orders from Verus, the Queen of the Angels, my family and I are temporarily residing in Purgatory, along with all our court. Since my people enjoy a medieval lifestyle, we've constructed cabins in Purgatory's Alighieri Woods. This morning, a dissolus broke free from our royal menagerie. Cue me chasing the monster through the forest while the earl follows behind.

Which brings me to the present moment and imminent death.

At last, my fingers brush against the creature's hard nucleus. *Yes!* Normally I give demons a chance to retreat before killing them. However, dissolus have the mental powers of paramecium. To them, attacking is nothing personal—it's just what they do.

Time to end this.

Tightening my grip on the nucleus, I yank with all my strength. The clear sphere breaks free from the gelatinous demon. For a moment, the dissolus quivers in place. Then—SPLASH—it collapses into a puddle of translucent sludge. The scent of rotten eggs fills the air. In my right hand, the nucleus transforms into a bright white orb before vanishing altogether. The gooey entrails covering the floor also disappear. Easy cleanup; that's one benefit of this demon type.

I exhale a long breath. "And *that's* how to kill a dissolus."

"Glad I was here to help," declares Aldred. "We make a great team." He moves to stand directly in the main aisle of the stables. In other words, blocking my departure. I've seen this action from Aldred before.

"Is there a particular topic you wish to discuss?" I ask.

"As a matter of fact, yes. Now that we've spent the morning together, I thought we could talk, man to man."

I tilt my head. "Go on."

Here it comes. Another discussion about my marriage contract.

For weeks, Aldred has been pestering me to sign a betrothal contract with his daughter, Lady Adair. At one time, I might have been interested. Now, not so much. The local residents of Purgatory are quasi-demons, and one of those ladies happens to be an excellent warrior named Myla Lewis. As of this moment, it's been eight days, six hours, and thirty-two minutes since I last saw Myla. At the time, she was fighting off Doxy demons in a nearby lake. Her battle technique displayed the perfect combination of beauty, intellect and lethal power.

Ah, Myla.

Long story short, I'm no longer interested in signing a marriage contract. Instead, my time's been consumed with researching a certain Miss Lewis. To that end, I've learned she's fighting in Purgatory's Arena tomorrow morning. I plan to sneak into an access corridor and watch her battle from a distance. The very idea makes my heart soar.

Aldred clears his throat, breaking up my thoughts. "Did you hear what I said?" he asks.

"No," I reply. Evidently, the earl was blabbing away while I contemplated Myla. Even so, I doubt I missed anything. There's only one topic of interest to Aldred these days.

My marriage.

"Please repeat your statement," I say.

Aldred makes a great show of scanning the stables. "I've news for you about Minister Devak." He narrows his eyes to conspiratorial slits. "Great information."

This is what humans call a *red flag*. Why the concern? I've been working on what I call an anti-Acca treaty. By uniting the armies of Kamal, Horus and Striga, I'll have enough warriors to make Aldred kowtow on any number of topics, including my marriage to Adair. Of all those houses, my negotiations with Minister Devak—and therefore the House of Kamal—are the farthest along.

"And?" I prompt.

"Devak's been asking around." Aldred lowers his voice. "About quasi warriors."

A chill rolls up my limbs. Can Devak be interested in Myla for some reason? When I next speak, it's an effort to keep my voice calm. "What is Devak's precise concern?"

"Wouldn't *you* like to know." Aldred smirks.

At this point, that smug grin of Aldred's tells me two things. First, the earl knows exactly what Devak is up to, and second, Aldred wants something in exchange for the information.

I stifle the urge to roll my eyes. "Name your price, Aldred."

The earl exhales a long-suffering sigh. "I might confide everything, but it's sensitive information … the kind you share with *family*, you know?"

Meaning: ink my betrothal contract and I'll tell all.

I chuckle. Aldred always overreaches in negotiations. However, what he lacks in finesse he more than makes up for in persistence. "I am *not* finalizing a contract merely to discover Devak's plans."

"Please; I never expected you to sign this very second," lies Aldred. No doubt, the man keeps the document in the folds of his tunic along with a quill, just in case. "But perhaps you can commit to spending more time with my sweet Adair? If so, then I might feel like sharing."

Aldred thinks he's being sneaky, but I already made this decision last night. "Mother is organizing a garden party at the Ryder mansion. My plan is to request Adair's company for the event." After all, I've said all of five sentences to the girl. We may be compatible. It's a long shot considering my blooming obsession with Myla Lewis, but there it is.

Aldred rubs his palms together. "Excellent, I'll tell Lady Adair today."

"Your turn," I state. "What about Devak's interest in quasi warriors?"

Aldred bobs his thick eyebrows. "No doubt, you're aware how the court itches to hunt local demons."

My eyes widen with shock. "No, I wasn't." A memory flashes through my mind.

I'm fifteen and late for monitoring a demon patrol in the Canadian Arctic. As I exit the transfer platform, a woman's screams echo through the cold air. I race out of the ice station and onto a sheet of white tundra under a grey sky. Freezing winds batter my body. Before me, a dozen Acca warriors tear apart a Vantys—a harmless she-demon who's equal parts human and

reptile. Aldred stands behind them, pumping his fist in the air. Fresh sprays
of blood darken the snow. I race over, my young voice bellowing.

"Stop!"

But the Vantys is already dead. And Aldred's men have placed her head
on a pike.

"This is disgraceful," I announce. "We are thrax, not a mindless mob."

Blinking hard, I try to wipe out that recollection. However, the image of a severed head stays seared in my mind. Thrax should act as ethical warriors, yet Aldred transformed them into something else. There's no avoiding the truth. With the wrong encouragement, my people can do terrible things.

And now, their baser instincts may be focused on Myla. I shudder. I'd been actively avoiding thoughts of any future with Myla. Contemplating her in the present was just too enjoyable. But now? I must consider the risk my people pose to her, myself included.

"You know us thrax," continues Aldred. "We're always seeking a new challenge."

Protective energy runs up my spine. I round on the earl. "The Queen of the Angels herself, the oracle Verus, sent us here to interact with the quasi population, not hunt them down."

"Bah." Aldred waves his hand dismissively. "It's only a matter of time before some quasi marches into our camp, looking for trouble. After all, they're semi-demonic. It's in their blood. And once those quasis come after us, then we'll have to protect ourselves. It's only right."

Images of Myla appear in my mind. She did indeed sneak into our compound, but only because she was on the trail of a mutual enemy, the Doxy demons. A weight of worry settles into my stomach. What if someone other than me saw her? Aldred is correct; my people would kill first and ask questions later.

"You still haven't shared specifics on Devak and quasis," I point out. "What did he say, exactly?"

"Devak's asking about Purgatory's Arena."

My heart sinks. *That means he's focusing on warriors like Myla.* "What's his interest?"

"My guess? Arena warriors are the best fighters. Here's the thing. Maybe you and I can team up." Aldred grins, showing off his mouth of yellow teeth. "Together, we could claim the first official quasi kill."

At those words, anger zings through my nervous system. "Let me make one thing absolutely clear." I prowl toward Aldred, my voice deep as thunder. "Hunting the local population is off the table, whether they are Arena warriors or not. If you or anyone else speaks of this again, I'll have you shipped back to Antrum and tossed into the dungeons." For every final word I speak, I tap Aldred on the center of his chest. "Do you understand?"

"All right." The earl forces another laugh. "No need to get sensitive."

I glare at Aldred with a look that says, *I'm done here.* "The dungeons, Aldred. I mean it."

Without waiting for a reply, I storm past the earl and out of the stables. Hunting quasis? *Outrageous!*

Suddenly, I wish my parents weren't away on a demon-hunting excursion. I'd like nothing better than to open a formal inquest, find out who's threatening quasis, and then fill our dungeons to overflowing. But starting an inquest is serious business. For the process to have teeth, my parents must sign off. And they won't return for at least four days.

Ah, well. Better to wait and do this correctly, much as I hate that fact.

All the way back to my cabin, my thoughts race through everything I've just learned: that Aldred is still pressing my marriage to Adair … the fact that my own people might be targeting quasi warriors … and how the entire situation could place Myla in danger. It all adds up to one terrible conclusion.

If I'm not careful, Myla might end up dead. That's not an option, so I take a silent oath.

With all my mind and body, I vow to protect the woman who already holds my heart.

—End Of Sample—

Order LINCOLN, Book 2 in the Lincoln series today!

APPENDIX

IF YOU ENJOYED THIS BOOK...

...Please consider leaving a review, even if it's just a line or two. Every bit truly helps, especially for those of us who don't *write by the numbers,* if you know what I mean.

Plus I have it on good authority that every time you review an indie author, somewhere an angel gets a mocha latte. For reals.

And angels need their caffeine, too.

COLLECTED WORKS

Angelbound Origins

About a quasi (part demon and part human) girl who loves kicking butt in Purgatory's Arena

1. Angelbound
2. Scala
3. Acca
4. Thrax
5. The Dark Lands
6. The Brutal Time
7. Armageddon
8. Quasi Redux
9. Clockwork Igni
10. Lady Reaper
11. Reaper Wars
12. Angry Gods
13. Phantom Corsair

Angelbound Lincoln

The Angelbound experience as told by Prince Lincoln

1. Duty Bound
2. Lincoln
3. Trickster
4. Baculum

5. Angelfire
6. Rixa
7. Mordred

Angelbound Offspring
The next generation takes on Heaven, Hell, and everything in between
1. Maxon
2. Portia
3. Zinnia
4. Rhodes
5. Kaps
6. Mack
7. Huntress
8. Gage
This is a finished series.

Dragon Bound
Stories from the dragon realm of Angelbound
1. Dragon Bound

Angelbound Xavier
Xavier's story
1. Archenemy
2. Archnemesis
3. Archangel

Fairy Tales of the Magicorum
Modern fairy tales with sass, action, and romance
1. Wolves and Roses
2. Moonlight and Midtown
3. Shifters and Glyphs
4. Slippers and Thieves
5. Bandits and Ball Gowns
6. Fire and Cinder
7. Fairies and Frosting
8. Towers and Tithes
9. Mirrors and Mysteries

10. Rapunzels and Powers
This is a finished series.

Witches of the Magicorum
Fairy tale retellings from the witch's perspective
1. Evil Queens and Goblin Kings
2. Mad Hatters and Manhattan Heirs
3. Goose Girls and Ghost Magic

Dimension Drift
Dystopian adventures with science, snark, and hot aliens
1. Scythe
2. Umbra
3. Alien Minds
4. ECHO Academy
This is a finished series.

Pixieland Diaries
1. Pixieland Diaries
2. Calla
3. Dare
This is a finished series.

Beholder
Where a medieval farm girl discovers necromancy and true love
1. Cursed
2. Concealed
3. Cherished
4. Crowned
5. Cradled
This is a finished series.

ACKNOWLEDGMENTS

If you're reading my freaking acknowledgements, chances are, I should thank you for something. So, for the record: you are awesome, dear reader.

That said, huge and heartfelt thanks must go out to my husband and son for their rock-solid support. Being an author means a lot of early mornings, late nights, long weekends, and never-ending patience. You two are the best guys in the universe, period.

After that, I must thank the extensive network of reviewers, friends and colleagues who helped me build my writing chops in general. Gracias.

Finally, deep affection goes out to my late, much loved, and dearly missed Aunt Sandy and Uncle Henry. You saw the writer in me, always. Thank you, first and last.

ABOUT CHRISTINA BAUER

Christina Bauer thinks that fantasy books are like bacon: they just make life better. All of which is why she writes romance novels that feature demons, dragons, wizards, witches, elves, elementals, and a bunch of random stuff that she brainstorms while riding the Boston T. Oh, and she includes lots of humor and kick-ass chicks, too. Christina lives in Newton, MA with her husband, son, and semi-insane golden retriever, Ruby.

Stalk Christina on Social Media

Blog:

http://monsterhousebooks.com/blog/category/christina

Facebook:
https://www.facebook.com/authorBauer/

Instagram:
https://www.instagram.com/christina_cb_bauer/

Twitter:
@CB_Bauer

VLOG:
https://tinyurl.com/Vlogbauer

Web site:
www.bauersbooks.com

COMPLIMENTARY BOOK

Get a FREE novella when you sign up for Christina's newsletter: https://tinyurl.com/bauersbooks

BEVERLY HILLS VAMPIRE

A NOVELLA BY CHRISTINA BAUER

BONUS IMAGES

"I dig out beautiful caves behind my characters; I think that gives exactly what I want; humanity, humor, depth." - Virginia Woolf

Dear Reader,

When I'm building worlds for my books, I often think about this quote from author Virginia Woolf. In my writing process, I definitely dig out a lot of caves. And they're deep ones, too. Even after more than forty books, I still only keep one chapter for every ten that I outline or write. And it's hard to cut this stuff. Yet, it's also a privilege to have this problem.

The good news is that these extra visuals now have a home in my books. On the pages which follow, you'll find some pictures that didn't fit into the main text, along with a brief description of each.

I hope you enjoy these bonus images from *Reaper Games!*

CB

CLOUD CARRIER

Cloud carriers are how souls are stored in ghost towers. I wanted a few big scenes where Xavier and Camilla showed their stuff and saved the day. Cloud carries played a big part.

Sadly, it was starting to become Xav and Cam's book. Since these two have their own series now, the tales of their exploits will have to wait.

CLOUD
CARRIER

DEMON DELEGATE

I outlined Cissy's contacts within the world of inter-realm diplomacy. Like the cloud carrier stuff, it was getting too big and distracting from the Myla and Lincoln Show.

Now, you can enjoy a picture of one of the demon delegates who attended the ghoul carnival!

DEMON DELEGATE

ARX HALL

I love this picture of Arx Hall. The palace itself looms in the tippy back pf the image while Lincoln stands in the foreground. How awesome are all the twisty stalactites that frame him? So cool.

In this case, I found I was writing weird excuses for him to go outside and just stare at his own house. This needed to go, but you can still see it here...

ARX HALL

ZELENE

I wanted to include another picture of Zelene pushing her way through the wall, but she was already getting a lot of real estate with her scream pictures.

Ah, Zelene. I still love you!

ZELENE

BETSY

*a*nd for the final image, I am pleased to share a picture of Betsy... along with some background. I grew up in Buffalo, NY, where there's a vibrant Polish immigrant community complete with traditional food, dancing and music. It's a true story that a friend of mine in high school really did have her junker's radio station stuck on polka music. Trust me, this stuff grows on you.

On a final notes, here are the lyrics for the *Too Fat For Me* polka. In case you're wondering, the definitive version is performed by Frank Yankovic.

Here's a silly ditty, you can sing it right away
Now here is what you say, so sing it while you may
Here's a silly jingle, you can sing it night or noon
Here's the words, that's all you need, 'cause I just sang the tune

Oh, I don't want her, you can have her
She's too fat for me
She's too fat for me
She's too fat for me
I don't want her, you can have her
She's too fat for me
She's too fat, she's too fat
She's too fat for me

I get dizzy, I get numbo
When I'm dancing
With my Jum-Jum-Jumbo
I don't want her, you can have her
She's too fat for me
She's too fat for me
She's too fat for me

I don't want her, you can have her
She's too fat for me
She's too fat
She's too fat
She's too fat for me
No, no, no, no, no

(Can she dance a quadrille?)
No, no, no, no, no
(Does she fit in your coupe?)
By herself, she's a group
(Could she possibly sit upon your knee?)
No, no, no

We don't want her, you can have her
She's too fat for me
And she's too fat for me
But she's just right for me
We don't want her, you can have her
She's too fat for me
Yeah, she's too fat, much too fat
But she's just right for me

She's so charming
And she's so winning
But it's alarming
When she goes in swimming
We don't want her, you can have her
She's too fat for me (ha)

She's too fat for me
But she's just right for me
So I sure want her, you can't have her
She's just right for me
(But she's too fat) she's not too fat
She's just right for me (ha-ha)

She's a twosome, she's a foursome
If she'd lose some
I would like her more some
I don't want her, you can have her
She's too fat for me
She's too fat for me (ha-ha)
She's too fat for me
I don't want her, you can have her
She's too fat for me
She's too fat, much too fat
She's too fat for me, hey

BETSY

www.ingramcontent.com/pod-product-compliance
Lightning Source LLC
Chambersburg PA
CBHW072124250626
47159CB00007B/2558